I0665055

KATE LARKINDALE

Evernight Teen ®

www.evernightteen.com

ISBN: 978-0-3695-0909-3

Cover Artist: Jay Aheer

Editor: CA Clauson

KATE LARKINDALE

DEDICATION

For my mother.

KATE LARKINDALE

Kate Larkindale

Copyright © 2023

Chapter One

The new jeans have that fresh-out-of-the-bag smell. I breathe it deeply before unfolding them and laying them across my bed. Oh, yeah. They're perfect. I step into them, squirming to get the stiff fabric up over my thighs. I have to lie down on the bed to get the zipper closed, but once it is, I can't help but love how the dark denim hugs my body. Why have I never had skinny jeans before? A glance at my phone tells me I need to get a wriggle on, so I throw my favorite t-shirt on over the jeans and allow myself one last admiring glance at my reflection. Damn, I look hot.

The familiar scent of coffee and toast greets me when I enter the kitchen. Teddy sits in his usual spot at the table, inhaling what looks, from the milk puddled around, like his third bowl of cereal. My stomach flips. I don't know how anyone eats so much in the morning.

"Good morning," Mom says, turning away from the blender and the bilious green liquid churning inside it.

"Would you like some super-shake?"

I glance across at Mama K who takes advantage of Mom's attention on me to dump her glass of swamp-water into the sink. She catches my eye and gives an almost imperceptible shake of her head. Her glossy black hair flies around her face for a second before settling back into her short, blunt bob.

"As delicious as always," she says, brushing past me to give Mom a long, lingering kiss on the lips.

Gross. It's too early for such blatant PDA.

I clear my throat and Mama K sits down at the table, pulling the newspaper toward her.

I eye the green sludge suspiciously as I edge past the blender toward the coffee machine. "No thanks, Mom. I'll just grab some coffee and a piece of toast."

"You really should try it," Mom says, pouring a little into the bottom of a glass. "It's so good." She shoves the glass in my direction. "Teddy? You will have some, won't you?"

Teddy's head shoots up in alarm as Mom sets green stuff down before him. It seriously looks radioactive. Nothing that color could possibly be good for you.

I wink at him. "I'll give it a shot if you do?"

Teddy picks up the glass with practiced slowness. He sniffs the liquid inside and wrinkles his nose. Stupid kid. He should know by now the only way to swallow these concoctions of Mom's is to hold your nose.

I gulp down whatever it is and make a face. Too much kale. Although, in my book, even waving the leaves over the top would be too much. "There. Happy now?"

Mom's eyes rake over me and she huffs, really looking at me for the first time since I stepped into the room. "What are you wearing?"

I spin around, showing off. "My new jeans. Aren't they gorgeous?"

"You can't go to school like that." Mom shakes her head. "Go upstairs and change."

"What?" I stare at her.

"Those jeans..." She makes a disgusted gesture, shaking her head with her face screwed up like she's tasted something bad. "They're obscene on you. You don't have the figure for them. Look!" She leans over and grabs the little roll of flesh spilling over the waistband of the jeans. "This is disgusting. Why do you girls insist on showing off the most unattractive parts of yourselves?"

I take a step back, pushing her hand away from the offending body part. I glance down at myself. I love these jeans. I love the way they accentuate every curve. Okay, so maybe I have a little bit of a muffin top, but my t-shirt covers it. Mostly.

Mom stands with her hands on her hips, glaring at me. Even in that pose she manages to be graceful and elegant. Her black leggings cling to legs a mile long, lean and well-muscled. Over them, her pink tank sits flat against her stomach. She wouldn't get any spillage over the top of her skinny jeans—if she wore them. Not for the first time, I wish her Russian genes were more dominant in me.

"Anastasia," Mom's voice takes on a warning tone. "Go change. Now."

"Mama K?" I plead, sliding my eyes over to my other mother.

She doesn't raise her head from the paper, just gives it a shake to tell me she isn't going to get involved in this one. Coward.

"I bought these jeans with my own money," I try. "I saved up for months."

"Why, Anastasia?" Mom's brow furrows as she

glares at me. "Why would you waste your money on something to make you look like a Georgian streetwalker?"

My jaw clamps down. "I like the way they fit." Or I did. Now I'm starting to see myself through Mom's eyes and I'm not sure I like these jeans as much as I did ten minutes ago.

Mom's jaw clamps too, mirroring mine. We do have *some* of the same genes. "Then you really can't see yourself. Go and change. Maybe if you stuck to your diet you might be able to wear skinny pants."

I want to argue more, but I know the expression on Mom's face. There's no arguing with it.

"Fine!" I stomp loudly as I leave the room. Which probably doesn't help my case at all. But it sure feels good.

Aren't mothers supposed to view their kids as gorgeous regardless of reality? I storm my way up the stairs. Now I'm going to have to skip breakfast if I'm going to make it to school on time. I bet Mom'll be glad. It's not my fault I'm not tall and blonde and willowy like her. Genetics are like that. She met Nana before she married my dad, so she must have known there was a whole lot of short, dumpy Polynesian DNA hanging around in there. Maybe she thought her own Russian genes were strong enough to overpower Dad's inferior Samoan ones. Well, sorry, Mom. Fail. I've been dieting my ass off for weeks and it makes no difference. My boobs and butt are naturally bodacious. And no amount of wishing otherwise is going to change that. No amount of dieting or exercise either.

****

I sprint up the school steps, the short skirt Mom hates almost as much as the skinny jeans flapping in the brisk breeze. I hold it down with one hand. Half the school mill around the quad below or sprawl on the stairs to catch a few minutes of early morning sun before the bell rings. I'd never live it down if I flashed them.

Vonnie leans against the wall half-way up. She has her phone tucked between her chin and her shoulder and babbles non-stop into it while at the same time applying eyeliner using a brass plaque commemorating some war as a mirror.

"Von." I step up and join her against the wall.

"Hey, Stas is here," she says into the phone. "Gotta go. Later."

"Who was that?" I gesture at the phone she dumps into the front pocket of her backpack.

"My cousin, Shay." Vonnie slings her bag across her shoulder again. "Thought you were going to wear those new jeans we bought over the weekend."

"Yeah, me too." Anger churns through my stomach and coats my throat. "I swear, my mom is such a bitch. You won't believe what she said when she saw me in those jeans."

Vonnie leans forward. "You're super hot in those jeans. They make your ass look incredible."

"Incredibly huge, apparently. At least according to Mom. She wouldn't let me wear them out of the house. Said she'd be ashamed to know I was out in public wearing them. She might even have called me a hooker at one point."

"Seriously?" Vonnie's perfect eyebrows shoot up under her bangs. "Did you argue with her?"

I stare at her. "Well, duh. I told her I paid for them with my own money and she has no right to tell me what I can and can't wear. Sometimes I feel like she still thinks I'm six or something. It took me months to save up for those. And now I'm not allowed to wear them because Mom's offended by a little muffin top."

Vonnie wrinkles her nose. "Seems extreme, even for your mom."

I groan. "I know. I can't wait until this stupid wedding is over. She's riding me all the time about my weight. She's the one who picked out those stupid orange dresses. I swear, I look like someone vomited a pumpkin in mine."

The first bell rings and I press myself into the wall to keep from being swept into the wave of kids surging toward the doors.

"Did K have anything to say about it?" Vonnie grabs my arm and we plunge into the crowd together. "You can usually count on her to be the voice of reason."

"Usually," I agree. "She's as crazy as Mom at the moment, though. I get they want to have the perfect wedding and all, but it's like nothing else even matters right now."

Vonnie giggles. "Did they agree on who's gonna wear the dress yet?"

"You've met my moms." I roll my eyes in her direction as we pass through the doorway and enter the school building. "They're both wearing dresses."

I stop at my locker and toss my books inside. I have English first period and realize, too late of course, my copy of *The Scarlet Letter* is still lying facedown on my bed. I slam the locker shut. It's going to be one of those days.

Vonnie accompanies me up the hall. "Well, don't worry about your mom. You can wear those cool-ass jeans this weekend. Shay told me about a party in Maytown. We have to go. And you have to wear those jeans."

"I can't." I shake my head. "It's my weekend with Dad. And I can't blow him off again. He's been making noises about changing the custody arrangements if I keep ditching his weekends. I'd die if I had to live with Dad full time."

"You'd get to go to school with Shay." Vonnie gives me a wicked grin as she peels off into her calculus classroom. "Best parties over that side of town, if you believe her."

"Later." I say, waving as I sail on down the hallway toward my own class. Maybe the best parties *are* over on Dad's side of town, but if I lived there, I'd never know about them. Parties are one of the seventeen billion things Dad now considers a sin. Skinny jeans are, no doubt, on the list too. His pastor probably thinks they're the root of all evil or something ridiculous. I groan. I guess I'm lucky to have involved parents in my life, but why do they have all these stupid rules?

Chapter Two

School is interminable, but finally the bus dumps me on the corner two blocks from my house. A strong wind gusts through the trees, shaking dry, brittle leaves off branches to scuttle aimlessly across the sidewalk. My hair whips around my face as I crunch through drifts of these fallen leaves toward home. Every few steps I have to spit out a mouthful and question why I keep my hair long. It's a pain in the butt. I grab a handful of the thick, wiry stuff and do my best to tie it into a ponytail with the elastic band I keep around my wrist. There. I bet it's not pretty, but at least I'm not choking on it now. And I can keep my hands free to hold down my skirt. My jeans wouldn't be blowing up and exposing my big, brown butt to the world.

By the time I reach my street, I feel like I've gone three rounds with Floyd Mayweather. My eyes tear with the grit blowing across them. Wiping at my damp cheeks, I drag myself across the lawn, skirting around the sign in the center that reads 'Varushkin School of Dance'. A photograph of my mother doing a perfect, beautifully extended arabesque en pointe sits next to the text. Like I do every time I walk this way toward the house, I give the image a little salute.

I push through the front door and almost get laid out by the Spiderman backpack dumped in front of it. "Teddy!"

I walk a short way down the hall and pop my head through the entrance to K's studio. The overhead lights are on as well as two lamps with high wattage bulbs. I have to squint in the brilliance.

"I'm home," I say quietly, not wanting to startle her. When Mama K is deep into her work, you could burn the house down around her and she wouldn't notice. That's why I'm supposed to keep an eye on Teddy after school. Technically he's never home alone because both Mom and Mama K are here, but Mom's studio is around the back of the house and she can't supervise him while she's teaching. And like I said, Mama K gets so lost in her work, if I'm not around, Teddy'll spend all afternoon playing on the X-box or watching things on TV he's not supposed to.

"Stas?" Mama K looks up over the top of her easel and pushes her glasses up onto her head. "Oh... Is it that late?"

"I just got home. You have a couple more hours. What are you working on?"

"Come take a look." Mama K gestures me over and I cross the brightly lit space to join her behind the easel.

"Do you like it?" Mama K sits back and studies her artwork.

I look at it for a long time. Mama K illustrates children's books and her unique blend of pen and ink drawings with watercolors gives every image a whimsical, dreamlike quality. This panel shows a little girl standing in the rain, water puddling at her feet and tears running down her face. A dog-lead hangs loose in her hand, the clip where it attaches to the dog's collar bent open.

"Poor kid," I mutter. "Bad enough to lose your dog on a fine day, let alone in that weather."

Mama K smiles at me. "You got exactly what I was going for. Thank you. Now I can move on. I've been tinkering with this one for about an hour."

"I'll leave you to it. Do you need me to do anything for dinner?"

She shakes her head. "Rennie has it covered."

"Great." I groan inwardly. More kale and quinoa, or something equally awful.

I groan more when I find the mess Teddy has made with his afternoon snack. Peanut butter, jelly, chocolate chips, and pretzels litter the table. I screw the cap onto a jar sticky with little-boy fingerprints.

"Teddy!" I yell. "Get your skinny butt down here."

I listen for his pounding footsteps and absently run a piece of pretzel through a blob of peanut butter. Where did Teddy even find this stuff? Mom's loathing of peanut butter borders on a phobia. Maybe we're not so different—I feel much the same way about kale. The sight of it makes me queasy.

"What?" Teddy stares up at me, all wide innocent eyes, a smear of jelly across one cheek like a sugary brand.

I return his look with one of my own, a glare I've borrowed from Mom. "What do you think?" I glance pointedly at the table.

"Oh," Teddy grins at me. "You want some?"

For a long moment I fight to keep up the mature, adult facade. But the saltiness of the pretzel and peanut butter on my tongue weakens me. Who am I kidding? "Yeah. I want some."

For a good ten minutes Teddy and I gorge in silence. When I'm stuffed, my mouth floury from too much salt and sugar, I sit back and watch my brother scrape the last of the jelly from the jar with a crust of bread.

Teddy looks nothing like me. At nine, he's still skinny as a string bean. I have no idea where he puts the food he eats. Given the mess on the table, this is his second round of snacking, and he ate as much, if not more, than I did. His hair is the color of the chocolate chips melting on the tabletop, his eyes a shade darker. They're Mama K's eyes, just a little less slanted than hers are, like her Korean genes were watered down by the Slavic sperm-donor she and Mom chose so their child would look like the pair of them. Teddy's looks are all his own. I've never seen slanted eyes and olive skin on someone with those high, Slavic cheekbones. But then, I've never seen anyone with my hair or skin tone sport that bone-structure either, and here I am.

"C'mon, Tedster," I say, hauling myself out of the chair, "We'd better get this stuff cleaned up before Mom comes in. Otherwise…"

Teddy grins and makes a throat-cutting gesture.

"Right." I rub the top of his head as I pass, marveling, as I always do, at the fine, soft texture of his hair. What I wouldn't do for hair like that instead of this coarse, wiry mess. Thanks for the genes, Dad.

****

Mom steps through the back door a few minutes after six, still in her leotard and tights. Her only concession to the cold wind whipping around the house is the oversized cardigan she's thrown over her teaching outfit.

"Good day?" I ask, looking up from the algebra homework I've been struggling with since Teddy and I cleaned away the evidence of our binge.

She crosses to the refrigerator and starts pulling things out, piling them on the countertop. "It was good. Except that witch Julianna has lowered her prices again."

Mama K wanders in, her fingers stained black with ink. "Again? How can she afford to keep doing that?"

Mom sniffs. "She has no standards. Fifteen, twenty in a class. How can they expect to learn anything in a class so big?"

Mama K crosses the room and cups a hand around the back of Mom's neck. "For most of them, it's just some fun. They don't want to learn much. If they do, they'll come to you. You already have more students than you have time for."

"I know. But if she's undercutting my prices so much, will any new students sign up?"

"Of course they will, Mom." I pack up my homework and dump it in the backpack I haven't managed to get upstairs to my room with yet. "You're the best teacher in town and everyone knows it."

"But maybe I should consider lowering..."

Mom charges more than most ballet teachers in the suburbs, explaining to mothers who balk at her prices she was trained at the Bolshoi and can teach stronger technique than any other local teacher. No one argues with her. There aren't any other ballet teachers around here who can claim Bolshoi training. I don't think there are any who can claim to have had a professional career even. So Mom can afford to charge more. She can also be picky about the students she takes on.

"No!" Mama K and I say at the same time. We've had this discussion before. Every time another teacher opens up shop or one of the existing studios lowers their prices, Mom panics. Because yes, she does lose a student or two each time. But never the good ones.

"I can't afford to lose even one or two students," Mom argues. "Not without replacing them. The school is barely profitable as it is."

Mama K starts filing through the assortment of vegetables and Tupperware containers Mom pulled from the fridge. "Rennie, you're being dramatic again. If anything, the school's more profitable now because the mortgage is paid off. You can't teach any more classes and you don't want to compromise on class sizes. The only thing you could do to grow the business is to hire another teacher so you can run classes in both studios simultaneously."

Mom shakes her head and reaches for a chopping board. "No. Another teacher couldn't teach like me."

"They wouldn't have to." I grab a carrot stick from the board, narrowly missing getting a finger chopped off as Mom hacks at the defenseless vegetable. "You could get someone in to teach tap or jazz or hip-hop. Ballet isn't the be-all and end-all of dancing, you know."

"My school is a ballet school," Mom says, dumping the carrots into a bowl and moving on to the zucchinis and peppers. "I have no desire to teach anything else."

I sigh. There's no point arguing with Mom. She has a stubborn streak about ten miles wide. And she's always right. "You wouldn't have to," I mutter. "That's why you have another teacher. God, you could hire Dad to teach contemporary and hip-hop. I'm sure he could use the money."

Both Mama K and Mom stare at me then, but it's Mom who speaks first, her brow knotted in concern. "Is there something you haven't told us? Is Tusi in trouble?"

I shouldn't have brought it up. I should have kept my fat mouth shut. Dad's as proud and stubborn as Mom. In fact, that's probably why they're not together anymore. Plus the fact Mom likes girls better than guys. But whatever the case, he wouldn't want Mom even suspecting things aren't going great for him.

"Stas?" Mama K flicks on a burner and sets a pot of water and rice on it to boil. "What's going on with your father?"

"Oh, nothing really." I try to stall, but there's really nowhere to go now. I've backed myself into a corner I can't get out of. "He just mentioned something about the theater being empty so much this year."

"I warned him," Mom says haughtily. "I told him when he bought that place the location was bad. I couldn't even get my students' families to go there to watch their kids dance. That's why we had to start using the University Hall for recitals even though the stage doesn't have the right surface for dance."

I say nothing. She's right, of course. Dad's theater is on the city fringe, not heading out toward the suburbs, but toward the industrial area to the north of the city. It's not the slums, but it's close enough I'd think twice about wearing any valuable jewelry or carrying large amounts of cash in his neighborhood. So Dad's stuck with a beautiful building in an area the people who patronize dance and theater are too scared to go.

"Talking about your father," Mom pauses to watch Mama K stir the rice. "You're going there this weekend?"

"Yeah." I sigh. "You said I had to."

"You do." Mom's voice is serious. "You know how he gets if he doesn't see you."

Unfortunately, I do. But that doesn't mean I have to like it. Don't get me wrong. I love Dad. But after Nana died, he found religion, and I don't often see eye to eye with his new buddy, Jesus. The dude's kind of judgmental, if you ask me.

"I know. How long is dinner? Should I get Teddy to come and set the table?"

Mama K gives the rice another quick stir. "Maybe five minutes for this? Oh! Rennie, did I tell you the florist called? They don't think they're going to be able to get the orange chrysanthemums you wanted. The woman suggested marigolds, but I told her I'd have to ask you."

I grab my backpack off the floor and head out the

door to the stairs, grateful the conversation has moved away from Dad and his business, even if it has morphed, inevitably, into wedding planning again. "I'll go wash up and send Teddy down."

But I don't think they've heard me. I've barely left the room and they're already kissing. As if the kitchen wasn't steamy enough.

Chapter Three

It's after 4:30 by the time the bus navigates Friday afternoon traffic and pulls up on the corner near Dad's apartment. I had to stand the whole way and my shoulder aches from the extra weight in my backpack. I keep clothes and stuff at Dad's for weekends, but there are always things I want to bring from Mom's. Like my new skinny jeans. I might leave them here after Vonnie and I crash the party Shay talked about. It's not like Mom's ever going to let me wear them out of the house. She made that pretty damn clear. I haven't seen Dad in a while, but he's never banned me from leaving the house in any outfit before.

The elevator in Dad's building is broken again, so I have to walk up the stairs, my bag heavier with every flight. When I reach the sixth floor, I'm breathing heavily. I take a moment to catch my breath before heading down the dingy corridor to Dad's apartment, number fourteen.

An envelope with my name on it is stuck to the door with a square of duct tape. I open it, hoping for a key; I find a note instead.

Hey Stas-Baby,

I'm at the theater. Come meet me there and I'll take you out for dinner.

Can't wait for you to see the new piece I'm working on.

X X X Dad

I groan. The theater's only a few blocks from here, but I don't feel like walking another step. Especially not with this bag on my back. It looks like I don't have a choice. Dad's never given me a key to his place. I make a mental note to ask him why. When I was a little kid and he used to pick me up from Mom's for our weekends, I didn't need one. I'm an adult now, or close enough. Surely I should have my own key. I've had one to Mom and Mama K's place—home—since I was ten. I've never lost it either.

Sighing, I tramp back down the stairs and onto the street. People crowd the sidewalks, everyone appearing to be in a huge rush to get wherever they are going. Most of the time I love being downtown, but tonight I'm tired and irritable.

It's a relief to turn down the narrow street the James Theater sits on. It's a low building sprawling across most of the lefthand side of the street. Behind it, the skyscrapers of downtown loom like specters. The front doors are closed today, no light shining through the glass. Like this, the theater looks small and shabby and insignificant. When there's a show on, the doors open wide and people and noise and bright light spill across the broad steps leading to the entrance. It's been a while since I've seen it like that.

I avoid the stairs and skirt the building to the stage door at the back. I know the theater like I know my own house. Hours of my life have been spent here, watching Dad and his company rehearse and perform. Almost as many hours as I've spent watching Mom dance or Mama K paint.

As I expected, the stage door is open. I slide through into the dimly lit corridor and follow the sound of music to the theater. I push through the double doors leading to the auditorium and I'm hit by a wall of noise so loud it almost knocks me off my feet. What pounds from the speakers is fiercely rhythmic, a series of competing beats driving relentlessly onward like a freight train hurtling into a tunnel. It sweeps me up and carries me forward to the stage.

Dad is alone up there, a single work light above him the only illumination. He's dressed in only a pair of sweatpants rolled to his knees. His skin glistens with a sheen of sweat. I sink into a seat in the third row to watch.

Dad's dancing is so different to Mom's. Ballet is all about escaping gravity, rising above the stage, and soaring through the air. Dad's dance embraces the earth. His feet remain firmly grounded and he uses the solidity of the floor beneath him to hold him, even rolling across it at one point.

Looking at him move, it's easy to understand what Mom saw in him. Even now, nearing fifty, Dad is a sexy man. The thought kind of creeps me out, even if it's true. There's not an ounce of extra fat on him, just hard, lean muscle.

The music thuds to a crescendo and Dad is barely visible as he whirls across the stage in a series of complex turns. He stops on the final beat by dropping to his knees, back arched, hands thrown over his head. I can't stop myself from applauding.

"Stas?" Dad climbs to his feet and squints in my direction through the light.

"Hi, Dad." I slide from my seat and walk up to the base of the stage.

Dad grabs a towel and runs it across himself. "How much did you see? What did you think?"

"It's great. Really dynamic. Love the music."

"Thought you might," Dad grins and sits on the edge of the stage, legs swinging below him. "It's some weird German industrial band. Great to dance to."

"For you..." I roll my eyes. Dad can find choreography in the weirdest places. It's kind of what he's known for. His company have always been on the cutting edge of contemporary dance, highly respected by critics and other dance professionals, but less popular with the general public who prefer something safer or prettier or easier to swallow and understand.

"For you too." Dad jumps to his feet and beckons me to come up. "Come on. I'll show you."

I shake my head. "Not now, Dad. I'm tired. And didn't your note say something about dinner?"

He sighs and shakes his head. "My little girl doesn't want to dance with me anymore."

"It's not you, Dad. I don't dance anymore. Period."

I quit dancing when I was thirteen and already wearing a C-cup. It wasn't that I didn't love it—I did. Dancing is a part of me. Genetics again, I guess. Maybe you can't have two dancers as parents and not inherit the gene. Nature plays some cruel jokes sometimes, and giving someone with a passion for dance a body like mine is only one of them.

Dad throws me a look. He knows dancing is like air for me. "Listen to this and tell me you don't dance."

Darting to the stereo, he thumbs his i-Pod until he finds what he's searching for. "I heard this on one of those access radio stations last week and thought of you. I phoned in to find out who it was. Listen and tell me you don't love it."

He presses play and a moment later the familiar strains of Tchaikovsky's Swan Lake fill my ears. I'm about to roll my eyes. Ballet music. Exactly what I want right now.

Before I get a chance to do more than draw in a breath, it changes. Under the orchestra, a Polynesian log drum comes in. Then another, counterpointing the first. I sit up straighter, listening in wonder to how well the two incongruous elements meld together. I love this. It's made for me. It's the two sides of my artistic family married together in a way that creates something wholly unique and individual. It's a musical me, half Russian classicism, half traditional island beats. After only a few bars, choreography spins through my head. Not ballet. Not quite modern or hip-hop either. A weird hybrid of them all. Pointe shoes and bare feet, tutus and tattoos. The whole production flits through my skull, right down to the palm trees in the background and dance-club lighting.

"So?" Dad raises his eyebrows in my direction. The gold cross hanging at his throat catches the light and flashes its brilliance into my eyes.

"It's okay." I give a noncommittal shrug. I can't let him see how inspired I am.

Dad sighs again and slings the towel around his neck. "Give me a couple of minutes to shower, okay? Then we'll go eat."

After he's gone and the doors to the green room clang shut, I climb onto the stage. I was lying. I do still dance. But only when I'm sure no one can see me. I sometimes sneak into Mom's studio at night and dance with the lights out so no one will know I'm there. Or I steal moments like this, when I'm alone in the theater.

I have only a few minutes, but this music is too special to ignore. I kick off my boots and socks and plant my feet on the sprung boards of the stage. I'm not warmed up so I need to take things slow. I set the i-Pod to repeat and let myself fall into the music. Moving almost in slow-motion, I revel in the way my muscles control the movement of my limbs as I contort them into shapes they were never meant to form. I'm not working on anything in particular, just using my body to channel everything going on in my life, all the conflicting thoughts and emotions I can't find words to express.

I dance out my anger at Mom over her comments

about my jeans and how I look in them. I glide through the guilt I feel about telling Mom and K about Dad's financial difficulties. I spin around my feelings about spending every second weekend at Dad's rather than with my friends. And finally, I wipe the floor with the all-encompassing plans for my moms' wedding.

I'm heading into a new section, the part where I deal with today's issues, when something breaks through the driving beat of the music.

A phone. I dive toward the front row and my bag, but my phone's screen is dark even while the ringing continues. I look around, finally spotting Dad's phone buzzing and vibrating at the edge of the stage.

I grab it and thumb the icon to answer without taking the time to look at the caller ID. "Hello? Tusi Nonu's phone."

"Hello?" The voice at the other end is deep and has the same island lilt Dad's has. "Hello? Who is this?"

"Stas," I say quietly. "Who's this?"

"Stas? It's your uncle. Ropati. How are you?"

I pull the phone away from my ear for a second and stare at it. Ropati? My father's brother Ropati? I haven't seen him in about four years. "I'm good. Dad's showering. Can I get him to call you back?"

"No. It's fine. I'm heading into a meeting in a minute. Can you just tell him I've finished the paperwork? He'll know what I mean."

"Um… Okay?"

"Thank you. I hope to be in town in the next few weeks. I'd love to see you again, Stas."

"Sure. That would be good." I have no idea if it will or it won't. I barely remember Ropati. Just small details like the scent of his expensive aftershave and how he keeps his hair trimmed close to his head so it never gets the wild, out-of-control look Dad's hair gets if he goes a few too many weeks between haircuts.

The magic of the music has gone after I've hung up the phone. I'm too wrung out to move though, so I slump in a chair and listen as the piece keeps playing on an endless loop. I should get up and change the settings on the i-Pod. I just don't have the energy.

By the time Dad slips back into the theater, my breathing has steadied and the sweat has dried into a salty crust across the surface of my skin.

Dad grins at me. "I knew you couldn't resist this."

I blush. "It's pretty cool."

Dad reaches for my hand and pulls me toward the stage. I shake my head and try to pull away, but he's too strong. So I end up back on the stage as the music starts over again. I can't help moving to it, my muscles warm now. Dad joins me, mirroring my choreography at first, then adding new movements. He takes my hand and spins me into him. I manage to stop myself before crashing into his chest. His hands spread around my waist, solid and reliable as he lifts me.

I love dancing with Dad. He's so strong, I'm never afraid to let my feet leave the ground. I trust he won't drop me. In Mom's classes, the boys were never big enough or strong enough to lift me. Partnering was an exercise in humiliation. I think that's a big part of why I quit.

When the music stops we're both breathless. Dad smiles and gives my shoulder a squeeze as he passes by me to grab the i-Pod from its dock. "You don't dance, huh?"

"Shut up." I can't help grinning at him.

The cold feels even more intense when we step out onto the street. It's dark and I wrap my scarf more tightly around my neck as we head toward the brighter lights beyond the alley.

"Hey, your brother called while you were in the shower," I say, then add, unnecessarily, "Ropati."

Dad frowns, his shoulders hunching toward his ears. "Did he say what he wanted?"

"He said to tell you he'd done the paperwork. Does that make sense to you?"

Dad nods, lips tightening as he does. Something like anger or terror flashes through his eyes, but it's so quick I can't be sure I actually saw it. I probably imagined it. I mean, why would Dad be angry or terrified of his brother?

"So, shall we go to Piccolo?" Dad asks, his voice too bright. "After that workout, I feel like I deserve lasagna."

I glance his way and there's no hint of the expression I think I saw a moment ago. I must have imagined it. It's dark and I can't see too well in the streetlights. "After a month on Mom's almost-all-kale diet, I feel like I deserve lasagna." I laugh so it doesn't sound as serious as it feels. Dad must hear the falseness in it because he turns and skewers me with his gaze.

"Stas, tell me the truth." His voice is low and holds a note of seriousness I don't usually get from him. "Is your mother forcing you to diet? Is she starving you? You've lost weight since the last time I saw you. Is this something you want?"

My head whirls. Starving me? No way. Mom only wants us all to be healthy. And as for wanting to lose weight, who doesn't? Even stick-thin supermodels moan in the magazines about how huge they are and how they have to slim down. Even Mom does. I'm no different to any other woman.

I shake my head. "I'm fine, Dad. Mom wants us all to look good at the wedding. She and K are paying a lot for it to be perfect."

Dad's face darkens. "There are more important things than looking good."

"I know. But sometime looking good helps you to feel good too."

In the harsh sodium glare of the streetlight above us, Dad's face twists into something terrifying and ugly. "How is it possible to feel good while living in sin?"

Chapter Four

It's after 10:30 when I manage to sneak down the fire escape and reach the corner of Albion and Masters where I'm meeting Vonnie. I settle myself against a lamppost and text that I'm here.

5 mins away. She texts back.

On the opposite corner a guy has set up drums and bashes away at them, seemingly oblivious to the crowd circling around to listen. A girl in baggy jeans, her hair tied up in colorful rags, moves into the circle of light cast by a streetlight and starts moving to the beat. It's not long before more people join her, bodies blurring into one as they catch the rhythm. My own foot starts tapping.

Before my hips start swaying to the beat, a horn sounds behind me.

"Yo! Hooker!" I whirl around, unsurprised when Vonnie's grinning face leans out the window of a car I don't recognize.

"Whose wheels?" I ask as I climb into the backseat.

"Mine." Vonnie's cousin, Shay, turns to look at me briefly.

I slap the palm she offers before she turns back to the wheel and negotiates her way through the crowd around the drummer.

"So, whose party is this?" I ask once we're crawling down the street in the direction of the hills.

Shay leans on her horn as a homeless-looking guy wanders across the road pulling an overloaded red wagon. "Some dude from school. He's cool. Should be a good party."

After winding our way up one of the streets snaking up and down the hills, and down a driveway almost as long as one of the streets, I'm lost. The houses up here are huge and modern, all glass and angles to make the most of the view over the city below. We park behind a sea of other parked cars and weave through them toward a house about three times the size of mine. A swimming pool glitters like a jewel at the side of the house, white lights casting rippling shadows across the trees and bushes shielding the house from the street and any neighbors.

"Swanky," Vonnie says, tugging down the tight, red miniskirt she's wearing.

"He's loaded," Shay says, clicking her keys to lock the car. "And his parents travel a lot."

"You've been here before?" I follow her through the wide open front door into a foyer that's almost the same size as Dad's whole apartment. This is an entirely new world.

"A couple of times," Shay says over her shoulder. "C'mon. Let's get a drink."

I raise my eyebrows at Vonnie who grins and shrugs before grabbing my hand and pulling me with her.

The kitchen is dimly lit and crowded with people. Music pulses from speakers tucked near the ceiling. Shay appears to have melted into the crowd so I keep hold of Vonnie's hand as she pushes her way through to a countertop where cups and bottles are stacked. A cooler of ice sits open on the floor and people dip their plastic cups in to scoop up ice.

"Want one?" Vonnie yells over the pounding bass.

I nod, unsure what she's offering. A moment later she shoves a cold cup into my hand. I take a cautious sip, surprised when sweetness spreads across my tongue. So different from the cheap, watered-down beer that's the staple at other parties I've been to. So much nicer too. I take a bigger gulp and move away from the counter to let someone else access the bottles.

Vonnie and I drift out the sliding doors and find ourselves on a deck. It's crowded out here too, but not so claustrophobic as the kitchen. More speakers pump music into the night and near the pool a group of kids are dancing. I sip my drink and take in the scene. When Vonnie heads down a short flight of stairs to a lower deck, I follow.

She's absorbed into a group of strangers almost immediately. I hang on the outside of the group, waiting for her to pull me in, but she doesn't. Aware I must look like a goober standing there, waiting to be noticed, I move away.

I lean on the railing of the deck and stare out over the city. It seems so quiet from up here, so peaceful. Strings of lights tangle together like beaded necklaces in a jewelry box. The noise and chaos and filth of the streets are invisible from here.

"Kind of different from being there, huh?" The boy's voice startles me so much I jump, my drink sloshing over the rim of my cup.

"I guess..." I wipe at the sticky liquid spreading across my new jeans.

He's tall, but carries himself with a confidence most tall guys our age don't possess yet. His arms are lean and well muscled under the sleeves of his gray t-shirt.

"I'm Zane," he says, taking a slurp from a cup the same as the one I've just emptied all over myself. Then he sticks out his hand for me to shake. I give him a quick once over—blue eyes, dark hair, the hint of a smile on full, pink lips.

I take his hand, shocked by the warmth of his palm and the strength in his long, tapered fingers. "Stas.

Anastasia, actually, but everyone calls me Stas. Or Stasi, sometimes, but I hate that." I'm babbling and I need to stop. I clamp my lips together to keep more words from spewing out.

"Cool name, Stas."

Is it? I've never thought of my name as being anything other than a pain in the butt. No one can spell it, and half the time people call me Stacey, which I hate. Almost as much as I hate being called Stasi. I never minded until we studied East Germany in history class and I found out how awful the secret police who shared my name were.

"Can I get you another?" Zane gestures at the empty cup.

I shouldn't. But then, I did spill half of the last one. "Sure," I say. "No idea what it was, so surprise me."

Zane grins and raises his eyebrows in my direction. "Brave girl," he says as he takes the steps two at a time.

Am I? Suddenly images of the posters in the gym flash before my eyes, warning me about taking drinks from strangers and date rape drugs. I probably shouldn't drink anything he gives me.

Vonnie breaks away from the group of kids she's been with.

"Who was that?" she asks, following Zane up the stairs with her eyes. "Jeans should be illegal on him. Did you get a look at his ass?"

Trust her to notice. "His name's Zane."

"He's cute."

"I know." I don't want to talk about him with Vonnie for some reason. And it's weird because Vonnie and I talk about everything. We always have.

"Vonnie?" Shay leans over the railing from the deck above us. "You down there?"

"Yeah. What's up?" Vonnie backs away from me and squints upward.

"There's some people you need to meet."

"You coming?" Vonnie drains her cup and starts toward the stairs.

I move to follow her, then stop. "You go. I'll wait for Zane and catch up."

"You sure?" Vonnie frowns and tugs at her skirt again. It's so short every step she takes makes it ride up so far she's practically flashing her panties.

I shake my head. I sound like Mom. Vonnie has a great ass and legs that go for miles. She rocks the skirt. "I'm sure," I say. "Just don't leave without me."

Vonnie grins. "Would I do that?"

"Yes," I say, but she's already gone.

Zane materializes next to me and thrusts a cup into my hand. "Hope you like vodka."

"Thanks." I forget my resolve not to drink it and take a sip. The same sweetness coats my tongue and flows down my throat. "Delicious."

Zane takes a healthy swig from his own cup. "Not bad."

"You live around here?" I turn my back on the city and face Zane. His eyes glitter in the light reflected off the swimming pool.

"No. I'm kind of a downtown guy."

"My dad lives downtown. I stay there most weekends."

"Yeah? Where?"

"His building is off Albion."

"And where do you live the rest of the time?"

I kind of don't want to answer. This cool downtown boy won't be impressed with Mom's suburbia. "The other side of town. Near Glenmont High."

"Yeah?" He lights up. "I go to Glenmont."

"You do?" I've never seen him there. And believe me, I'd have noticed him.

"I'm new," he explains. "Just started on Thursday."

Weird time of year to transfer, but what do I know? "Must be quite a commute from downtown. How come you don't go to Beaufort?"

"My aunt said Glenmont was a better school."

That sends my eyebrows shooting up my forehead. In no universe ever has Glenmont been a better school than Beaufort. This is a Beaufort High party and I bet more than half the kids here live in houses as large and opulent as this one. Sure, there are Beaufort kids who come from crappy buildings like the one my Dad lives in, but the majority of them are rich. Capital 'R' rich. Glenmont is more middle class.

"Sorry, but your aunt doesn't know what she's talking about."

Zane laughs. "That doesn't surprise me."

"So, you live with your aunt?"

"Yeah." Zane's voice tightens. "I needed a break from my folks, you know?"

"Doesn't everyone?" I chuckle, but Zane doesn't join me.

"You don't get along with your parents?" Zane takes another slurp from his cup.

I go to do the same, surprised when I discover the cup's nearly empty again. Do I have to answer him? It's so complicated, and I just met this guy. I don't want to scare him off with my psycho family before we've even got to know each other. So I shrug. "Do teenagers ever get along with their parents?"

Zane's face hardens and his eyes go blank. I've said the wrong thing. Why do I always have to say the wrong thing?

"Sorry," I say hurriedly, face blazing with heat. "You don't have to answer that."

He remains silent, his face shadowed and stony. I drain my cup for something to do, wincing at the loud slurping sound I make.

Zane's head rises. He glances at my now-empty cup. "Want another?"

I nod uncertainly. What just happened there? I make a mental note not to ask about his parents again and follow him up the stairs.

The kitchen and upper deck are even more crowded now. I catch a glimpse of Vonnie's red hair outside the sliding doors. She laughs loud enough I can hear it from where I'm standing and leans in toward a tall guy wearing a leather jacket. As I pass them on my way into the kitchen, I notice the ring sparkling in his lip, more laddering his earlobes, and punched through his eyebrow and nose. While I stand in line with Zane, waiting for our turn at the bottles and cooler, I watch him wrap her in his arms and bend to kiss her. She giggles and swats him away, but he isn't put off and a moment later they're glued to one another.

I wonder vaguely what it's like to kiss a guy with a lip piercing. Does it hurt?

"More vodka?" Zane doesn't wait for me to answer before sloshing some into a cup and topping it off with some 7-Up from the cooler. "Ice?"

I nod and he drops a few cubes in. He hands me the drink before turning back to make one for himself.

The music is louder by the time we've pushed our way back outside. The group dancing by the pool has grown. The beat is infectious and my toes tap along to it without me even thinking about it.

"Wanna dance?" Zane takes my hand and pulls me toward the tiled area that's become the makeshift dance floor.

"No, thanks." I pull away. "I don't dance."

Zane tosses me a skeptical glance. "Not at all? Ever? Seriously?"

I shake my head. I want to dance with him. I want to dance with him about as much as I've wanted anything. He looks like he might know how to move and I want to feel how our bodies might move together.

But I won't. He doesn't need to see this fat ass jiggling away, these boobs bouncing along half a beat behind. That would be one quick way to turn him right off. And I think I kind of like this guy.

Chapter Five

I take a long swallow of my drink. Everything looks very bright and sharp all of a sudden, the lights, the people, the edge of the house.

"C'mon." I tug Zane's hand and head toward the pool. Not to where the dancers are, but to the other side of it where the deck continues and several recliners litter the poolside.

It's darker over here, away from the floodlights attached to the house. I lie back on one of the loungers and stare up at the sky. A moment later a creaking sound tells me Zane's settled himself on the lounger next to me.

"Aren't the stars pretty?" I say, staring up at them.

"They're okay," Zane replies. "But there's too much light pollution to get a real sense of how many there are up there. It's better away from the city."

"Aren't we away from it?"

Zane chuckles and the sound makes my insides feel warm. "Here? No way. I'm talking miles away. Like in the country. You can see a billion stars when you're out there."

"A billion?" My tongue stumbles over the number and I giggle before trying again. "A literal billion?"

"Maybe even more."

I lie back and consider. I can't understand the number. How many stars would it be? I take another sip of my drink while I try to make sense of it. It doesn't help. My head spins. I sit up, hoping it will clear my head.

"I'm not great at math," I say, looking over at where Zane has sprawled out. "I can't imagine a billion stars."

"You don't have to imagine them. They're there.

They're real. I'll show you sometime."

"Yeah?" I move closer to where he's lying. His eyebrows are heavy above those wide, blue eyes. I want to run my finger along them, to discover what they feel like. To keep myself from acting on this urge, I take another slurp from my cup, disappointed when I discover it's almost empty again.

"Damn! These cups are too small."

Zane laughs. "Or maybe you're drinking too fast. Want a refill?"

I nod. Why not? Vonnie's occupied with Mr. Leather Jacket and I haven't seen Shay in hours. But they'll find me when it's time to go home.

Zane gulps down the rest of his drink and stands up. It takes me two attempts to untangle myself from the lounger and I only manage it after Zane takes my hand and drags me to my feet.

"You sure you want another?" he asks as we bully our way through the crowd to the kitchen.

I hold up my hand, fingers only an inch or so apart. "Just a teeny one."

"As you wish."

While Zane busies himself with the drinks, I glance around, searching for Vonnie. It doesn't take long to find her. She and the piercing guy are still kissing, more passionately now. His hand has crept up her skirt and she's clinging to him like she's drowning, both of them pressed up against the wall of the house.

Zane hands me a cup. "Sure I can't get you onto the dance floor?"

I take a sip. I do like this song. A lot. It has a beat you can't not move to.

Zane must take the unconscious swinging of my hips as an answer. Before I have time to think about it, or answer his question, he's drawn me to the edge of the dance area and I let myself fall into the music.

I wasn't wrong about him. This boy can move.

I don't know if it's minutes, hours, or weeks later that Vonnie taps my shoulder.

"Shay wants to go now," she says, her voice soft and blurred at the edges. Kind of like my vision. Where's the sharp brightness I was admiring before?

"Huh?" My head is fuzzy and thick.

"Time to go."

"Oh..." I untangle myself from Zane whose body I seem to have melted into. When did that happen? How? "I gotta go."

"It's getting late." Zane looks around blearily until he spots our cups where we dumped them on a low table. "Guess I should go soon too."

"Need a ride?" I ask.

Zane hesitates and looks over the crowd. "Nah. I'm good."

"Okay..." I don't want to leave him. I don't want tonight to be over. I've had fun. Far more than I usually do at these parties.

"See you in school?" Zane holds my drink out to me and I take it without thinking about it. I'm hot and thirsty from dancing so drain the cup.

Did I detect a note of hope in his voice? Does he want to catch me in school? Now there's something to look forward to. My face warms up. "Yeah. See you Monday."

His eyes meet mine and everything melts away. "I hope so," he murmurs.

"Yeah..." My face heats up. Does he mean it? I know I do. "Me too."

"Come on!" Vonnie drags at my arm. Her hair is disheveled and her lipstick smudged. She looks happy, though. And less drunk than I suddenly feel. God, how much did I drink?

"Bye…" I slur as I follow Vonnie a little unsteadily up the path. Was it this crooked before? I don't remember. Why did Vonnie have to yank me away so quickly? Didn't even give Zane a chance to kiss me. If he wanted to. I wanted him to. But if he wanted the same thing, wouldn't he have done it when we were dancing? We were pretty close for a while there. Maybe that was only because my legs don't seem to work properly anymore. They won't take me in a straight line. And my feet must have grown. I keep tripping over them.

"So, did you have a good time?" Shay asks when we reach the car.

"That guy is so hot!" Vonnie exclaims. "And he can kiss like…"

"Do you even know his name?" Shay asks, a teasing note in her voice.

"Uh…" Now it's Vonnie's turn to blush. "It didn't exactly come up…"

"It's Robbie." Shay turns to me as I fumble with the seatbelt in the back, my fingers suddenly too thick and clumsy to manage the simple procedure. "What about you? I didn't see you all night."

The seatbelt clicks into place and I lean back against the seat, letting my eyes drift closed for a second. "Oh, yeah." I sigh. "I had fun."

****

I'm woken way too early on Sunday morning by a banging on the door. Burying my head under my pillows, I try to fall back asleep.

"Stas?" Dad's voice comes to me through the covers. "You can't still be sleeping. You went to bed so early last night."

That's what he thinks.

My head is heavy and the stale, syrupy taste of

vodka clings to the back of my tongue. My eyes burn with exhaustion, the lids so weighted it's an effort to keep them even half open.

"Stas?" Dad calls again, this time rattling the handle. There's a lock, thankfully.

"What?" I call back. "It's the middle of the night."

"It's 8:42," Dad corrects. "I'd like you to come to church with me."

My stomach rolls and for a moment I think I might puke. Church? Are you kidding me? "Uh... Not today."

"You say that every time, sweetheart. I'd really like you to come. Everyone is always asking about you. And..." He stops, hesitating like he's unsure if he should say what's actually on his mind. "And, well, I can't help but worry about your eternal soul. I pray for you, living in a den of iniquity."

That wakes me up. I can't believe I've just heard those words. Den of iniquity? Is he serious?

"Dad?" I climb out of bed, wincing as my bare feet hit the cold, wooden floorboards, and pad to the door. "Are you okay? What are you talking about?"

Outside the door, Dad's dressed in his Sunday best, a knife-sharp crease running down the front of his pants, his shirt starched and ironed, a silk tie knotted expertly around his neck. He's clean-shaven and his usually bushy mop of hair has been tamed with coconut oil. He smells like the beach.

"Please come to church with me," he says again. "It's important to me that we do something to save your soul."

Does he know about last night? I eye him carefully, looking for a sign he might realize I'm still a little drunk from the party. My breath probably smells as bad as my mouth tastes so I keep my face turned away when I speak again. "My soul's fine, Dad. I'm not perfect, but nobody is, right? It's not a sin."

"I'm not talking about you," he says, his voice as sharp as the crease in his pants. "It's your mother and that … that … woman." The word is spat like he can't stand the taste of it crossing his tongue.

I've always known Dad doesn't like Mama K, but he's always managed to be civil about it before. Today his anger and disgust spill out, showing me a side of him I've never seen before. He usually limits his disapproval to the odd disparaging comment. When I think about it, they have been getting more vicious over the last few months. More frequent too. Maybe that's why I've avoided coming here the last few weekends, using my friends and homework as excuses to stay away.

Or maybe it's the pressure to go to church when I don't believe in it.

I sigh. I'm not getting out of it this time. Dad's not kidding around when he says it's important to him. The guy genuinely wants to save my soul. He's not going to accept any excuse I come up with for not going with him today. "Let me grab a shower," I say.

****

Dad's church is big and loud and seethes with people. He seems to know everyone, stopping to shake hands with half the congregation as we search out a pew with enough room for the pair of us. I've been here before, both with Dad and with his mother, Nana. Back then, Dad rarely came with us and Nana used to pray for him the way he now prays for me.

Since Nana's been gone, the place has lost any magic it may once have held. I used to love coming here as a kid, the singing and clapping captivating enough I could ignore the long, boring sermons. Since Nana died, the atmosphere seems to have changed. Even the music isn't uplifting like it used to be.

I keep a smile pasted across my face as I shake hand after hand, nodding as I'm introduced. I spot a pew with a couple of butt-widths free and grab Dad's hand to drag him over. I sink down onto the hard wooden bench gratefully. I've brushed my teeth and rinsed with mouthwash, yet the stale flavor of last night's booze still lingers in my throat. My stomach flip-flops lazily. If I make it through the whole service, I'll be lucky.

The preacher, an older man with wild white hair and glasses so big they cover most of his face, steps up to the pulpit and the congregation stills. The quiet doesn't trickle in like it does when a teacher steps into a noisy classroom, it falls like a heavy blanket over a bed. Even I sit up straighter.

This isn't the man I remember from when I used to come with Nana. I liked him. This pastor hasn't even spoken and already I know I'm going to hate him.

"Welcome," he intones, the word less like a greeting than a curse in his gravelly voice. "Let us pray."

Before the sermon is half over, I have to question whether Dad told the pastor I was coming. The whole piece is a veiled assault on the new laws allowing my two moms to marry each other. He has a commanding way of speaking, a way of saying hateful things that makes him sound reasonable and tolerant. Maybe it's his accent which has the same familiar lilt my father still speaks with. The congregation nod and mutter their agreement on almost every point, the whole church humming with the sound of their approval.

"Hallelujah!" An older woman with a flowered hat perched on top of an impossible up-do throws her hands skyward.

"Amen," says another person, setting off a chorus

of 'hallelujahs' and 'amens.'

I wish I understood what Dad gets out of being here. Nana always talked about church as somewhere she found strength and peace. A sanctuary where she could relax and be herself.

I feel like we're an army being mobilized against our will.

My jaw clenches and my hands crush into fists in my lap. I can't believe I'm in a room with so many people who believe this bigotry. I can't believe there are this many people in the city in this day and age who think like this. My chest aches with the knowledge my moms and so many of their friends have lived with this level of hatred directed toward them for so long. A bright spark of anger surges through me. How can Dad sit here listening to this? How can he sit and nod and mumble words of assent? He's a dancer. Half his company is gay. Does he not recognize the hypocrisy? Is he so unhappy Mom has moved on with her life? It's been over a decade. And he's had other partners over the years. Briefly. How can he get tied up in knots about it now? Because Mom and K are getting married? Why does he care?

I'm so grateful when the sermon ends, I let out a great gust of air. My face throbs with tension from grinding my teeth. I can't wait to get out of here. The sunlight slanting through the garish stained-glass windows, combined with the press of bodies, makes the room oppressively hot. I wonder vaguely if that's the intention—to give us a taste of Hell. Because surely this is Hell—an overheated building full of people whose ideas are so far away from my own there might as well be an ocean between us.

When the choir stand to sing the final hymn, I feel like I'm the only one who sees any irony in the fact the singers are belting out a chorus including the line 'we have to love each other like we love ourselves.'

As soon as the preacher steps down from the pulpit, I push my way from the pew. I hurry out of the building, my feet moving faster and faster as I near the doors. I throw myself at them and run through the dimly lit foyer to the main entrance and the parking lot beyond.

Once I'm outside, I manage to breathe again. I walk through the maze of parked cars until I reach the edge of the lot and the thick line of trees cutting the church-grounds off from the highway. I climb over the low wooden fence and sit down with my back to the building. House of love, huh? More like a house of hate.

I suck in great gusts of green-smelling air and will my heartbeat to slow. My anger tastes like pepper, the heat coating my throat and making it hard to swallow. I have to control it. I can't talk to Dad or anyone else here until I've managed to fold this away. I have a right to be outraged, but this is not the place to express it.

****

After an uncomfortable lunch at the diner a few blocks down from the church, Dad drops me home.

"Stas," he says as I climb out of the car. "You know my door is open for you anytime."

I nod, eager to get away. "Sure, Dad. But I'm good here. See you in a couple of weeks, okay?"

He sighs, his eyebrows knotting together over eyes that look both tired and tortured. "Okay... Love you."

"Yeah. Me too." I grab my bag off the backseat and swing it over my shoulder. "See ya."

I climb to the porch without a backward glance. When I open the front door, he still hasn't driven away. I glimpse the way his head rests on the steering wheel and have to question if he's crying. For a second I consider going to him. He looks so alone. Maybe his good buddy

Jesus didn't show up to hold his hand today.

"You're home." Mom appears in the doorway and wraps an arm around me. "Did you have a nice time with your father?"

I lean into her, breathing her faint citrus scent. "Not really..." I don't want to elaborate. My parents don't fight. They're not best friends. Their interactions tend to be brief and civil. But I can't imagine Mom keeping her cool if she had to listen to the crap the idiot pastor spouted this morning. The crap his congregation seemed to lap up.

"Did he mention if he was coming to the wedding?" Mom draws me further into the house, closing the door behind us. "I sent him an invitation, but he has not yet responded. We'll need to know for the catering and place-settings."

I give Mom a quick hug before moving toward the staircase and the sanctuary of my room. "He didn't say, Mom. But my guess is he's a no..."

Chapter Six

I wait for Vonnie in our usual spot on the school stairs. For once I arrive first and climb up to sit on the wall overlooking the entrance. My gaze scours the torrents of students flowing across the lawn below and swarming up the steps. I should be seeking out Vonnie's distinctive red hair, but instead my eyes land on every dark-haired boy. After Saturday night, I was kind of hoping Zane would be waiting for me this morning. Or at least looking for me.

"Yo!" Vonnie spots me from the bottom of the stairs and starts pushing her way up.

I hop down off the wall after one last survey of the area. No sign of Zane. Disappointment sits heavily on my gut, almost displacing this morning's slimy blender concoction. This week Mom's added beets to her list of miracle ingredients. They aren't great on an empty stomach, believe me.

"Wasn't the party epic?" Vonnie's eyes shine with excitement. "And you won't believe it. You know that guy I was talking to? The tall guy with the piercings? He called me last night."

"Really? You gave him your number?" I know I was drinking Saturday night, but I'd remember that. The dude was cute, but he looked kind of dangerous too, with his tortured hair, leather, and piercings.

Vonnie laughs. "That's the best part. I didn't. Shay must've given it to him. Which means he likes me enough to actually chase it down. Pretty cool, huh?"

"Yeah," I manage. "Cool." Sometimes Vonnie's brand of logic can be exhausting. Or maybe I'm just bitter because a cute guy has never gone to those lengths to get my number. Zane hasn't even bothered to try and find me. Maybe he doesn't even go to school here. But why would he lie?

"How was the rest of your weekend with your dad? Did he try to get you to go to church?"

"He did get me to go to church." I roll my eyes. "And yeah, it sucked."

"I bet. You must've had a wicked hangover. I've never seen you so wrecked."

"The hangover was about the best part of the whole experience."

She winces. "That bad, huh?"

"Worse."

The bell rings over our heads and we slip inside to escape its insistent blare. As I spin the dial on my locker, I catch a glimpse of Zane farther down the corridor and my heart takes a flying leap into my throat. I watch him glide through the crowd, his green t-shirt snug against his chest, not stopping to talk to anyone. When he turns to go through the door of a classroom, he pauses and looks my way. I take a step forward, rising on my toes to catch a glimpse of him through the throngs of bustling students hurrying to their first period classes.

Our eyes meet and the noisy hallway falls away. The people bumping and shuffling against me disappear. All that remains are Zane's blue eyes holding onto me. They bore through my skin, seeing things no other human eye has ever seen, reading the secrets written across my soul.

"What are you doing, you stupid bitch." Someone shoves me hard enough I fall into my still-open locker. The world crashes back in on me, the voices louder and more strident than before. By the time I pull myself out of the narrow space, Zane's gone. I mutter a curse at the person who crashed my daydream, but whoever it was has already moved on.

I look for Zane at every class change, but don't catch sight of him again. By fourth period, I'm beginning to wonder if I imagined everything that happened at the party, that I read more into the look in the hallway than was actually there.

I ponder this through the beginning of my history class. I muse on it through math. Instead of solving the equations the teacher has scribbled on the whiteboard, I scribble his name across blank pages in my notebook, finding new and interesting ways to intersect the four letters making up his name. Z - A - N - E.

Vonnie's chatter distracts me briefly during lunch, but when I sit down in front of my easel in art class, the thoughts come flooding back. They remain through gym and I'm still trying to figure out the meaning on the bus home.

This is so unlike me. Oh, I've been obsessed with boys before. When I was twelve I practically fainted every time Michael O'Reilly walked into the studio. A single glance in my direction was enough to set my heart racing and sweat beading along my brow. I don't think I ever spoke to him. I didn't need to. His perfect face filled my dreams and fueled endless fantasies. When he quit dancing for hockey, I don't think I was alone with my disappointment. The dressing rooms were full of soft sniffles and carefully concealed tears.

But this is different. Zane isn't an older boy I can only fantasize about. He's real. And I don't believe I've imagined the connection between us. I just wish I understood what those jolts of energy mean. I sigh and dump the pile of envelopes in the mailbox into my backpack.

****

I'm about to head up the three steps leading to the porch when a figure appears on the lawn, squinting at the sign sitting in the middle of it. I pause and the person in the yard looks up at me. My heart does another of those death-defying leaps.

"Zane?" I take a few steps toward him.

"Uh..." He glances around like he's been caught shoplifting and is searching for a way to get out. "Oh. Hi. Stas, right?"

He forgot my name? I guess it is unusual. And we were drinking.

"Yeah. Stas. Are you stalking me or something?" I chuckle like it's a ridiculous thought.

"Stalking you? No. What are you doing here? Are *you* stalking *me*?" Zane studies the quiet street behind us for a second then turns back to examine the sign between us. "Do you go to classes here?" Zane gestures at the words 'Varushkin School of Dance' on the sign.

I laugh. "Do I look like a dancer?"

Zane takes the time to look me over, his eyes traveling across my body with such agonizing slowness it's like being dissected. I'm not sure if it's invasive or magnificent to be looked at like that, to be really seen. "What does a dancer look like?" he asks finally.

A shiver rolls down my spine and I have to fight to keep my voice steady when I say, "Like that." I point at the photograph of my mother. Even as I do it, I know it's not true. That's what a ballet dancer looks like. Not all dancers do ballet and not all dance requires that particular body type. Just dancers in my house.

"So, if you're not a dancer, what are you doing here?" he asks.

"I live here." I point to the photograph. "That's my mom."

For a second Zane looks confused, his brow knotting together between his eyes. Then it smooths out and he smiles. "Oh. So you're adopted? Cool."

I shake my head. "No. Not adopted." Wow. Even this almost-stranger can't believe I'm related to Mom. No wonder she has such a hard time with the idea I'm her own flesh and blood. "My dad's Samoan," I explain.

"Oh." Zane's face reddens. "Sorry."

It's time to change the subject. "What are you doing here? Since we've already ascertained you're not stalking."

Zane gives an embarrassed shrug. "I Googled dance schools in the area, and this one came up. Would your mom have space in one of her classes?"

"You dance?" I can't believe I hadn't figured it out. Zane has the poise and bearing of a ballet dancer. And those long, lean muscles can only have come from hours at the barre. Having been around dancers all my life, I recognize the body type. No wonder I loved the way he moved at that party.

"Yeah. I've been away from it a few months though, and I'm out of shape. Now I'm here and settled, I want to get back into it. Think your mom might take me on?"

I think my mom might die of happiness if he walks into the room. Boy dancers are few and far between even in big city ballet schools. At Mom's tiny suburban studio, she's lucky if she has four boys on her roll at any given time. And boys over thirteen or so are even rarer. She'd probably have more if she taught other styles of dance alongside ballet, but Mom won't consider it.

"She'll probably want to watch you dance first," I tell him. I want to see him dance. Not the wiggling and shaking we did at the party, real dancing. Ballet. I hope he's good. I'd be disappointed if the quiet self-confidence he exudes isn't based on real talent.

"That's cool. I brought my shoes." He taps the

battered backpack slung over his shoulder. "So, do you dance at all? Living here, I'd imagine it's kind of hard to get away from."

I nod my head in the direction of the studio behind the garage, indicating he should follow me. "I used to," I say. "But I quit."

Zane looks like he wants to ask more, but clamps his mouth shut.

I like that he knows when to quit it with the questions.

As we round the garage, the sound of piano music overtakes the noise of the wind. I don't have to look through the windows to know what the class is doing. Without my wanting them to, my feet twitch, wanting to move to the music, to trace the familiar pattern of steps the music dictates.

I lead the way through the double doors into the narrow space in front of the classroom. A handful of mismatched chairs cluster at one end and a group of mothers sit there amidst a clutter of abandoned book bags and street clothes.

"So? What now?" Zane stands inside the doorway with his hands jammed into his back pockets. His eyes travel the room, taking in the low ceiling and the worn carpets covering the bare floorboards. He takes a step forward until he reaches the glass doors to the classroom. I follow and watch the group of little girls in their tights and leotards as they finish their class with curtseys to Mom and Mrs. Archer, the pianist who has sat behind the battered upright for as long as I can remember.

"Thank you, girls." Mom's voice travels through the closed doors. "Until next week."

I wait until the horde of pre-teens has spilled out the door before pushing my way into the studio. The familiar scent of sweat and rosin and hard work fills my nostrils.

"Anastasia?" Mom strides toward us. "Why are you here? Is something wrong? Is it Teddy?"

"Hey, Mom." I shuffle forward. "This is Zane. He just started at my school and is looking for a dance class. Can you help?"

Chapter Seven

Mom's eyes scan Zane in much the same way he studied me. He stands and takes it, his gaze not wavering from hers.

"I have ten minutes," Mom says. "Show me what you can do."

I slide away to the side of the room, making myself invisible. Mom doesn't let anyone inside the studio. The glass panels in the doors are her only concession to the over-eager moms who want to see their little darlings' every move. Some days there are five or six of them pushing and shoving for a view through the two narrow panes.

Zane strips off his jacket and boots. I'm surprised when the t-shirt he's wearing isn't the same green one he wore in the hallway at school. Surprised, and, well, a little disappointed. That t-shirt fit like a second skin. And how the hell did he have time to go home and change before he came here? Didn't he say he lived downtown?

He pulls a pair of soft, black ballet slippers from his backpack and slides them onto his feet. He rolls his jeans to his knees, revealing calves knotty with muscle. Mom watches all of this with a practiced eye. She knows what she's looking for.

"Barre," she says. "Warm up."

Zane goes to the barre and works his way through the familiar warm-up routine of plies and tendus. His strength and grace are apparent even in these simple exercises. My heart thuds in my chest, heavy with excitement. Why do I feel like I'm the one auditioning? It's not like Zane is some prodigy I discovered. He found Mom's school on his own. That I came home just at the moment he showed up was luck, nothing else.

Mom gestures for him to come to the center of the room after he's done what I guess she considers enough to be warmed up. "Do you have something you can show me?"

Zane nods. "Do you have a CD player?" He bends over his backpack again, coming up with a CD in a cracked case.

Mom points to the stereo sitting on the floor.

After setting up the CD, Zane hurries back to the middle of the room. He stands in a perfect fourth position, head up, chin jutting skyward as he waits for the music to start. When it does—a spare, simple piece played on a thin, reedy instrument that sounds almost Eastern—he moves.

Oh boy, does he move.

His arms and legs whirl with precision, filleting the air. He leaps as if he has springs in his feet, soaring over the floor to land surely and without more than the softest of thuds. I can't tear my eyes away even though I'm desperate to know what Mom's face looks like. She can't help but be impressed by this.

The music stops and Zane darts across the room to stop the CD. "Sorry," he says a little breathlessly. "I'm out of shape. I haven't danced in a few months."

If this is Zane out of shape, I'm not sure what he'll be like when he's in shape. The thought sends a weird quavering feeling through me and I'm glad I'm leaning against the wall. My legs have become suddenly liquid.

"You're good," Mom says. "Who was your teacher? And why did she let you stop dancing for months?"

Zane blushes and throws his jacket back on before bending to slide the ballet shoes off his feet. "You wouldn't know her. I moved here from Rosemont. And she didn't want me to stop dancing. There were…" He pauses and a shadow passes over his face. "There were circumstances." He shrugs and gives her a smile so forced it has to be painful.

"Wednesday, Thursday, and Saturday." Mom says. "At five. Okay?"

Zane nods, his shoulders relaxing. "Perfect. See you on Wednesday, then."

I notice he doesn't ask how much the classes will be. Mom doesn't mention it either.

Zane and I have to push through a gaggle of girls to get out of the studio doors. Once we're clear of them and outside the low, wooden building, Zane grabs my hand.

"Thank you." He squeezes my fingers. "You have no idea how much I appreciate it."

I shrug, trying not to focus too much on how warm and tingly my hand feels inside his. "It's no big deal. I'm just pleased she agreed to take you on. But not surprised. You're good."

He shakes his head and drops my hand. "I'm usually better. My flexibility sucks right now. I felt it a lot in the jetes."

"Well, you on a bad day dances circles around most of the guys around here. Most of the girls too. How come you quit?" I saw him dance for about five minutes, but it was enough to see the talent oozing from every pore. And he looked like he loved every second of his performance. He didn't give up willingly, I'd bet my life on it.

Zane shuffles his feet against the loose stones on the driveway. "I…" He stops and looks away from me. "Just some stuff going on at home."

"Oh." I try to catch his eye. "Bad, huh?"

He looks back at me, a pained smile twisting his

full, beautiful lips. "Yeah. Pretty bad."

I don't want to push him, but I don't want to go inside either. Who knows what carnage Teddy will have caused today. "Well," I say, my voice far too bright and chirpy, far too eager, "If you need someone to talk to..."

"Thanks." He reaches for me again, this time resting his hand on my forearm as we make our way back into the front yard. "I might take you up on that."

I hope he does. I want to know more about this boy. I want to understand the sadness in those blue, blue eyes. But most of all, I want to dance with him. Not the drunken booty shaking we did at the party, but real dancing.

"I guess I'd better head in," I say once we've walked as far as the sign on the lawn. "See you around."

Zane grins, but the smile doesn't reach his eyes. "I hope so."

This would be the time to turn and walk away, yet somehow I can't. My feet are rooted to the spot, my eyes fixed on Zane's. Did he really say he hoped to see me again? Didn't he say the same thing on Saturday? Yet he didn't find me at school.

"Yeah. Me too," I manage to choke out.

Zane looks down, breaking the eye contact I've been drowning in. He runs the toe of his sneaker through the dusty trough under the sign.

"Guess I'll see you tomorrow?" I say in a way I hope doesn't sound too eager.

"Yeah," he says too quickly. "I'll catch you at school, huh?" Zane turns and heads toward the street, walking so fast he's almost at the corner before I realize he's moving.

****

The rest of the evening passes in a happy blur that can't even be dampened by Mom's tofu and spinach dinner.

"Yuck," Teddy whispers when he sits down at the table and sees the plate piled in front of him. "What is this?"

"Dinner," I tell him.

He gives me a skeptical look, but digs in.

Mom reaches over and gently wipes a smudge of blue paint from under Mama K's left eye. "Did you get them all sent off today?"

Mama K nods. "Everything except the cover. The publisher sent some notes on that, so I'll have to try and work them in tomorrow."

"Is that going to be easy?" Mom asks.

Mama K shrugs and runs her fork through a puddle of sauce, leaving three parallel tracks running through it. "It shouldn't be too hard. But you never know... How was your day?"

Mom smiles and glances my way. "Stas brought me something special this afternoon."

"You did?" K swivels her head to look at me.

I shrug. It's not like I discovered him or anything. "A guy from school was looking for a dance class. So I introduced him to Mom."

K turns back to Mom. "He's good?"

She nods. "Very good. Excellent, even." She turns to me. "But don't you dare tell him that. I don't need that kind of ego."

"You don't think he already knows he's good?" I shovel some spinach into my mouth.

"I hope not," Mom says darkly.

"And you were worried you wouldn't get any new students," Mama K says.

Mom gives a wistful smile. "This one I'd take without fees." She turns on me again. "But don't tell him that, either."

I roll my eyes. "Maybe I just won't talk to him ever again."

Mama K gives me a wicked grin. "Probably the best idea."

My face burns and I know I'm turning red. Stupid face. I can't keep anything from anyone. And now my Moms and Teddy all know I like this guy. I steel myself for the relentless teasing I know is coming.

"I have to watch a science documentary on TV tonight," Teddy says, saving me. "It starts at seven, so can I be excused?"

"TV as homework?" Mom clucks her tongue against her teeth.

"It's a documentary." Teddy picks up his half-full plate and heads out of the room. I wonder where I'll find his tofu dumped later on. Hopefully somewhere I can find it before it starts rotting and stinking up the house. Teddy has gotten a little too resourceful when it comes to not eating Mom's cooking.

I decide to try following his example. "I have a ton of homework too. Can I be excused?"

Mom looks at my plate, which is still almost as full as it was when I sat down and sighs. "You can be excused."

I get up and scrape my uneaten food into the compost bin. Thank goodness wasting food isn't as big a sin in my house as being fat. I do feel bad there are starving kids out there, but even someone close to death from starvation would think twice about eating Mom's tofu.

Once I'm in the safety of my room, I call Vonnie.

"Guess what?" I say as soon as she answers.

"What?"

"Zane came over this afternoon."

"What?" her voice is so high-pitched it almost

whistles. "Tell me everything."

So I do.

I tell her about his dancing and about him saying he wanted to see me again.

"He'll ask you out before the end of the week," Vonnie promises.

"You think?"

"I'd bet money on it."

It takes six pages of my history text before my heart feels like it's settling back into the place it's supposed to sit.

I'm about to give up on homework for the night and take a bath when Mama K's head appears around the door.

"Argh!" I recoil, blinking in horror before I realize the brown goop covering her face is a mud mask. "You look like the creature from the black lagoon."

She grins, cracking the mud around her mouth. "You think I look bad? Don't tell your mother. She's next."

"No, thanks. Did you want something? Other than to scare me out of my skin?"

"I did." K gives me her best puppy dog eyes. They don't work so well when her face is caked with mud. "It's garbage night and I forgot. You're still dressed. Can you put it out at the street?"

I glance at the clock. It's just after nine. Teddy will be asleep. What a pain in the butt. Garbage should be his job. "Yeah, I'll do it."

There's a lot of garbage and it takes me two trips to get the bags down to the street. I'm sweating a little as I head back up the driveway. I pause half-way up to look up at the sky. It's a clear night and the moon is large and yellow as it hangs near the horizon. But I'm not looking at the moon. It's the stars I'm interested in. All billion of them.

I'm about to head back into the house when movement catches the corner of my eye. I whip my head around and glimpse a figure rounding the corner of the house, cutting across the lawn, and heading for the street.

"Hey!" My heart leaps into my throat for the third time that day, but this time it's not a good feeling. It sits there, throbbing sickly against my tonsils.

The figure turns, the whites of their eyes gleaming in the moonlight. "Stas? What are you doing out so late on a school night?"

"Dad?" I take a few cautious steps across the lawn. "What are you doing here?"

"I needed a word with your mother," he says smoothly. "But I'm leaving now. Goodnight, Stas."

"Goodnight," I say, distracted. Why didn't Dad talk to Mom yesterday when he was here? It would have been easier than driving across town again. But then, he came from the direction of the studio, so maybe it was dance business he came for. Weird. Maybe Mom took my suggestion he teach here seriously.

That would be a first.

Chapter Eight

Despite the wind whipping around campus, Vonnie and I decide to eat lunch outside. It's only October, but already the air has a crispness to it, a bite that tells me cold weather isn't too far away. While it's even vaguely warm enough to eat outside, I want to make the most of it. I hate winter.

I pull out my lunch, eyeing the Tupperware containers with suspicion.

"What have you got?" Vonnie peers at the weird brown goo filling one of the tubs.

"No idea." I crack the lid and give a cautious sniff. It might be leftovers from last night, but I really can't tell. Mom must really want me to look emaciated in my bridesmaid gown.

I poke at the slimy stuff with my fork, then take an experimental bite from the pot. As I expected— tasteless, but with a texture I find slightly nauseating. I snap the lid closed and toss the container back into my backpack.

I make a face at Vonnie. "Maybe the whole idea behind this diet is the food's so horrible, you don't eat it and lose weight."

"Here." Vonnie hands me half her sandwich. "It's not fancy, but it looks a whole lot better than that shit."

I bite into the warm peanut butter and jelly. "You're a lifesaver, Vonnie."

A shadow falls across us and instantly the scant heat is gone. I shiver as I glance up to see what's stolen my sun.

"Um… Can I join you?" Zane shifts awkwardly from foot to foot, like he's ready to run if we refuse him.

"Of course!" Vonnie slides over and pats the

space she's made between us on the narrow bench. "I'm Vonnie, by the way."

Zane sits. Vonnie hasn't left a whole lot of space and his thigh presses against mine. "Zane."

"Nice to meet you, Zane." Vonnie jams the rest of her sandwich into her mouth and jumps up, stuffing her trash into her backpack. "I just remembered! I'm supposed to be meeting someone in the library. Catch you after school, okay, Stas?"

"Um…" Before I have a chance to say a word, she's gone, leaving me sitting there, pressed up against Zane like I'm trying to wear him.

"Your friend seems nice," Zane says after the silence has gone on too long to be comfortable.

"Vonnie? Yeah, she's great. We've been besties forever." I'm way too aware of Zane's leg and the way its warmth seeps through his jeans and my leggings. How firm it is. Now Vonnie's gone, I feel like I should shuffle over and give Zane more space, but he doesn't move, so I stay where I am, trying hard not to hyperventilate.

"Must be nice to have a friend like that."

I glance in his direction. He isn't looking at me. His eyes are forward, looking out at the trees shedding their leaves and the line of pale blue sky beyond them.

"I can't imagine life without her," I say finally. He must be lonely. He must have friends he left behind at home, maybe even someone like Vonnie. "Do you miss your friends back home?"

Zane shrugs. "Some, maybe. Others, not so much."

I bite my lip. So much of what comes out Zane's mouth feels carefully measured, like he's answering questions, but only giving as much information as he's comfortable with. And in some cases—like this one—that's very little.

He looks over at me and sighs. "Being a boy ballet dancer isn't always easy. Especially in high school."

He doesn't need to say anything else. I know what he means. I know where he's coming from. I've seen the way the male dancers from Mom's school get treated in the hallways. I've heard the abuse they've had to endure. Girl dancers tend to be awful to each other because the competition for roles and places in schools, programs, and companies is so fierce. Boy dancers take most of their crap from outsiders who don't understand what it really takes to be a dancer. You have to be pretty goddamn determined to bear all that and keep going. Determined and way more confident in yourself than I'll ever manage to be.

"I know," I say.

"Yeah. I guess you do." He gives me a watery smile before diving into his backpack and pulling out a granola bar. "So, while I do miss my friends, there aren't a whole lot of them to miss."

I don't know if that makes it easier or harder for him. "You've made some here, though, right? I mean, you came to that party with someone, didn't you?"

He nods slowly. "I've met a few people. I don't know if I'd call them friends yet, but they're okay to hang out with."

I wonder if I'm included. I look down and find I'm still holding a chunk of sandwich between my fingers. I'm not hungry anymore, but I jam it in my mouth anyway, letting the peanut butter glue my tongue to the roof of my mouth so I don't say anything that might frighten Zane away. Sometimes my mouth gets a few steps ahead of my brain.

"What do you do for fun?" he asks after a moment. "After school and stuff."

I swallow the lump of sandwich which seems to stick somewhere toward the middle of my chest. "I have to look after my little brother after school, so that kind of eliminates doing anything really fun. But I'm free on the weekends. Well, except when I have to go to my dad's place..."

I stop and bite my lip. If I want this guy to ask me out, I need to shut up. I keep talking this way, I'm making myself seem way too high maintenance.

"So, if I asked you to go bowling or play mini-golf or something, would you come?" Zane smiles.

"Bowling's fun?" I ask, the words spilling out before I know they're even in my head.

Zane stares at me. "You don't think bowling's fun?"

"I ... I don't know. I don't remember the last time I bowled." I don't know if anyone at this school has bowled since we were in about the third grade.

"That does it then." Zane balls up the wrapper of his granola bar and tosses it toward the trash can on the far side of the path. It arcs beautifully and would go in, but a gust of wind catches it and sends it rolling toward the gym. "I'm taking you bowling. Are you free on Friday?"

I nod, my tongue suddenly unable to shape words. Vonnie said he'd ask me out before the end of the week. She always knows more than me.

The bell rings and we stand, grabbing our backpacks from the ground as we turn toward the school building.

As we push through the doors, Zane grins, the first genuine smile I've seen on him. "Awesome. I'll pick you up at seven?"

"Sure." I'm grinning too. I can't help myself. Vonnie was right. Jeans should be illegal on him. And suddenly bowling, something I haven't had any desire to do for the last eight years, seems like the most exciting thing ever.

****

The house is quiet as it always is on the Tuesday nights when it's Mama K's turn to carpool Teddy and his friends to Scouts. I take my time over the dinner dishes, mentally cataloguing my wardrobe for something I can wear bowling with Zane on Friday. Now I wish I hadn't left my new jeans at Dad's.

"Stas?" Mom's voice startles me out of my thoughts and I spin around, soapsuds flying off my hands to settle in melting drifts on the brown tiled floor. "Sorry, darling. Did I give you a fright?"

I scrape the remaining suds from my fingers. "Daydreaming, I guess."

"I'm going out to the studio," Mom says. She's in her dance clothes under the stretched cardigan knotted around her waist. "Want to do a barre with me? I was late this morning and missed it."

I shake my head. "I have a ton of homework."

She nods and heads to the back door, hands expertly knotting her hair into a bun as she goes. She hesitates before going out, turns and looks back at me as if she is about to say something else, but changes her mind and slips out into the night. I plunge my hands back into the warm soapy water as I watch her hurry down the dimly lit path to the studio. Her slender silhouette stands out against the brightly lit doorway for a second before disappearing into the building. A moment later the lights in the main studio flick on.

I finish cleaning up the kitchen and settle down at the table with my history text. I've read about three paragraphs when my phone rings. I glance at the screen, half hoping it will be Zane. More than half hoping.

"Stas?" Vonnie's voice is high-pitched with excitement. We already debriefed on the Zane situation after school, so whatever is going on, it's something new. "Guess who's going to see Sidewalk Regrets this weekend?"

"You? But that show's been sold out for weeks."

"And you!" She giggles. "Robbie's sister's best friend is dating the guitarist and can get us in."

"Who's Robbie?"

Vonnie gives a dramatic sigh. "The guy from the party, Stas. Don't you ever listen to anything I say?"

"Oh! Piercings, right?" I listen. I've had a lot on my mind. Well, a lot of Zane.

"I can't this weekend. The wedding? Remember?"

"It's Sidewalk Regrets…"

Now it's my turn to sigh. Typical that my favorite band is playing in town on the one night I can't go. "It sucks, I know. But you don't want me hanging around on your date, do you? You like this guy, right?"

Vonnie's silent for a second, her breath loud in my ear. "I think I do…"

"He's hot," I add, trying to remember more about him than black leather and silver jewelry.

"*So* hot," Vonnie agrees. "And cool, too, if he's into Sidewalks." She rattles on. I wonder if Zane likes Sidewalk Regrets. Would he be impressed if I told him I could get him into their sold out show?

We keep talking until my phone's battery has slipped into the red. "I gotta go," I shout over Vonnie. "Phone's gonna die any second. See you on the steps."

"Yeah, okay. See ya." Vonnie hangs up before I do.

My charger is plugged in by my bed. As I climb the stairs, I try to figure out a way it might work. Mom and K's wedding is at two. The reception is after that, but it'll be over by 8:30. Maybe I can still make it to Sidewalk Regrets. They won't start until after nine and even the biggest party animals at the wedding will probably be fading by then.

It's only after I've plugged my phone in to charge I realize the house is still quiet. I press my phone's button again, surprised when the time flashes up 8:23. I start back down the stairs.

"Mom?" I call. "Are you back?"

She isn't, though. She would have come through the back door and I was in the kitchen the whole time. No way could she have made it in without me noticing. I cross to the kitchen windows. The main studio light is off, but the entryway still blazes with light.

"Mom?" I call again.

Mama K will be back with Teddy any minute now. Mom must have lost track of time. Or she's in her office. I shove my feet into my boots and open the back door. The night air gives my face a cold slap as I step outside. Wrapping my arms around myself, I trot down the familiar bricked path.

When I reach it, the studio door is ajar. I frown at it as it swings forward and back in the wintery breeze. Mom wouldn't leave it open like that. She keeps the door locked unless class is in session, not because there's anything much of value to steal in there, but because more than once we've found homeless people sacked out in the corners of the studios. It's been a few years since the last one, but you can't be too careful.

"Mom?" I slide through the door and close it carefully behind me. "It's almost 9:30, Mom."

Music drifts from the studio ahead of me. But it's dark. It makes no sense. I thought I was the only one who danced in the dark. And that's only because I don't want

Mom knowing I'm in there, don't want her knowing I still dance.

I take a few steps toward the studio then stop. Something isn't right. I can't put my finger on what it is, but the hair rises on the back of my neck. I take a deep breath. There. That's it. That smell. It's not the familiar scent of rosin and sweat. That's there, but over it is another scent. Sharp. Metallic.

I reach my hand out and find the panel of switches on the wall. I don't stop to fumble for the right one, just press them all down. Light explodes around me, making me blink and throw my hand up before my eyes.

As I do, I catch a glimpse of something red.

When I dare to lower my hand, I realize the red is blood. A puddle of it. A thick, viscous puddle spreading across the blond wood floorboards.

And my mother lies in the middle of it.

Chapter Nine

My hand jerks out and hits the light switches again. This isn't real. My eyes are playing tricks on me. This can't be real.

Cautiously I press down on a single switch this time, not wanting to blind myself. The studio lights brighten to reveal the same crimson pool, my mother's form still sprawled in the middle of it.

I can't breathe. Air stays trapped in a painful lump somewhere toward the middle of my chest.

This isn't real.

It's a dream.

A bad, bad dream. I'll wake up soon.

My lungs contract painfully, and I bark as the air escapes in a single gasp. And then I'm breathing again, the coppery tang of fresh blood searing the inside of my nostrils with each labored breath.

"Mommy?" My voice is too small. Too haunted.

That can't be Mom down there. Mom's never still. Mom would never let her bun sit askew, tendrils trailing across her neck and cheeks. Mom was all grace. She would never lie with legs and arms splayed in awkward, unattractive angles. She would never look at me with glassy, staring eyes, the pale blue iris already starting to cloud over.

She's dead.

I don't need to touch her to know that.

I don't need to get any nearer.

My hand trembles as I reach into the pocket of my jeans for my phone. I have to call someone. Mama K, maybe? No. That's not right. Vonnie? The police.

The thought ricochets through my skull at the same time I remember I don't have my phone. It's back in the house, sitting uselessly on the charger. I start toward the door, my legs soft as cotton wool. I have to get my phone. I need it. My phone. My phone.

I stop at the door. The wind whips the trees around so their shadows seem to dance across the patches of light spilling into the yard. My hand freezes on the doorknob. What if whoever did this is still out there? I can't force myself to take another step.

The office.

There's a phone in the office.

A sob of relief escapes my trembling lips. I stumble down the hallway, away from the shell of my mother on the studio floor, away from the scent of blood.

The office is dark, the door closed, blinds drawn. That's normal. Mom always keeps the blinds drawn if she's not in there. The thought isn't reassuring, though. Anyone could be hiding behind the door. Anything.

My whole body shakes as I stand in the dimly lit hallway. I can't go in. But I can't leave either. The world I felt comfortable moving through minutes ago has suddenly become terrifying and dangerous.

I glance around and catch sight of a fire-extinguisher mounted on the wall. Without thinking, I grab it, tearing it free and raising it before me. It's surprisingly heavy and its weight and heft make me feel braver. Brave enough to kick open the door to the office, anyway.

I burst into the tiny closet-like room brandishing the metal cylinder before me. Behind the desk a pair of filing cabinets loom, shadowy sentries.

There's no one there.

The fire extinguisher hits the floor with a clang and rolls away under the desk. I dive in the same direction and snatch up the phone. My hands shake so much it takes me three goes before I manage to punch the numbers.

"Hello? Police?" I shout before the phone has even started ringing. "Hello? Hello? Police?"

****

I can't stay in there with Mom, but I can't leave her alone either. So I end up pacing the covered entryway while I wait for the police to arrive. It doesn't take long. It feels like only seconds before a car pulls up the driveway and paints the night with flashes of red, white, and blue. Two uniformed police officers climb out of the vehicle. With their heavy belts laden with tools and weapons, the men are too large when they join me in the confined, covered space.

"Can we…?" They gesture at the studio door and I step aside to let them in. I should follow, but I can't force my feet to move in that direction. The wall I'm leaning against seems to have softened and threatens to swallow me whole.

The door closes behind the police and I sink further into the wall. Maybe it will let me fall through. Maybe on the other side is a world where this hasn't happened. A world in which my mom isn't dead.

An engine slows and I look up. Mama K's car pulls into the driveway behind the police car. It's barely stopped before she's out and running toward me.

"What happened?" she cries, her eyes wild and frightened, her mouth twisted into a grotesque shape by worry.

"Mom…" I can't go on. How can I tell Mama K she's dead? My mouth won't shape the words. My lips keep repeating the same word over and over again. "Mom. Mom. Mom. Mom."

Mama K gives up on me and pushes me aside as she busts through the doors. More police cars are arriving. An ambulance. Radios spit and crackle through the night air. Teddy's white, frightened face peeks out the window of Mama K's car. He catches my eye and pales even more. I start toward him, but he ducks down below the window before I reach the vehicle. When I reach for the door handle, he punches down the lock and drops back into the footwell.

"Teddy?" I rap on the window with my knuckles. "Let me in, Teddy."

He curls up tighter.

"Please, Teddy? Please?"

For a second I'm sure he's not going to move, but slowly, very slowly, he raises his hand and pulls up the lock button. I open the door and climb in, careful not to step on him as I do.

"What happened?" he whispers, his voice trembling.

I open my mouth to tell him, but nothing comes out. The words have dried into husks in my throat. I don't know what happened. I just know what I saw. How can I tell my baby brother our mom is dead?

"I…" I shrug helplessly.

He's only eleven. Not a baby anymore, but far too young to have to face this. I'm barely coping. I'm not coping. How the hell can Teddy deal with this?

He climbs out of the footwell and sits beside me. Right beside me. I feel the way his ribs expand with every breath. It's like suddenly I have an extra body part attached to mine.

"I'm scared," he whispers.

I want to comfort him. I want there to be something I could say that would help. There are no words that could make anything better now. There are lies and there's the truth. Neither feels like the right decision. So I hug him and for once he lets me.

****

Teddy and I sit together a long time, looking at the people moving in and out of the studio through the open car door. I don't understand anything being said, simply watch the weird waltz as people mill around.

Nothing catches my attention until Mama K is led out by a pair of cops. I sit up straighter, my arms tightening around Teddy, pressing his head into my side. Mama K's head is bowed, her shoulders slumped so far she looks like she's folding in half. She doesn't glance our way, doesn't protest when the policemen lead her to a car and help her into the backseat. The door closes behind her, the other two cops move around to the front doors and get in. It's only once the engine roars to life I realize what's happening.

"No!" I extricate myself from Teddy's heavy, clinging limbs and struggle my way out of the car. "Mama K! Mama K!"

The car eases out of the driveway and I follow. My legs tingle with pins and needles after having Teddy's weight on me for so long. I stagger like a drunkard, falling to one knee before scrambling back to my feet and running after the vehicle. It's too late, though. By the time I reach the street, the police car has roared away, lights flashing.

"No!" I cry again, a sharp stab of loss piercing my chest. I already lost Mom. They can't take Mama K too.

Two men sidle up to me and take my arms, not roughly, but in a way that supports the legs threatening to collapse under me at any second. They're not dressed as cops, but something about them screams cop at me.

"Are you Anastasia Nonu?" one of them asks. He's the shorter of the two, but makes up for his lack of height with the broadest shoulders I've ever seen. A thin, reddish mustache creeps across his upper lip like an anorexic caterpillar. "I'm Detective McMillan and this is my partner Detective Allan."

"Yes," I manage. They asked for Anastasia Nonu. Were they expecting someone else?

"What's going on?" My heart thumps too hard against my ribs.

The other detective steps forward with his hat in his hand, his head bowed. "Is your mother Irena Varushkin?"

I nod, a sick feeling rising in my throat.

"And you found her tonight? You called the police?"

I nod again. They don't think I did it, do they? They don't think I killed her?

I notice tiny details about the man standing in front of me—the small, fish-hook shaped scar near the corner of his left eye, a fresh shaving nick on his chin. His mouth moves, but I hear nothing.

"...Anastasia?" My name breaks through the fog. Someone touches my shoulder. The one called Allen crouches by me, his eyes level with mine. The world rushes back, louder and more confusing than ever. "Do you need a drink of water, Anastasia?"

Water. For a second I can't think what it even is. "No." My voice sounds strangled and strange, not at all like mine.

"Anastasia?" The police officer with the mustache, McMillan, leans toward me again. "When you're ready, would you to come with us? We need to get some information from you."

Information? I stare up at him. What kind of information? And talking of information, there's some I'd like too.

"How... How did she..." I swallow hard, the word 'die' stuck inside me with barbs so sharp they pierce the lining of my chest. I try again. "How. Did. She.

Die?"

I saw her. I saw the blood. I have ideas and images in my head. But I need to hear it from them. I need to be certain I'm not imagining this.

Detective Allen shuffles his feet and tugs at the belt-loops of his ill-fitting pants. "It's really too early to say. We're investigating the scene to get a better idea what might have happened. But from the looks of it, I think we have to consider it might be murder."

****

Murder?

I stare at the detective, my eyes straining with the intensity of my gaze. Murder? Mom? The two things make no sense together. Who would murder Mom? She had no enemies. At least, not that I know of. Sure, there are people out there who might not agree with her lifestyle choices—I'm not exactly a fan of her bizarre diets—but murder?

"H-H-How?" I manage finally. But I don't really want an answer. There was blood and with blood comes pain. However she died, I already know she suffered.

"The cause of death is yet to be ascertained," McMillan says. "The victim sustained stab wounds to the chest and abdomen, but until the autopsy has been performed, we can't assume it to be the cause of death."

I hate the way he talks. Victim. That's my mother you're talking about, pal. And believe me, she's no one's victim. Mom's tough. She got out of Russia, didn't she? She made it as a dancer, which has to be one of the most highly competitive professions there is. She divorced my dad when she fell out of love with him. That takes guts.

"Is there anyone you'd like me to call for you, Anastasia?"

"Mama K?" I choke out, blushing at how childish the name sounds. But I *was* a child when Mom and K got together, and I couldn't pronounce her given name, Kyung-Seok. She's been Mama K to me ever since. And because that's what I called her, Teddy started calling her Mama K too. Now even Mom calls her K. Everyone does. "Where'd you guys take Mama K?"

"Would that be Kyung-Seok Lim?" Detective Allen coughs and stares down at his shoes. I follow his gaze and study the scuffed brown brogues he wears.

"Yes." I nod.

"We took Ms. Lim into custody." McMillan's voice is too smooth, too sure of itself.

My head snaps up. "Why?" Mama K is in jail? It makes no sense.

"As the closest person to your mother, we need to question her. She may know something about what happened."

"You don't think..." I trail off. I can't even finish the thought. These people can't possibly think Mama K had anything to do with this. She'd never do anything to hurt Mom. They never even fight. Sometimes their lovey-dovey stuff makes me want to gag, but there's no denying how much the pair of them care about each other. I mean, god! They're days away from getting married. "She wasn't even here. She was with my brother. They just got back now."

McMillan stiffens his shoulders before he looks my way again. "At this point we have to chase any lead. Most murders are committed by someone the victim knows, and more often than not, by someone close to them."

If that's the case, why aren't they questioning me? I was here. Kids fight with their parents, sometimes even kill them in a fit of rage. How can they know I didn't kill her? I guess I must look too stunned, too shattered, too something for them to even suspect me.

This cannot really be happening. I pinch my thigh, grabbing as much flesh as I can between my nails and squeezing as hard as I'm able. The sharp, bright pain makes me gasp. But the two cops are still there. I'm awake, and this is real.

My stomach hollows out.

"Teddy?" I ask, flicking my eyes between the two policemen. "I need to get my brother. He doesn't know yet. I didn't tell him. Do I..." The words stick in my throat, too thick and heavy to swallow or spit out. "Do I have to tell Teddy?"

"You don't have to do anything," Allen says in a surprisingly comforting voice. "If you'd rather we broke the news, we can do it. Or we can wait until Teddy is with his mother. I believe Kyung-Seok is Teddy's mom?"

I nod. K is Teddy's birth mother. Because Mom had already experienced the joys—or trials—of childbirth, when she and K decided they wanted a child of their own, one they wouldn't have to share with anyone, they also decided K would carry the new baby. But there was never any question of Teddy being only K's. He is their kid, Mom and K's, even if none of Mom's genetic material is in his make-up. The same way I'm their kid. The only difference is my dad is someone we know, someone Mom used to love, whereas Teddy's dad is an anonymous sperm donor. It doesn't make us any less of a family.

My legs feel like soggy noodles. I don't want to be here anymore. I still feel like the scent of Mom's blood clings to me. My lungs struggle to expand enough to draw in air. I don't care if I have to go to the police station to answer questions. I just want to be with my family. I need to make sure Mama K is all right. I need to protect Teddy from this news. I need to figure out who might have done this to my mother.

Chapter Ten

The police station is loud and bustling. Teddy clings to me as we walk through the heavy glass doors and find ourselves in a corridor lined with long wooden benches. A desk sits at one end and a stern-looking female cop sits behind it, eyes roving across anyone entering the building. Any time one of the people sitting on the benches moves, she pins them back into position with a glare that could freeze fire. I shiver. This place gives me the creeps.

"Where's Mama K?" Teddy asks me, his voice far quieter than usual. "I want Mama K."

I keep an arm wrapped around him. "She's here somewhere," I tell him. But where? In a cell somewhere? I hope not. Teddy shouldn't ever have to see his mother in a jail cell. I shouldn't have to see that.

Allen and McMillan stride to the counter and lounge against it while they speak to the terrifying woman cop. I hang back, keeping Teddy close to me. One of the guys on the bench is either really drunk or insane. He shakes his head and mutters to himself, hands gesticulating wildly as he explains something only he can understand to the air. One of the others, a bulky guy with a shaved head and a tiny star tattooed at the corner of his eye, leers at me. When he catches me looking in his direction, he winks and makes a suggestive gesture at his bulging crotch.

Gross.

I turn away to face the wall, but it doesn't make me feel a whole lot better. I can feel his eyes on me, prying at my clothes as if trying to tear them off with the force of his stare. My skin crawls. I wish I could take a shower to wash away the slimy tracks of disgust and shame his gaze leaves as it scrapes over me.

"Come on through." Allen appears by my side and puts a hand on my shoulder to guide me past the desk and through the heavy doors beyond it. I breathe a sigh of relief once they close behind me.

We walk through a maze of corridors. The walls are all painted a uniform, dull gray that blends with the stark concrete floors and ceilings. It's like being in a bunker or something. Or inside a storm cloud.

The two cops stop outside a door painted a faded, olive green. McMillan knocks once, then again a second later. The door swings open to reveal a small room with a table and several uncomfortable-looking folding chairs. A thick-hipped female cop with what Mom would call a lesbian haircut fills the doorway. Behind her I catch a glimpse of Mama K, her head bowed against the tabletop. What did they do to her? What did they ask her?

"Mama!" Teddy cries and bolts from my side. I reach for him, but he dodges my hand and ducks under the policewoman's arm to run across the room.

At the sound of his voice, Mama K lifts her head. Before Teddy has even reached the table, she's standing, arms open for him to rush into. He hurls himself into her embrace, burying his face into her shoulder. She holds him so tightly I'm surprised he doesn't turn purple. She turns and looks my way, her face chalky, eyes bloodshot and red-rimmed. Her lips are white from being pressed so tightly together. I'm sure mine match hers. My jaw aches from the pressure of holding in the howls of grief forcing their way up my throat.

"Stas…" She chokes out my name and unfolds one arm from around Teddy to reach for me. "Oh, Stas…"

Tears cling to her eyelashes and she blinks them back. My own eyes burn, but I fight the desire to give in to them. Not here. Not now. Not with Teddy watching. With all these cops.

I stumble across the floor and into Mama K's arms. She draws me close, pressing me in against her and Teddy. I have a million questions I want to ask her, but they're stuck in my throat, trapped behind the billiard-sized lump swelling there.

"Who would do this?" she whispers into my ear. "Who could hurt my Rennie?"

My chest hollows out at the sound of her nickname for Mom. Only K calls Mom that. To everyone else she's Irena or Ms. Varushkin. Or to her students, Madame. Those names suit Mom with her erect posture and severely tight bun. If there was a fun-loving Rennie inside, only K knew her.

"Ms. Lim?" The female cop clears her throat and swaggers her way around the table to join us. "Thank you for your time. If you can think of anything else that might help us with the investigation, please call me on this number." She hands Mama K a card. "Rest assured we will be doing everything within our power to find out who did this."

Mama K gives an almost imperceptible nod and begins moving Teddy and I with her toward the door.

"Your mother is on her way," McMillan tells K from the doorway. "If you'd like to wait in the lounge? I think you might find it more comfortable."

Mama K gives another vague movement of her head. She's in shock. She's not functioning right. And who could blame her? The woman she loves, the woman she's given the last twelve years of her life to, is dead. And she's had to sit here for god knows how long being questioned about it.

"This way," McMillan says gently.

Mama K allows herself to be led through the

doorway, Teddy still clutched against her like a baby possum or something. When the female cop holds me back from following them, Teddy's eyes widen in fear.

"Anastasia?" The woman runs her fingers through short, choppy blonde hair. "Could you stay for a moment? I'm Marcia Adams, and I'd like to ask you a few questions."

There's a steeliness to her words I can't fight against. I have the right to say no to her and her questions, but her tone tells me doing that wouldn't make me any friends around here. Besides, I have nothing to hide.

"I don't know anything," I say as I cross to the table and lower myself onto the cold, hard seat behind it. I wish I could say something more, wish I knew something that would help them find out who did this.

****

Marcia Adams doesn't sit down right away. "Can I get you a drink? Coke? Coffee? Water?"

I shake my head. My stomach churns so wildly I wouldn't be able to keep anything down. I stare at the now-closed door, willing it to open again, for Teddy and Mama K to be back here with me. I don't want to be alone in here with this woman and her questions. I have too many questions of my own.

"Are you sure?" Adams studies me. She's not dressed like a cop. At least, she's not wearing a uniform. But I can see the tell-tale bulge of a gun under her dark blue blazer.

I nod, and this time she seems to accept it. She sits across from me, taking off the blazer and hanging it across the back of her seat. I was right about the gun. It's in a holster under her arm. I wonder if she's ever shot anyone.

She catches me staring at it. "Sorry. It's

intimidating, I know." She shrugs out of the holster and sets it aside, hanging it under the blazer so it's out of my sight. "I never thought I'd get used to carrying a weapon, but I feel naked without it now."

I don't know what to say. I've never touched a gun, let alone fired one. I wonder again if she's ever shot anyone. And if she enjoyed doing it if she has. That thought leads me to Mom. Did someone shoot her? No. Stab wounds. That's what the guy said. Multiple stab wounds.

My head gets very light and floaty, like it might fly off my shoulders at any second. I clap my hand on top of it to keep it in place. Shockwaves reverberate through my skull. The room swims then settles back in place. The familiar weight is back, now with the added bonus of a throbbing knot somewhere toward the center. Guess I don't know my own strength.

The room is silent for a long moment before Adams clears her throat and looks directly at me. Her eyes are brown and full of sympathy. My throat thickens again.

"I'm sorry about your mother," she begins. "I realize this must be a very difficult time for you, but I need to ask you a few questions, now, while everything's still fresh in your mind."

I nod. I've watched *CSI* and those other crime shows. I know the procedure.

"When was the last time you saw your mother?" Adams has a looseleaf notebook in front of her, a fine-tipped felt pen poised over it.

"Tonight. I was in the kitchen when she went out to the studio."

"This was at the house on North Garrett?"

I nod and she scribbles something down.

"What time did she leave the house?" She taps the

pen against her lower lip as she looks expectantly at me.

I shrug. "Around 7:30, I guess? Maybe just after?" I don't wear a watch. I know Teddy and K left right after dinner because Scouts starts at 7:30.

"Was there anything unusual the way she left? Did your mother act any differently than usual?"

I rub my fingers across my eyebrows, trying to remember. I picture the kitchen, me at the sink up to my elbows in dishwater. Nothing feels wrong or out of place about the scene. "No. It was normal. She asked me to come and dance with her and I said no. Same as always." I recall the way she looked at me when she asked me to dance with her. Would she be alive now if I'd said yes? My stomach wrenches and for a second I think I might puke.

Adams continues to probe. "So, you were in the kitchen when she left. How much longer were you there?"

"The rest of the night," I'm more certain this time and the words come out more powerfully. "I started my homework, then my friend Vonnie called and we talked until my phone's battery died. I went up to my room to put the phone on the charger and that's when I realized Mom hadn't come back inside."

"So you went looking for her?"

"Well, yeah. I needed to ask her something. And it was weird she wasn't back yet because a barre usually takes about forty minutes at the most. But Mom's maybe a little more intense at the moment, because she's stressed about the wedding. I know dancing helps when she's anxious, so I wasn't really worried or anything."

"Ah, yes. The wedding. Coming up on Saturday, right?"

It's that soon, isn't it? I was just talking to Vonnie about it. It seems impossible it's this week. No wonder

Mom's so psycho. A wedding in five days, and her daughter still a blimp who's going to ruin all her photos by looking like a beach ball.

"Saturday," I confirm, then realize it won't be happening on Saturday. I won't be wearing the ugly orange dress. Mom and K will never be married. The thought hits me like a fist to the gut and I find it hard to suck in my next breath.

"Pretty brave of your moms to be putting together such a big wedding, huh?"

"Brave?" I stare at her, still struggling to breathe.

"I just mean, so soon after the law change. A wedding like that. It's kind of a big screw you to the conservatives who have kept same-sex marriage out of legislation for so long." She eyes me cautiously. "A lot of people aren't happy with the law change."

"I know." I feel my lips twisting into a wry smile. "Like my dad."

"Your dad's not happy about the wedding?" Adams pounces on the idea like a puppy on a treat.

Uh oh. What did I just get myself into? "Well, not exactly…"

"Can you tell me anything more about your father?"

"What do you want to know?" I raise my eyebrows. She can't think Dad had anything to do with this. He and Mom aren't best buddies, but they're still mostly friendly. Civil, anyway. When their relationship ended, I don't think it was terrible. I was only four, but I don't remember shouting and screaming or anything traumatic about that time. I've always thought theirs was a love that burned too brightly at the start, then faded to ashes.

"How long were your parents together?" Adams asks.

"Um… Not too long. I think about five years. They met when Mom was on tour with the Bolshoi. They're both dancers, but really different dancers. I think that was what ended things. Not to mention the different worlds they came from."

Mom's told me this story over and over. When I was a kid it was my favorite fairy tale. Mom, the prima ballerina with the Bolshoi, arriving here, hungry for knowledge of the world outside the narrow walls of her company and her country. She saw Dad dancing on a street-corner by her hotel and was captivated by the rhythm and the acrobatics he performed as part of his act.

When they danced together, sparks flew.

But where there are sparks, there's fire.

"When the relationship ended between your parents, was Kyung-Seok on the scene already?" Adams flips over the page in her notebook. Her handwriting is narrow and even, filling each line from beginning to end.

I shake my head. It was almost a year before K stepped into our lives. "K and Mom met later. At a yoga class. They were friends a long time before it became more."

I remember the day Mom told me K was coming to live with us. She'd already been around so much, it didn't feel like a big deal. Mom was so much happier than she'd been in a long time, and I liked seeing her smile, hearing her laugh. I liked K too, because she snuck me candy when Mom wasn't looking and let me read comics when we went to the library. I felt so lucky to have two moms. It wasn't until later, at school, I realized it made me different.

"Has your father ever expressed anger or resentment at your mother's relationship?" Adams's eyebrows pull together.

Now that's a tricky one. "I was pretty young at

the time…" I don't know how to answer this. "I mean, I don't think he was thrilled, but what guy would be if his ex shacked up with a woman? He's never rude to K, though."

I don't quite know how to express my thoughts. My mother's dead. That thought overwhelms everything else. Thinking back, remembering her, makes the ache in my chest worse. But at the same time, I cling to those memories. They're all I have of her now. All I'll ever have.

"You mean, your father felt threatened by K?"

I pick at a loose thread in my skirt. "Not exactly. Maybe…" What guy wouldn't feel threatened when he was replaced? Especially being replaced by a woman. Kind of a big kick to the manhood. And if there's one thing Dad is irrationally proud of, it's his masculinity. Maybe it's because he's a dancer and dancing is so often considered a feminine thing. Or it could be part of his Samoan upbringing. Nana always said if he'd stayed in Sava'ii, he would have been a chief.

"Has your father said anything about the wedding?"

Has he? I roll my eyes. "Oh, yeah. He has very definite opinions."

Adams cracks a wry smile. "And I'm guessing he's not for it?"

"No. Not really. Dad's started going to church a lot more since my Nana died. And if the sermon last time I went was anything to go by, his church is definitely not behind the new laws." My throat tightens at the memory. Does Dad actually believe the shit the pastor spouted? I wish I knew. I wish I'd asked him. How hard would it have been to question him about his beliefs? But Dad and I don't talk like that. Not anymore.

"Thank you." Adams gets up and gestures me to

follow her to the door. "You've been very helpful. You can go and join your family now."

As I follow her directions to the lounge down the hallway, I can't help thinking I've just dumped my father into a world of trouble.

Chapter Eleven

Mama K and Teddy are squished together in an armchair too small for the two of them when I reach the lounge. Teddy's thumb is in his mouth the way it always was when he was a baby. It took years for my moms to get him to stop sucking it. Yet K doesn't even seem to notice it's plugged back in there again.

K's mom—we call her Halmoni, a Korean word for grandparent—sits on the couch across from them, her face a mask of anguish as she threads a tissue through her fingers. Here's someone who has definitely never liked Mom and K's relationship. It's only been in the last couple of years, since K's dad died, that she and her mother have been on speaking terms again. Her family basically disowned her when she came out in college. K told me once she'd known she was queer since she was about twelve, but it took until she was twenty-one to finally act on it. I can't imagine what it must have been like. I guess I'm lucky to have grown up in a time and place so much more tolerant of difference.

Just not tolerant enough.

"Are they done with you?" K asks finally.

"I think so." I perch myself on the arm of the chair, rubbing my palm across Teddy's fine, soft hair. He slaps me away. He might be sitting here sucking his thumb, but he's not going to let me treat him like a baby.

"We should go then. This place gives me the heebie-jeebies." K gives Teddy a squeeze. "C'mon, Champ. We're going to Halmoni's."

K has to sign all kinds of paperwork to get us away from the police station. I zone out after a while, listening to the low, droning voices giving list after list of instructions and directions. There are apparently a huge number of things we need to do. Things I don't even want to think about doing. The numbness that washed over me is wearing off now, and loss jabs at my gut. I can't get my head around the fact Mom's gone. I need to go home. I need to see for myself she's not there. Until I feel the empty spaces she usually fills, I know I'm not going to believe she's really gone.

Halmoni drives us home to pick up clothes and pajamas and toothbrushes. The yellow crime tape surrounding the property sends a wave of sickness rolling through me. My hand freezes on the car's door handle, and for a moment I'm certain I can't get out. Nausea rises in my throat, sour and acidic. I swallow it back with difficulty and step out of the vehicle. My legs tremble and tears prickle against my eyelids as I catch sight of the stupid sign in the middle of the lawn, my mother's graceful body in its perfect arabesque appearing to mock me.

A policeman lifts the tape to allow us entry and follows us as far as the porch. I can't tell if it makes me feel better or worse to know there's someone here guarding the place Mom was killed. Isn't it too late now? If he'd been there...

No. I can't think like that. No one has guarded our property for the last seventeen years. And no one has been murdered here either. And who's to say a guard could have stopped it happening even if there had been someone here? I was here and I couldn't stop it. I wasn't even aware it had happened. Shouldn't I have felt something? The connection between us breaking, or something?

I dash upstairs to my room, keeping my eyes from wandering away from my path. Without much thought, I chuck jeans and sweaters and underwear into an old gym bag I find in my closet. The house feels wrong. Empty.

Abandoned. How can so much have changed? Can it really have been only hours ago I last saw her?

I drift to the window and look down at the buildings below. All the lights are on. More yellow tape surrounds the studio, a red notice plastered across the glass doors. Taking my bag with me, I slip from the room and creep down the stairs. From somewhere behind me, I hear sobs but can't tell if they're K's or Teddy's. My throat tightens. I don't want to know.

I let myself out the back door so I don't attract the attention of our police-guard. The path from here to the studio is so familiar, I could walk it in my sleep. Yet it feels different now. The last time I walked this path I had a mother. I stop at the police tape and stare across at the doors. The red notice warns people not to cross the crime tape, that this is the scene of an ongoing investigation, that tampering with evidence or crossing the line is punishable by law.

I stare beyond the notice, into the studio itself. The dark shadow on the floor catches my eye and my gut turns cold. It's not a shadow. It's blood. Her blood.

The vomit I swallowed back earlier spews out of me in one great acidic glurt. I drop to my knees, not even feeling the gravel bite through the worn fabric of my jeans. There can't be anything in my stomach, yet that doesn't stop my body from retching up bile until I'm so weak I can barely hold myself upright.

I close my eyes and all I can see is the patch of darkness on the floor. All that's left of my mother is a pattern of blood across the boards. I wish I could be in there, that I could scoop up every drop and push it back into my mother's body. It will have cooled by now, may even have dried in places, but I don't care. It's still her blood, and even if it can't bring her back to life, it belongs inside her body. The body lying in the coroner's office, possibly already sliced open as they do the autopsy to find out exactly how she died.

I stare at the blood. That's how she died. How can there be any question about it? Someone came into the studio while she was alone and hurt her until her blood pooled on the floor. While I sat in the kitchen gossiping to Vonnie about boys and music and all kinds of other meaningless crap. How could I have been so close and not heard anything, not felt the moment her life was snuffed out?

"Stas?" K calls my name. "Stas? Where are you?"

I hurry toward the back door. K can't see this. The blood will ruin her. Or has she already seen it? She probably did when she raced in there after coming home to find police cars in the driveway.

"I'm here." I push through the door and find the others on the front porch. Wind blasts through the open doors, creating a tiny tornado in the center of the kitchen. School notices and bills whirl into the air and float to the floor in haphazard patterns. I slam the door behind me, stilling the cyclone.

"You found her?" K asks in a low voice after she joins me on the porch.

I nod. "Did you see…"

She shakes her head. "The police stopped me."

Thank god. No one should ever have to see something like that. I doubt I'll ever get the grotesque image out of my consciousness. It'll wait for me every time I close my eyes.

"I have to go and identify the body, though." K's voice wobbles. "I don't know if I can do it."

I swallow hard. "Do you want me to come with you?" I have no idea if I can do it either, but I have to try. Even after seeing her sprawled body and the drying blood, I can't accept Mom's gone. Maybe viewing the body somewhere else will make it real to me, will make this feel like something more than a bad dream I can't wake myself up from.

Time has become screwy. We've been at the police station all night. The sun hangs in the sky like an inflating balloon as we haul our stuff into Halmoni's tiny house. Once we're done, Halmoni distracts Teddy with cartoons and candy while K and I slip back out.

At the car, K tosses me the keys. "I can't," she says simply.

I slide behind the wheel and adjust the seat. Halmoni must be tiny. The seat sits so far forward my boobs press painfully against the steering wheel.

"Okay?" K fastens her seatbelt and stares bleakly through the windscreen. "You know the way to the hospital?"

I nod. Of course I do. I spent too much time there with Nana.

I wonder if Dad has been hauled into the police station. Is Adams questioning him the same way she questioned me? What will he say? That it's a just punishment from god? Did he wish this on her? On us? Did he do it?

"No." I say aloud. "No way."

K raises her eyebrows. "Huh?"

"Nothing." There's no point voicing my fears. Dad and K aren't best friends anyway. They tolerate each other because of Mom and me, but there's certainly no affection between them.

We drive in silence. Is K's head as jumbled and chaotic as my own? Mom's dead. I say the words over and over, but they don't ring true. They don't make sense. Mom can't be dead. All I can think about is the stupid fights we've had. About jeans and kale and other things totally meaningless right now. I should have been nicer to her. I shouldn't have been embarrassed by her Russian accent. I shouldn't have answered her in English every time she tried to speak to me in her native tongue. I shouldn't have refused her invitations to the movies or the theater or just to go shopping at the mall. The regrets pile up in teetering stacks to weigh down my soul.

I should have kept up my dance classes.

It would have made her so happy. Even if we both knew my body isn't perfect for ballet, the love of dance was something we shared. I realize now how little we had between us once I refused to come to class anymore.

Chapter Twelve

We don't have to enter the main hospital doors to get to the morgue. There's a small, almost secret, side entrance. We miss it twice because the bushes lining the path are so overgrown they conceal the fact a door even exists. When we finally reach it, we have to push a bell to be allowed in and declare our names to the disembodied voice squawking through the intercom.

A tall, thin man meets us at the door. He has a grey mustache and a hunch. His white lab-coat is too big for him and flaps around his narrow frame like a bedsheet.

"You're here for Varushkin?" he asks, squinting down at the clipboard he's holding.

"Yes," K says and her voice wobbles. Other than the flat, glazed look in her eyes, it's the first sign of emotion I've seen from her. I wonder if, like for me, the reality is only just beginning to sink in.

"You'll have to wait until the police get here, so take a seat." He leads us to a cramped waiting area consisting of three worn couches. They look so decrepit and dirty, I don't want to sit on them for fear of catching something.

K sits. "I didn't realize the police had to be here."

"Oh, yeah." The man fingers his mustache. "For identifications, anyway. If it's a social visit, I'm enough."

Social visit? How social can visiting a dead person be?

K gestures for me to sit next to her, so I drop down gingerly, trying not to let any bare skin touch the couch. It's cold in here. Even with my jacket on. And it smells weird. Like alcohol and bleach and something slightly sweet that makes my stomach turn over sickly.

I jump when the buzzer goes off, announcing the police arrival. The thin man hurries off to admit them and I'm not surprised to recognize the same two cops who spoke to me in the driveway.

"Anastasia." McMillan nods at me when he enters the room first.

I return his nod, not trusting my voice all of a sudden.

My mother is behind those bolted metal doors at the end of the room. My dead mother.

Cold sweat oozes its way down my spine. My hands tremble so much I have to sit on them to keep them still. I don't really need to see this, do I? I already saw her. I already know she's dead.

"Right this way." The thin man punches a code into a keypad on the wall and the heavy doors swing open. K gets up from beside me and follows him, Detective Allen trailing behind.

McMillan pauses and looks over his shoulder at me. "Coming?"

I swallow hard and struggle to get off the couch I never wanted to sit on. My legs shake almost as hard as my hands. Do I really want to go in there?

"You don't have to, if you don't want to." McMillan's voice is gentle. He's speaking like that to make me feel better, but somehow his niceness makes me angry.

"I want to." The words come out far louder than I mean them to. "I'm coming."

Pushing in front of him, I hurry to catch up with K. She shouldn't be alone when she does this. I'm not sure I'll be able to offer much in the way of support, but I can be there. I've already seen Mom once, so this shouldn't be such a shock to me. Shouldn't.

The thin man stands in front of a bank of what

look like large filing drawers. I guess that's what they are, really. The thought doesn't do anything to slow my heart's rapid pounding. He reaches up and pulls on the handle of one. The drawer glides open without a sound, a sheet-draped figure lying inside. Without a pause, the thin man lifts the sheet off the figure before stepping away to give us space to view it.

K doesn't look right away. She stares at the ground and her shoulders heave as she sucks in deep breaths. When she does shuffle forward, she keeps her gaze downward until she's almost touching the metal drawer.

"Stas," she whispers, turning and reaching a hand out to me. "Please…"

Gulping, I take her hand and let her draw me forward. Now I'm staring at the floor too, at the worn, green linoleum scored with wheel-marks from a thousand gurneys.

"I can't do it," K whispers. "I can't look."

I glance over at her and see how pale and drawn her face is. Hollows seem to have been scooped out under her eyes. I squeeze her hand and nod. I'll do it. I'll look first. I raise my head, keeping my face turned away. I want to be ready for this. I breathe five or six deep, steadying breaths before I allow my head to turn.

The first thing I see is her hair. It's loose and lies in a tangled mass across the pillow. I wonder vaguely why they've given her a pillow. It seems odd to offer comfort to someone who's dead. I trace the length of a single blonde strand to her face.

Her face is the color of chalk and her lips, still bearing a coat of the blood-red lipstick she never went without, are twisted into a grimace. I know her eyes reflect the anguish and pain she clearly felt in the moment she died, but thankfully they're closed this time so I don't have to look at it.

And she's dead.

Seeing her lying there makes it real. Really real. My mother was never still. She fluttered her hands when she spoke. She never sat for long, always preferring to speak while moving about, doing some other chore while holding a conversation.

Now she's still. Permanently still.

"Is this Irena Varushkin?" McMillan's voice startles me at my shoulder.

"Yes."

K makes a small noise in her throat. She throws herself at the corpse, her body heaving with the weight of the sobs convulsing through her. She rains kisses on my mother's cheeks and claws at the sheet covering her body.

After a minute or so, Allen and McMillan pull her away. They have to support her as they lead her from the room. I stay where I am, my gaze drawn back to the lifeless body. With the sheet pulled away, I catch a glimpse of the wounds that killed her, four wide gashes open across her chest and stomach. It's only a glimpse, though. The thin man darts in and pulls the sheet up before I get a chance to see anything more.

"Enough?" he asks, holding the sheet up, ready to cover her face again.

I shake my head. I don't want her face to be covered. I want to say here and stare at it until every detail is branded into my brain. I never want to forget the thin arch of her eyebrows, kept that way by careful plucking in the bathroom mirror. I want to remember the high, aristocratic cheekbones and the hollows underneath. The nose she always thought was too big, but complimented her slightly over-generous mouth. I want to commit all these things to memory, singly and as part of the whole.

"It's time." McMillan re-enters behind me, his heavy footsteps echoing off the room's hard surfaces and angles.

I nod, but don't move away. This is the last time I'll see her. And it's not really her. It's a shell. It doesn't even really look like her. Not with the hair loose like this. Not with her being so still. It's like looking at a waxwork model or a storefront mannequin instead of my mother. All the parts are there, but she isn't. She's gone.

I give a small nod and the thin man drapes the sheet over her face again. I turn and follow McMillan into the depressing little waiting area. I manage not to cringe when I hear the soft thud as the drawer slides back into the wall. It's a sound that speaks of finality, a door closing on a future permanently shut down.

****

It's noon by the time we get back to Halmoni's. K is quiet now. Too quiet. She sleepwalks her way into the house and collapses onto the couch, curling up into a ball around one of her mother's many throw pillows. I wish I knew what to do for her. But I don't have the first clue.

Teddy's at the table, a plate of food untouched in front of him. I catch the scent of the broth Halmoni cooks his favorite noodles in and my stomach growls.

Halmoni jumps up and hurries to the stove. "You need to eat."

I shake my head. "No, I'm fine." My stomach twists and writhes so much, I'm certain I'll never keep anything down. Even though those noodles do smell amazing.

"You must eat," Halmoni insists. "Keep strength up."

For what? It's too late for strength. Whoever did this to my mom is long gone. And she was strong. Didn't do her much good.

"You okay, Tedster?" I sit next to him and accept the bowl of noodles Halmoni sets before me.

"Did you see her?" Teddy pulls a single noodle from his bowl with his chopsticks then lets it fall back into the soup with a splash.

I close my eyes and the image of my mother's corpse is embossed across my eyelids. I have a feeling it's going to be there a long time. I may never close my eyes again. "Yeah. I did."

"Is she…" He stops and looks up at me, his face haunted in the lamplight.

I nod. "She is. She's dead, Teddy."

And that's when it becomes real.

Teddy drops his chopsticks and they roll off the table to clatter on the floor. He ducks his head, tucking his chin in against his chest. Tears swim in his eyes, and he blinks hard to keep them at bay. I push my chair closer and wrap an arm around him. I'm a little surprised he doesn't shrug me off. Instead he knocks his head against my collarbone. I pull him in tighter. His chest and shoulders heave. Tears paint salty tracks along my neck.

My heart aches at the sound of his crying. Teddy hasn't cried in front of me for years. I bet he hasn't cried at all. He's a tough little kid. I've seen him come off his bike and lose half the skin on his elbows without a tear falling. I'd take a full body road-rash over this pain any day.

When Teddy finally pulls away, my shirt is damp. He won't look at me. He bends to pick up his chopsticks and wipes at his face. He keeps his back to me as he goes to the sink to rinse the implements. He returns to the chair, drops his gaze to his bowl and shovels food into his mouth like he's suddenly starving.

"Teddy…" I have no idea what I want to say to

him. I'll always be here for him? He shouldn't be embarrassed by his tears? It's okay to cry when your mother is murdered?

He doesn't respond. He finishes his noodles, tucks the bowl into the dishwasher and disappears out of the room. I get up to go after him, but Halmoni takes my arm and presses me into my seat.

"He be okay," she tells me. "Leave him."

I try to capture a slippery noodle between my chopsticks. I hope she's right.

Chapter Thirteen

The next several days are a blur of meetings, phone calls and visits from strangers. McMillan and Allen show up on a regular basis, but so far they haven't caught the monster who killed my mom. They don't even seem any closer to figuring out who might have done it.

"It's possible it was a drifter," McMillan tells me as he sips coffee at Halmoni's kitchen table. "Perhaps your mother surprised someone who had broken into the studio for shelter."

I raise my eyebrows. Just the other day he told me most murder victims know the person who attacks them.

"Isn't there any evidence?" I can't believe whoever did this didn't leave a trace of himself—or herself—at the scene. I can't dismiss the fact the killer could have been a woman, no matter how much I want to.

Maybe Mom had another lover somewhere, a woman she spurned once and who never forgave her for it. Or someone who was in love with her from afar. A former student, maybe? Ballet dancers are famous for their bitchiness, but I've never heard of it leading to murder. Disfigurement, maybe… Didn't that happen to the artistic director of the Bolshoi not too long ago? Some pissed off dancer threw acid over him because she didn't get the part she wanted or something equally lame?

"Forensics are working on it." McMillan drains his cup and gets up to set it in the sink. "Because the studio was used by so many people, there's a lot of material to work through."

I bet. There would be a minimum of fifty dancers passing through the school on any given day. And if each of them only dropped one strand of hair, it adds up to a lot of hair to test over a week. Mom had a guy who came in every couple of days to sweep and mop and wax the floors, but I bet there were still corners where hair and other stuff piled up.

"Is Dad in jail?" I haven't been able to think about my father. That he could commit murder is incomprehensible. It's impossible. Yet he has no real alibi. He claims to have been at the theater at the time Mom was killed, yet no one saw him there and there was no rehearsal scheduled. So he could have done it.

But he couldn't have. I know he couldn't. Not Dad. My father wouldn't even flush a spider down the drain if it decided to hang out in the bathtub. He'd catch it and set it outside on the deck or let it crawl through an open window. My mind can't accept he could have done this.

I want to understand. The cops get up and head for the door without answering my question. "We'd better get back. Just wanted to assure you all we are continuing to work on the case. We'll be in touch again soon."

"Yeah, okay..." I find their visits both frustrating and comforting. On the one hand it's nice to know they're out there, working on this, trying hard to find an answer for us. On the other, it's infuriating that two days have passed and the only person they appear to suspect is my father. There has to be someone else.

Once they're gone, the other things I've been trying to ignore flood back. The house is too quiet and silence presses on me like the walls are shifting sheets of lead. I get up from the table and cross to the door the policemen just exited. It's mid-morning and I'm in Halmoni's warm bungalow. I should feel safe here with sunlight streaming through the windows, geraniums in pots lining the sills. I peek through the glass in the back door as I lock it, testing the handle twice to be sure it really is locked.

Usually I love having the house to myself, but I don't think I'd be any more comfortable being alone even if I was in my own house. Apart from a quick trip to pick up more clean clothes, none of us have been back there. I'm not sure we ever will. I can't imagine living there again, the studio looming behind us like an overgrown specter. I'll see Mom in every shadow. She'll appear in the corner of my eye as I pass open doors or climb stairs. Her ghost will live in the very air we breathe. No, we can't live in that house. We can't stay here forever either.

K and Teddy have been bunking in Halmoni's room—K sharing the bed with her mom while Teddy sleeps on the floor next to them instead of in K's old bedroom at the end of the hall. I've had the couch. Not that I've slept much. My eyes are unwilling or unable to close. Every time my lids start drifting shut, they pop open again and I jerk awake, heart pounding, adrenaline pumping through my veins with such force I'm alert for at least another two hours. I spend my nights prowling the house, eyes glued to the windows as I seek out any movement, any threat.

A car turns into the driveway and I dart to the windows, ducking beneath the sill before I peer over the top to find Halmoni's car pulling into the garage. I breathe a sigh of relief. They're back. They've made it out into the world and survived.

The tightness in my chest eases. I've become such a paranoid bitch. I want my family to stay here, safe behind locked doors. I can't leave. Out there is too dangerous, too threatening. That's why I'm here alone while they all went to the airport to pick up my mother's sisters.

I watch them climb out of the car, two women, one tall like Mom, the other short and thick around the waist. They both have Mom's blonde hair, though, and when they near the house, I realize they have the same distinctive nose too.

They burst through the front door almost before Halmoni unlocks it.

"Anastasia? *Zaika*? Where are you?" one of my aunts calls in Russian. The familiar tongue brings tears to my eyes. *Zaika*. Bunny. It has been so long since anyone called me that. Mom loved to talk to me in Russian. I rarely answered her in anything but English. Listening to the familiar lilt and rhythm makes me homesick for her in a whole new way.

I wipe my eyes and straighten my spine as I walk through to meet them in the living room. "I'm here," I say, the Russian vowels unfamiliar and awkward on my tongue. I can't even remember when I last spoke it, yet the words spring effortlessly to mind.

My aunts surround me, smothering me in hugs. I want to hug them back, but I can't move. I stand there, stiff as a board, letting them pull me every which way as they smother me in their oversized bosoms. They smell sweet, like they've shared the same perfume or cologne on the plane.

"How was your flight?" I ask once they finally let me go long enough for the words not to be swallowed up by their voluminous clothing.

"Fine, fine, *lyubov moya*. You mustn't worry about us." It's the tall one who says this. I know one of the sisters is Galina and the other Zoya. Never having met them, I'm not sure which is which.

"*Tetya* Zoya," I begin, watching to see who might react. "Please sit. You must be tired after your long trip. Can I get you anything?"

The shorter one smiles broadly and pats my cheek. "Such nice manners. Just like a Russian girl. Even if you look like a *negr.*"

Zoya's use of the word shocks me so much I step backwards. It must show on my face because K is suddenly there, standing next to me.

"What?" she says, looking at me with her brows knitted together in concern.

I turn away from my aunts. "She just said I look like a nigger."

K's face darkens. "Are you sure?"

I shrug. It's not a word I've heard in Russian before. Even at their worst Mom and Dad never resorted to name-calling. Much. I'm pretty sure Mom's muttered *svin'ya* at Dad a few times, but there's a big difference between calling someone a pig and a nigger.

Galina must notice my distress because she swoops in and pulls me closer. "Please, don't be offended. You are a beautiful girl. Very exotic and lovely. You will turn heads everywhere you go in Tobolsk."

Tobolsk. I recognize the name. It's the town in Siberia where Mom grew up. She left at fourteen, though, to join the Bolshoi's ballet school in Moscow. Why would I be in Tobolsk to turn anyone's head?

"Huh?" I must sound completely stupid. I'm beginning to wonder if my Russian is even rustier than I initially thought. I must have missed something. A grammar construction I've forgotten or a colloquial phrase I've never heard before.

Zoya's face crumples and she looks around the room in obvious distress. "Did no one tell Anastasia? Did no one tell her she will come to live in Russia with Galina and I?"

Chapter Fourteen

My head whirls. What did she say? I'm going with her? With them? To Siberia? No way. No fucking way!

I turn to K who doesn't look at all concerned.

"Don't you have anything to say?" I throw at her.

Now it's her turn to look confused. "Huh? About what?"

I gesture toward my aunts before it dawns on me. She doesn't speak Russian. She has no idea what they just said.

"She said I'm going to Tobolsk with them. Were you planning to tell me any time soon?"

K's face falls. She stumbles to the couch and sits down, dropping her head into her hands. My heart speeds up. It's been a mammoth effort to get her out of bed. The last thing we need is for her to fall apart all over again.

"Sorry..." I sit next to her and rub at her shoulders. "What's happening?"

"They want you to go home with them," she mumbles. "Nothing's set in stone yet, but Stas..." She stops and looks up at me with eyes too big and too dark for her pale face. There's real fear in them. Is she scared of me?

"What?" I trace circles across the back of her shirt.

"Weren't you listening while the social worker was here?"

Halmoni bustles into the room, sees K and I talking, and uses a mixture of English, Korean, and sign language to usher my aunts into the kitchen. A moment later I hear them exclaiming in loud Russian over Teddy. Mom never spoke to him as much in Russian. I guess by the time he was born, she was further from her roots, more assimilated into her new culture. Plus, she shared Teddy with K who doesn't speak Russian. Thanks to Halmoni, Teddy speaks a bit of Korean, but his Russian is limited to a few words and phrases. The aunts will be so disappointed.

"Which one was the social worker?" There have been so many officials of various types showing up at the house, they've become one gigantic blur in my mind. Only Allen and McMillan remain individuals. And that's only because they came first.

"The woman who came yesterday," K says. "You really don't remember?"

I shrug. Is she so surprised my mind wandered? My mother is gone. I've spent the last few days trying to deal with funeral arrangements and police questioning, trying to keep her from having to do things I know will be painful. Maybe I wasn't even there when the social worker came by. What do we need a social worker for anyway?

"What did she say?" I ask impatiently. Why is K stalling?

K sighs. She looks at me, her expression is heavy with sadness. Not grief now—not exactly. "I'm not your mother," she says finally.

"Yes, you are." I stare at her. She may not have birthed me, but she's still my mother. She and Mom have always been my mothers. Mom and Mama K. Since I was four. I barely even remember life before she was around.

"Not according to the law…"

My stomach clenches and turns cold. I want to say something, ask a question. My tongue is frozen in place, though. What does the law have to do with it? We're a family. We stick together. Now, even more than in the past.

"What does that mean?" I manage to choke out, my lips thick and clumsy as they try to shape the words. My head spins like I'm on the carnival ride that presses you into the walls with the force of its movement.

K takes my hand and squeezes it between hers. "I have no legal right to you, Stas. Even if Rennie and I were married, I wouldn't. We'd talked about it. After the wedding we were going to start adoption proceedings to make you and Teddy ours."

"I am yours." I tear my hand away from hers and get up from the couch. I can't sit still. I have to move. I have to think. This is crazy. Mama K is my mother as much as Mom is ... was. Mom was as much a mother to Teddy as K. He's my brother. We're a family.

Mama K stands up now too. She follows me as I pace the floor. "And you're mine. You're the child of my heart. Unfortunately, the law doesn't look at it that way. I'm not a blood relative. Neither is Teddy. Your aunts are." She makes a helpless gesture toward the kitchen door.

How could she have gone to the airport this morning knowing this? Did she know?

"I... I..." I can't say anything. I can't think. I can't even breathe. "I gotta go."

Without even grabbing my coat, I pull open the front door and run.

****

I take the front steps in a single leap, hitting the sidewalk with a jolt that sends spikes of pain through my ankles. It doesn't stop me, though. I keep running until I've put Halmoni's house and her entire neighborhood behind me.

When I stop, it's because I can't run any further. My chest aches with the need for air and I double over, sucking in what I can. I'm out of shape. Already. Sweat pools between my breasts and trickles down the nape of my neck. Salt stings my eyes. Sweat? Maybe. Or tears. Or a mixture of both. I hurl myself down on a grassy verge, chest heaving with the effort of breathing. Blood roars in my ears and my pulse beats heavily at my temples.

They can't take me away from Mama K. They can't. Fuck the law. Family is bigger. It has to be. I've never even met Galina and Zoya before today. They've been names. A handful of faded photographs. A card on my birthday if I'm lucky. K has been there for me. She's brought me soup when I was sick. She's bandaged hundreds of skinned knees and elbows. She's given me the courage to face Mom if my report cards didn't show the straight As she always expected of me. She's ... I can't even list all the things she's done for me. Read me books at night, held me after nightmares left me too scared to sleep, gave me advice when I fought with friends. Supported me when I wanted to quit ballet. She's been a mother to me with all the highs and lows that come with the job. Surely no social worker would discount that.

"Stas?" A voice startles me so much I sit bolt upright, eyes snapping open with an audible click. "Is that you?"

Zane squints down at me, shielding his face with his hand. "What are you doing here?"

I run my hand over my face in the hope there are no errant tears there. I'm a mess. I should care if Zane's seeing me at my worst. Right now it doesn't feel very important.

"Yeah. It's me." I drag myself to my feet.

"I heard about your mom. I'm sorry." He looks down at his feet.

I haven't a clue what to say so I keep quiet. The

only sound between us is the noise of my hand rubbing back and forth across the fabric of my jeans.

"She was a really good teacher. I bet she was a great mom too."

The lump swells in my throat. "She was," I whisper.

"I miss my mom too." Zane won't look at me now. He jams his hands into the pockets of his jacket and walks in tight circles on the sidewalk.

"Is she dead?" I ask. The sweat drying on my body is cold. I wrap my arms around myself to keep from shivering.

Zane sighs and shakes his head. "Might be better if she was," he mutters.

"Huh?"

"My parents are splitting up," he explains. "It's messy. Too messy. I got pissed off with being used as a bargaining chip by them both and came here to live with my aunt."

"Oh…" I'm not sure what to say. My grief is too fresh and raw to understand how he can say it would be better if his mom was dead. I wouldn't wish this agony on my worst enemy. And Zane isn't. I'm not sure exactly what he is, but it's not an enemy.

"Where are you going?" he asks.

I shrug. "I don't know. Away. I can't deal with being there right now." I don't think I'll ever be able to. How can I go back knowing there are people there who want to take me to Siberia? How can I stay away when my mother's funeral is on Saturday?

"It gets to be too much, doesn't it?" Zane gives me a look of such sympathy it makes me want to cry all over again. "I've been there. I know what it's like not to want to go home."

It's too cold to stand still any longer so I start

walking again. Zane falls into step with me and it seems perfectly natural when he turns the corner alongside me. A couple of blocks later, when he slips his jacket around my shoulders, that feels natural too.

"Do you like it here?" I ask finally, the silence between us growing too long.

He shrugs. "It's better than being at home."

I wonder if the home situation is why he quit dancing for all those months. My stomach turns cold when I realize he's quit again. He's lost his teacher just when he'd found someone to work with. My mom's death is going to affect so many people. I've been so focused on my own pain and my family's, I haven't thought outside, to the wider community who will be devastated by her loss. The toddlers who come in the mornings to bounce along to music. The elementary schoolers doing their first pliés at the barre, getting their first taste of what ballet is really about. The older kids, the ones who haven't been tempted away from dance by boys or cheerleading or football. And the talented ones. The ones who might have a chance at a career in ballet. The ones like Zane. They'll miss her the most. Her harsh criticism and her relentless correction of their technique, but also the stories and advice she could share. War stories from her own days in a company.

We've reached the little shopping center a few blocks from my house—the one I lived in with Mom, K, and Teddy. Zane blows on his hands. "Cold out. Can I buy you a hot chocolate?" He gestures at the little coffee shop on the corner, its windows bright in the flat gray light.

I shiver. Zane must be freezing without his jacket. "Sounds good."

Chapter Fifteen

We duck through the cafe doors as the first drops of rain splatter against the windows. It's warm in there, steamy with the scents of coffee and sugar and baked goods. Zane leads me to a table tucked away in the far corner and pulls the chair out for me to sit. What a gentleman. Mom would be so impressed by his manners.

The thought sends a fresh wave of sadness through me and I have to close my eyes for a moment to keep tears from flowing down my face again. Will it ever get easier? I won't make it through a day if anything I see or hear or experience reminds me of her. I remember being sad when Nana died, but that sadness was gentle compared to the brutal assault this grief brings down upon me at every turn.

"Hot chocolate?" Zane looks down at me. "Or do you prefer coffee or tea?"

"Chocolate is perfect." I force myself to smile. I barely know this guy. He shouldn't have to deal with an emotional breakdown.

"Be right back." The smile he tosses in my direction disarms me. It changes his face, brightens it until he seems to glow. I can imagine what he must be like on stage. No one could keep their eyes off him.

By the time he returns with two mugs of hot chocolate, marshmallows scattered across the saucers instead of in the liquid, I've composed myself. A little, anyway.

"I wasn't sure if you took marshmallows," he says, handing me one of the mugs. "Most of the girls I know are dancers and wouldn't eat a grain of sugar if you paid them."

Normally I'd scoop up the marshmallows and

deposit them in my mug, ignoring Mom's chastising look in my head. But this time I can't. I pick one up and squeeze it between my fingers, letting its soft inside spill out through the powdered coating.

Zane carries on with his own drink, dunking the marshmallows briefly into the chocolate before popping them into his mouth one by one.

"Guess sugar isn't a problem for you, then?"

He shrugs. "I don't go crazy on it, but I figure a marshmallow every now and then won't kill me."

I like that. But male dancers are never as obsessive over their bodies and diets as girl dancers. At least, none of the ones I know. Dad keeps in shape, but he loves a good creamy pasta dish or a plate of fried chicken as much as the next guy. That's one of the reasons I used to love going to Dad's as a kid. I could count on getting real food there whenever Mom was on one of her kooky food crusades.

I drop two marshmallows into my own mug and push them to the bottom with a spoon. I like my marshmallows melted to nothing but a sugary froth.

"So, what's so bad you had to run away?" Zane sits back in his chair and studies me. A faint whisper of a milk mustache lingers above his lip. I'm shocked at how much I want to lean over and brush it off. Or maybe even lick it.

"My aunts arrived from Russia." Just saying the words returns the panic to my throat, metallic and poisonous. "I've never met them before. And they said they wanted me to come home with them."

"To Russia?" Zane's face creases with concern. "Do you want to go?"

I stare at him. "No. I don't want to go. I don't know them. And I want to stay here with Mama K and Teddy. But Mama K doesn't think they'll let me."

"Who's Mama K?"

"My other mom."

Zane looks impressed. "Two moms, huh?"

"Yeah. But K isn't my birth mother. Mom is. K's Teddy's birth mother—my brother." I can't explain all this right now. My family is so complicated and weird. "Anyway, Mama K apparently has no rights toward me. Because she and Mom weren't married yet. Or something."

"What about your dad?" Zane's elbows are on the table now and he's leaning toward me.

Dad.

I don't even want to think about Dad.

I shake my head. "Dad's ... I think Dad's in jail." My face heats up. The cops didn't actually say, but their silence spoke volumes.

"Oh ... I'm sorry." Zane lowers his gaze to the tabletop and runs his fingers through a line of sugar spilled there. "Is... Is it because of..." He trails off, obviously not wanting to ask.

I nod. "They think he did it."

Zane looks right at me and the directness of his gaze is disarming. "Do you?"

It's the first time anyone has asked me outright. I've been asked about Dad's movements, his likes and dislikes, his politics, his attitudes, his moral code. I've been asked about things I couldn't possibly know about another person. Yet no one has asked me that one, obvious question. I don't think I've even asked it myself.

Zane's eyes don't waver even as the silence between us lengthens. I feel like he's stripping off my skin with his gaze. Like he's seeing everything inside me. I hope it's not as black and ugly and twisted as it feels.

Very slowly I shake my head. Dad can't have done it. He had far too much respect for Mom. Even if he did disagree with her "lifestyle" as he chose to call it, he wouldn't kill her over it. It's not like the relationship between her and K is new. They've been together almost twelve years. If he was going to kill her over that, it would have been years ago.

Wouldn't it?

A nagging thought won't leave me alone. The old Dad wouldn't have done it, but how well do I really know the new, religious Dad? If I hadn't skipped so many of my weekends, maybe we'd be closer. Maybe he would have told me how he really felt.

"No." I say, my voice coming out louder and more firmly than I intended. "He wouldn't do something like that. My dad's a dancer!"

Zane nods. "Tusi Nonu, right?"

I look up, surprised for some reason he'd know. "Yeah. You know him?"

Zane flushes. "I don't know him. But I know *of* him. I mean, he's one of the most significant choreographers in the country, right? You can't dance and *not* know Tusi Nonu."

Huh. Dad's a little famous around here. I hadn't realized people outside our little corner of the universe might have heard of him.

"Do you think he did it?" I ask. The words surprise me as soon as they escape my lips. How can I ask him that? Zane's never even met Dad.

Something flashes outside the window and Zane turns to look. I follow his eyes, watching a police car crawl down the street. Its lights aren't flashing and its siren isn't on, but Zane stiffens, pushing himself away from the table so he's sitting as far from it as he can without getting up and moving away.

"Zane?" I lean toward him, uncertain what's going on.

He ignores me, eyes still glued to the window, following the cop car as it pulls into a parking space a little further down the block. When a single cop climbs out and starts walking toward the cafe, Zane explodes out of his seat like there was a rocket beneath him. His hand rakes through his hair, making it stand up in crazy spikes. A look of utter desperation crosses his face before he turns and bolts out the cafe's side door.

****

The bells over the cafe door jangle in protest as Zane slams out it. He's past the corner of the street before I manage to extricate myself from behind the table. What did I say? My head reels. Everything seemed to be going so well. I thought we were getting along. What the hell just happened?

I stand up, pushing the remains of my hot chocolate aside. When I push the chair in, I realize he left his jacket. I slung it over my seat after we came in. I put it on and hurry out the doors.

Once outside, I'm not sure where to go. I glance down the street in the direction Zane ran. Should I go after him? He's nowhere to be seen. No. He will have had too much of a head start. I'd never catch him. Even if I had an idea where he might go. I don't even know where he lives. Downtown is a big place.

Zipping his jacket against the cold, I turn and walk the other way, my feet taking me toward my own house as if on autopilot. Where he lives. I have to figure out where he lives. I have to return his jacket. It's too cold for him to be without it.

The yellow crime tape surrounding our house sags and flaps in the wind. Pieces of it have torn free, leaving gaps in the perimeter fence. It gives the place a shabby, abandoned feel. I shiver as I stand on the sidewalk, looking up at it. Will I ever call this place home again?

My heart constricts. This was a happy home. Sure, we had our squabbles and arguments, but overall, this was a place of warmth and joy. Now I can't look at it without fear and grief tangling through my soul.

Dragging myself away from the sidewalk, I follow the path around to the studio. The crime tape has been reinforced here, several layers stretching across the path to the main doors. Ignoring it, I duck beneath and come close enough to the entrance my breath fogs the glass. I punch in the code on the box under the sign saying 'Varushkin School of Dance' and lift out the key hidden inside.

My hands tremble so much it takes several tries to get the key into the lock. When I do, I freeze, unable to take the next step. Breath catches painfully in my throat. I won't look, I promise myself. I'll go in, but I won't see the blood. I won't go near the spot my mother died. I only need to get into the office.

Bolstered by my own promises, I manage to turn the key. The door springs open easily and a moment later I'm inside. The room smells familiar—of rosin and sweat—but a darker, bitter, metallic scent hangs over the top of the more homey ones. A scent like a dead animal. Blood. It's the scent of blood.

It takes every ounce of will I possess to take a step into the gloomy near-darkness. Shadows lurk in every corner, and in every one lurks the shape of my mother's killer. My pulse beats loudly in my ears—so loud I'm certain I'd miss the sound of footsteps behind me, or another person breathing. And this does little to allay the panic creeping into the pit of my stomach.

I cross to the tiny office space behind the dressing rooms and flick the switch by the door. Bright, golden light fills the room, banishing any ghostly assassins that might linger there. The bitter taste in my throat recedes a little and my pulse slows.

The filing cabinet sits behind the narrow desk. I pull it open, wincing at the rattling sound the old drawer makes as I slide it out. Hundreds of manila folders queue inside, lined up in rows, each with a student's name on the top left. I stare at them all, realizing I have no idea what Zane's last name is. If I have to go through all these files, I'll be here all night. I flip through the first ones and recognize names I haven't heard in years. She hasn't even got these organized by current and past students. They're all here, lined up in alphabetical order. Joanne Abbot, Fiona Abercrombie and on and on. Five drawers all together. I don't have a chance in hell of finding Zane's quickly. Unless…

I slam the drawer closed and cross to the desk. A few notices about upcoming dance contests litter the desk along with some unopened mail. I slide aside an electricity bill and find myself looking down at another manila folder. In the top left is the name Zane Talbolt. I smile. Some luck for once. It would have taken me eons to get to the Ts.

Flipping open the file, I find the standard enrollment form tucked inside. My mouth curls in a smile when I see Zane's middle name is Edward. Zane Edward Talbolt. It's a strong name. An important name. But that's not what I came for. What I need is an address.

I grab a piece of scrap paper from the pile on the corner of the desk and scribble down both his address and phone number. I don't have my phone with me, but it may come in handy some other time. Especially if he's not home when I show up. I close the file on the desk and am about to put everything back where I left it when I decide to file the folder instead. Mom's not coming back to do it, so I should tidy up her paperwork. If anyone wants to take over the school, they'll appreciate it.

I turn back to the filing cabinet and bend to open the bottom drawer. I expect it to slide as freely as the other drawer I pulled on, but this one sticks. I tug harder, but the drawer doesn't budge.

"Damn it!" I breathe, bending further and inserting my fingers into the space beneath the drawer to try and figure out what it might be stuck on. Probably another file that's fallen out the back of one of the drawers. I expect my fingertips to brush against paper to cardboard, so when they find cool, sticky plastic, they recoil.

"What the…" With one hand I raise the drawer slightly, using the other to jiggle the plastic-wrapped package until it jerks free of whatever it's caught on.

I straighten and peer through the clear plastic wrap.

It takes a second for me to understand what I'm seeing. My hands shake slightly, my palms suddenly slick with sweat.

"What the hell?" I whisper, dropping the package to the floor with a thud and taking a step back, wanting to get as far away from it as I can.

But the room is too small to get away from the neatly wrapped stacks of banknotes.

Chapter Sixteen

I stare, uncomprehending at the bundle of money. Where did it come from? Whose is it? Why is it here? The questions race never-ending laps around my skull as I poke the plastic wrap with the toe of my boot. A little tears away, revealing what I already suspected: they're not singles.

With shaking hands, I bend down and pick up one of the bundles that's come free of the plastic. It takes only a second for me to ruffle through it. All hundreds. A lot of hundreds. My hands tremble too much for accurate counting, but there have to be at least a hundred notes in this stack. And there are several layers of them still in the plastic.

There has to be thousands and thousands of dollars here.

I drop the bundled notes like they're hot and pull at the drawer above.

This one slides free easily. When I reach underneath it, I don't find anything unusual. Just the cold metallic base of the drawer.

Nothing nestles beneath any of the other drawers either.

Is this Mom's money? It can't be. If she had access to this amount of cash, why would she have been so concerned about losing pupils or another teacher's prices? Why would she and K have gone with their third choice wedding venue because the top two were out of their budget range?

Is it K's?

No way. K could never deny Mom anything she wanted. If there was any way she could pay for it, K would have booked the venue in the mountains both she and Mom fell in love with when they visited. She would have bought Mom the hand-embroidered silk dress she coveted.

No. This doesn't belong to either of them. So whose is it? Teddy's?

My mouth twists into a humorless smile. Teddy can't hold onto a dollar for more than a day without spending it.

Is this money what got Mom killed?

A chill rolls up my spine and makes the hair on the back of my neck rise. The police searched the studio. If they didn't find this package, either it was really well hidden or it's been put in the drawer since, And if that's the case...

I snatch up the package and stuff it back into the cabinet, feeling the hollow beneath the drawer above and finding the brittle torn edges of the tape that must have held the package in place. Maybe the police search disturbed it and the tape broke after the drawers had been slammed closed again. Maybe the money had been there for years, since Mom bought the battered old file-cabinet at a garage sale.

I close the filing cabinet and check to make sure the room has been left in order. I don't want to be there any longer. If someone's looking for that cash—and I'm sure someone is—I don't want to be the one getting in their way. I need time to figure out what to do with it, whether to tell anyone it's there.

I step toward the door and my foot comes down on something that makes me slip, sending me off balance. I grab hold of the wall to keep from falling to my knees. When I've recovered, I bend and pick up the small notebook that was responsible.

It's just a notebook. One of those little ones with a cardboard cover like the ones I used to write my spelling words in when I was in grade school. The front cover has been torn off, but the back one clings on, secured by a single staple. I thumb through it, finding columns of numbers and letters, all in careful block letters, some written in pencil, some in pen. The same scent that drifted from the banknotes clings to this notebook too. I guess it was wrapped in the same package.

None of it makes any sense to me, but if it was in with the money, I have to assume it's some kind of account book or something. The key, perhaps, to why the money is there, whose it is, what it's for.

I jam the notebook into my pocket to look at again later. Maybe when I'm calmer I'll be able to decipher it. When I'm thinking straight. I shiver, suddenly wanting out of this place. Flicking off the lights once more, I take a deep breath before sliding out the door.

As I do, a beam of intense white light shines through the window and forces me to shield my eyes.

"Who goes there?" a harsh voice shouts through the glass.

I freeze. Someone stands outside the window, a flashlight aimed through the glass and pinning me to the wall.

"Don't move," the voice says in a tone too serious to argue with. I stay where I am, barely breathing, while I listen to the door rattle and creak as someone outside lets themselves in. I left the key in it. I only expected to be a few minutes so I left the key in the door. How stupid can I be?

"In the back," the guy outside with the flashlight shouts and seconds later footsteps pound down the hallway toward me.

Crap. I'm cornered. My eyes dart around the room. There's nowhere to go. Not with the flashlight's beam nailing me where I stand.

The footsteps slow as they near the doorway. A figure enters the room, another flashlight joining the one already pouring through the window. A second later, the light goes on and I drop my arm.

"Who are you?" A uniformed police officer has a gun raised in one hand, the flashlight in the other. I stare into the black eye of the gun's barrel and shiver. "Name! Now!"

"Anastasia Nonu," I stammer out.

The gun drops and disappears into a holster on the cop's belt. "What are you doing here? This is a crime scene."

"You okay? What's going on in there?" The first cop's voice drifts through the glass.

"Just a kid," the other one calls back.

"I live here," I say. "This is my mother's office."

"It's still a crime scene. Didn't you notice the tape outside?"

I nod. "I needed something."

The cop frowns. "Let's get you out of here. You didn't touch anything, did you?"

Does he know about the money? Did he catch me toying with it through the glass?

"Out there, I mean." He jerks a thumb in the direction of the studio.

I shake my head. "No. I … I don't want to go in there."

He snorts. "Let's get you out." He hurries me out of the office and down the hallway, careful to keep me walking in a straight line down the middle of the floor. When we reach the main doors, I can't help risking a glance over my shoulder and catch a glimpse of the now-dry bloodstain marking the studio floor, an irregular dark patch that swallows every rivulet of moonlight dripping through the windows.

A small noise escapes my throat. I hadn't actually forgotten she was dead, but seeing such a stark reminder brings the horror flooding back. Mom's dead. Over at Halmoni's house, my aunts are waiting to sweep me off to Siberia.

I pull Zane's jacket tighter around me. It smells good. Like his woodsy cologne, fresh air, and clean water.

"Out," the cop says, shoving me through the doors and out into the cold. Wind rustles the leaves overhead, throwing them off their branches to spiral down toward the ground. I wonder vaguely if a leaf knows it's dying when it tears loose from its branch. Did Mom know she was dying as she lay there with her blood pooling beneath her?

The two cops stand before me. "You can't come in here," the one who brought me out says. "If you need something from inside the house, you need to inform us. We can accompany you inside to ensure the integrity of the crime scene isn't compromised."

I stare at him. He sounds like an actor on *CSI* or something. I didn't think real cops talked like that. It sounds scripted.

"Sorry," I mumble. "Won't happen again."

"Now, can we take you somewhere? It's cold." The second cop ducks his head as a gust of wind blasts past. They don't know about the money. If they did, they'd suspect me of going in there to get it and probably of killing Mom. I wish I knew what that meant.

I pull out the slip of paper with Zane's address on it. "I'm going to Grivas Close," I say with as much authority as I can. "To a friend's."

"We can drop you there."

****

It's a short drive to Grivas Close, a tiny alleyway off one of the streets behind the high school. I peek at the piece of paper in my hand. Number 12. Didn't Zane tell me he lived downtown? I wouldn't call this downtown.

"This is it," I say as the cop car eases past the mailbox.

I have to wait for the second cop to open the door before I can get out. No door handles in the backseat of cop cars. TV got something right.

"Thanks," I say.

"Stay out of crime scenes." The cop grins and tips his hat as he climbs into the cruiser. I watch them continue down the lane until the dead end and turn. I wave as they sail past on their way back up to the street.

Taking a deep breath, I push open the gate to number 12. A flagstone path leads to the front door. A horseshoe bolted to the center of the red front door acts as a knocker. I hesitate a moment, and before I can rap it against the piece of iron beneath, Zane is beside me.

I spin around, confused by him appearing from behind me, rather than from the door in front of me. But my surprise is nothing compared to the look of shock in his face. It's probably only been an hour or so since he ran out of the diner. Yet it feels like centuries have passed. Maybe I'm an old, gray-haired lady now and that's why he's looking at me like this.

"You forgot your jacket," I say, holding it out to him.

"How'd you find me?" He glances over his shoulder before pulling me away from the house to stand on the sidewalk in front of it.

"You don't want to know." I mean it to sound like a joke, but it doesn't. It comes out sounding almost hysterical and I realize how close to the edge I really am. I found thousands of dollars in my mom's studio. A policeman pointed a gun at me. If he's smart, Zane will run as far away from me as he can. My legs weaken and I have to grab hold of his arm to keep myself upright.

"Whoa." Zane reaches for me, taking my shoulder to steady me.

I ease myself down onto the curb and put my head into my hands. I force myself to breathe. In. Out. In. Out. My racing heart slows a little and I feel like I might be able to stand without passing out.

"C'mon." Zane helps me up and keeps a steadying arm around me as he guides me toward a tiny blue car parked a few yards up the street. Zane digs through his pockets until he comes up with a key.

"Get in," he says, swinging open the door for me and tossing the jacket I returned to him into the backseat. "I'll take you home."

Home.

Where is home? Home was always Mom. Her scent. Her hair. Her voice. Those were the things I called home. Our house isn't home anymore. I just about got arrested for being there. And I'm not even sure I knew my mom at all. Not if it's her money hidden in the filing cabinet.

"Does anyone know where you are?" His voice is low and gentle. "I mean, will people be worried about you?"

My head snaps up. It hadn't occurred to me. Mama K is probably worried about me. Teddy too. Maybe even the aunts and Halmoni, but I don't care so much about them. I look over at the clock on the dashboard and am surprised to see it's after six. The day has melted away. Where has it gone?

"How about I take you home now." Zane sounds so reasonable.

"Okay." I find myself agreeing with him without

argument. I don't want to go back there. I don't want to see those two Russian witches. I can't let K worry about me. Not at a time like this.

I give Zane directions to Halmoni's house, and we're there in less than ten minutes. When he pulls up outside, I don't move. The wind whooping around the car and the hypnotic drone of the engine has lulled me into a state of calm.

"Do you want me to come in with you?" Zane's eyes glitter in the light from the streetlights overhead.

I swallow hard, looking up at the windows, lit up like there's a party inside. "Do you mind?"

Without a word, Zane shuts off the engine and swings open his door. I follow, a little more slowly, ducking my head against the wind.

Halmoni pounces on us as soon as I push open the door.

"Where you been?" she screams. "We so worried about you. We have guests. You very rude and inconsiderate girl."

I cringe away from her tirade, backing into Zane who stands awkwardly in the doorway. "Sorry," I murmur.

"You will be sorry." Halmoni puffs herself up like one of those weird, angry fish. She seems so much bigger than she really is. "Everyone so worried. At time like this too! And you off with boyfriend?"

My face pounds with blood. "Zane's not ... um..." I can't go on. I want the floor to open and swallow me. I want to be anywhere but here.

"I should go." Zane gives my shoulder a final squeeze. "I'll call you tomorrow, okay?"

I turn to him, seeking out his eyes. "Promise?"

He nods, a small smile playing on his lips. "I promise."

I'm holding his hand, his long, tapered fingers curled around mine. It's warm, and when I pull mine away, I miss the heat of it.

He disappears out the door, closing it behind him without a sound. I push past Halmoni and prepare to face the wrath of Mama K.

She leaps to her feet as I walk into the living room. "Stas!" She runs to me and hugs me far too tightly. "Thank god you came home. I've been so worried."

I relax against her, letting her stroke my hair and run her warm hands across my shoulders. It's so familiar being here, the slightly acid scent of her skin filling my nostrils. This is home.

"I'm sorry," I murmur.

"Sh." Her hand brushes the side of my face and she looks right into my eyes. "I was worried, yes, but I understand. We'll work this out, Stas, I promise. I don't want this any more than you do."

Her eyes are dark and steady as they hold mine. She means it. This is as important to her as it is to me.

"Where are they?" I look around, surprised Zoya and Galina are not still sitting there.

"The aunts?"

I nod.

"They've gone to a hotel. There isn't enough room for them to stay here, and our place isn't exactly an option."

I shiver. Don't I know it. I almost got shot or arrested for going there. Yet already the experience has taken on a dreamlike quality. Maybe it never really happened. Maybe I didn't find a king's ransom hidden in a filing drawer. Maybe I didn't stare down the barrel of a gun. Maybe I didn't hold Zane's hand as he delivered me back here. Maybe I never actually left at all.

Maybe I imagined all of this. The aunts, Mom's

death, the whole lot of it. Maybe it's all just a long, terrible hallucination.

I wish it was.

As I sink down on the couch, a clock on the mantlepiece chimes. I glance up. Seven o'clock. My mouth twists. In another lifetime, Zane would be picking me up to go bowling around about now.

Chapter Seventeen

Saturday morning dawns clear and cold. I lift the curtains behind the couch and look out at the street, still painted with the pastel colors of sunrise. It's so beautiful. The sun peeks over the horizon like it's checking if it's okay to come out. I don't want to encourage it.

I wrap the quilts more tightly around myself and let the curtain drop. Mom and K were supposed to be getting married today. If that was happening, I'd be rejoicing at the sunshine. Instead we're burying my mother and it feels wrong the sun should be out.

It's only a little after six, but I know I won't sleep any more. Keeping the quilt draped over me, I climb off the couch and head for the kitchen. If I'm going to make it through today, I'm going to need coffee. Lots of coffee.

I put the coffee machine on and sit down at the table to wait for it to do its magic. My phone sits in the center of the table amidst a jumble of pamphlets and flyers I got from the police yesterday. Apparently I can't just go visit Dad. There's all kinds of red tape to go through first, the most important being Dad putting me on his visitors' list. Which he hasn't. It feels the same as him not giving me a key to his house. Like I'm a part of his life, but only on his terms. Or maybe he doesn't want me to see his guilt.

I grit my teeth and get up to pour myself a cup of coffee even though the liquid hasn't finished draining through the filter and hisses and spits on the hotplate. I can't wait any longer. And I need to distract myself from the furious thoughts invading my brain.

"Up early." Halmoni steps into the kitchen in a startlingly red kimono. "Couch not comfortable for sleep?"

I shake my head. "It's fine. Just couldn't sleep."

Halmoni bustles about, putting the kettle on and pulling small boxes of tea leaves from the cupboard. I watch, fascinated, as she measures out small amounts of each tea into a delicate china pot.

"What kind of tea is that?" I ask once she's finished with the leaves.

"Different kinds," she says. "Today will be difficult day. Sad day. So need tea to relax mind and give strength. I use Iron Lady as base and blend with chamomile, peppermint, and other herbs. You want some?"

I shrug. I don't think any tea is going to give me the strength to get through today. I'm not sure even whiskey would do the trick. Even morphine would have a hard time dulling this pain.

"Try," she insists, putting a cup that matches the pot in front of me. "Better than that poison." She throws my coffee cup a distasteful look. I wonder how K ever became the coffee fiend she is now if her mother was such an ardent and obviously knowledgeable tea drinker. Maybe that's why. Don't kids always rebel against their parents? I mean, I gave up dancing when I knew it was the most important thing to my mother. Even though quitting hurt me, I always knew it hurt her more. God, I'm a bitch.

K comes into the kitchen while I'm blowing the fragrant steam away from the surface of my tea. Her hair is a tangled mess and dark circles ring her red, puffy eyes. Halmoni fusses over her, making her sit and pouring more of the now pungent tea.

"Thanks, Mom." K yawns and leans over the tea to sniff at it before shoving it away from herself. "I'm going to need coffee today."

"It's not so bad," I say, taking another sip from

my teacup.

K wrinkles her nose and gets up to pour herself a generous mug of coffee. "I'll take your word for it."

Halmoni tuts, but says nothing. She pours herself tea and sits down at the table. "Teddy still sleeping?"

K nods. "He's in my bed. He's been having nightmares."

"Haven't we all?" I can't keep the bitter words from sliding from my lips.

K glances my way and sighs, letting her eyes drop to the tabletop. "Can you help with Teddy today?" she asks. "I don't think I'll be much good to him."

My heart cracks when she says this. Today was supposed to be the happiest day of K's life. She and Mom put everything they had into planning this wedding. It was going to be a celebration of their love and that they now had the same rights as other people in love. They'd planned every detail so it would run perfectly, both as their own personal event, and as a huge fuck-you to the people who denied them that right all those years. I may have bitched about the orange dress and having to diet to fit into it, but underneath, I'd been looking forward to the wedding. I was so damn proud of them both for doing it large. No timid little scurry to the registry office for them.

"Of course." I grab K's hand and force her to look up at me. "Whatever you need."

She manages an insipid smile that doesn't get near her eyes. "Thanks, Stas."

I squeeze her hand. The aunts will be there. I've only seen them briefly since they arrived, but of course they will be there for the funeral. It's why they came. My stomach churns and I shove both cups away from me. I'd better not put anything more down there. It won't stay put long.

****

The funeral is not held in a church, and I'm glad. Mom's attitude to religion was barely tolerant. I didn't understand it until I studied the Soviet Union in high school and discovered how people who practiced religion were treated under the communist regime. No wonder Mom was wary. And of course Dad's family were all super-religious. Not Dad so much, but Nana and his brothers and sisters and cousins. Then all that changed and Dad was suddenly the most religious guy around. His new-found fervor makes his family look like heathens. And god only knows what that makes me. Satan's right-hand, probably.

Instead, it's held in a large room behind the funeral home. We get there early and sit in the seats reserved for us at the front. I try to keep from staring at the simple wooden box sitting on a podium at the front. Mom's in there. It's closed, thankfully, but I can't help glancing at it and imagining her lying inside, hands folded over the simple white silk blouse and black pants I picked out for her to wear on her eternal journey.

I snort, then snatch my hands up to my face to keep more giggles from escaping. Eternal journey. I sound as corny as the brochures the funeral director handed us the first day we came here. I don't believe in heaven or an afterlife. Mom's not on a journey. Her travels have been halted. And all that's left is for her corpse to be dropped into a hole in the ground.

"Anastasia." My head snaps up when I hear the Russian pronunciation of my name. Zoya stands over me, eyes already brimming with tears.

"Hi," I say, shifting in my seat so I'm closer to Teddy. I wish I could move. I don't want to be near these two people who want to rip me out of my life. But at the same time, I feel a little sorry for them. They don't seem to speak English. It must be hard for them to be here.

They shuffle into seats the row behind me and sit, sniffling loudly.

"Is she really in there?" Teddy points toward the coffin, eyes huge and haunted.

"Yeah," I say. "But just her body. That's not really her. The part of Mom that made her Mom, it's gone. What's in the box is a shell."

I hope he gets it. Mom left days ago. What we're burying today isn't Mom, just the vessel she lived in for forty-six years.

"Like a hermit crab?" Teddy screws up his face.

"Kind of." I like the analogy. It implies Mom has moved on, gone to find some other shell now she's outgrown this one. I guess that's what the Buddhists believe with all their reincarnation stuff.

Teddy nods, accepting this. I'm relieved. He has to have a million questions, but he's not asking them.

Next to Teddy, K is quiet. Her eyes are closed as if she's praying. Her hands writhe in her lap, fingers twisting around each other, knuckles white. I want to reach out and still them, but I don't.

I turn to face the back of the room. People have started drifting in and arranging themselves in the seats set up in regimented lines. I recognize some of Mom's students, current and past, but many of the faces are unfamiliar. Vonnie steps through the doors, flanked by her parents. In the simple blue dress she's wearing, her wild red hair tamed in a single thick braid down her back, she doesn't look like my friend. She catches my eye and gives a tiny wave, her eyes brightening in a way that shows me she's still in there. I return the wave, but am distracted by another figure stepping into the room behind her.

The man is tall and well-built with a neatly trimmed mustache. His charcoal colored suit is pressed and obviously expensive. His eyes scan the room until they rest on me. He nods in my direction before sliding into a seat near the rear of the room, followed a second later by a slender woman with a lot of gold jewelry glistening against her ebony skin.

Ropati.

His name springs to my mind. Dad's brother. Unlike my aunts who returned to Samoa after college, he still lives here. I wonder why he's here. Has he seen Dad? Does he know if Dad did it?

Music starts playing, drowning out the confusion of my thoughts. A somber woman in a tailored black suit steps up to the podium and adjusts the microphone. The low murmur of conversation from behind us quiets.

"Irena Alexandrova Varushkin," she intones, using my mother's full name. "Mother, partner, ballerina, and teacher. She has touched so many lives, in so many ways. Today we will celebrate that life."

Celebrate? My jaw clenches. The wedding was supposed to be a celebration. This is a funeral. It's a time to reflect on her life, maybe. To mourn the way it has been cut short in such a dramatic fashion. It's no time for celebration.

Anger surges into my throat, hot and poisonous. I choke it back, but it leaves a nasty flavor coating my mouth. I hate sitting up here, every eye in the place prickling the nape of my neck. It's not fair when I can't look back.

Gritting my teeth, I slouch down in my seat and wait for it all to be over.

The service goes on too long. Too many people get up to speak about how much Mom meant to them. I find myself resenting each and every one of them. She was my mother, not theirs. When the woman in the suit—would she be called a celebrant, or is that solely for weddings? I can't help thinking this is the same woman Mom and K had booked to preside over their wedding—asks me to come up and speak about Mom, I can't move. My butt is glued to the seat. I give my head a small shake and look down at the floor.

Behind me, the aunts cluck and mutter endearments at me in Russian: *lapochka* and *myshka*. I want them to shut up. I'm not a bunny or a mouse, and neither of them has the right to call me that, to pat my shoulder as if it could give me any comfort. In the awkward silence that follows the invitation, Zoya rises and goes to the microphone.

"It has been too many years since I saw my sister," she says in Russian. "She was always the brave one, the adventurer. Galina, my other sister, and myself, we have never traveled. This is our first trip out of Russia. Irena was so much braver than us. She left home at fourteen to go to ballet school. We knew then, she'd never return to Toblosk. To Irena, the world was an exciting place to explore, not somewhere to settle. Her journey has been an unusual one, but for her family, that was not unexpected. Galina and I thought we were coming here to take her home to be buried with her family. Since arriving here, we have discovered Irena's family is the people she has here. Her roots are maybe in Toblosk, but this is her home, and she should stay here amongst the people she now calls family."

Tears run down Galina's face and I turn in my seat to reach out and touch her hand. My anger has faded. How lovely they have seen this, they understand family isn't only the people you share blood with. If they have changed their mind about taking Mom's body home with them, have they also changed their mind about taking me?

Chapter Eighteen

The service at the graveside is short. Far fewer people show up at the sprawling cemetery than were at the funeral home. Teddy clings to me and sobs as we drop clods of earth onto the coffin, each hitting the wood with a hollow thud. My heart grows heavier with each one, sinking lower and lower in my chest until it sits like a lump of rock somewhere near my waist, still and silent.

K is last to throw her dirt. She's said nothing since we arrived at the funeral home. She hasn't cried, though, and for that I'm grateful. Teddy has cried enough for all of us. His face is puffy and swollen from the intensity, his eyes so red they'd glow in the dark. I wish I could cry. A lump the size of a basketball pulses at the base of my throat, but I can't cry.

I watch K step to the edge of the grave and look down at the wooden box, now scattered with dirt. She clutches the clod in her hand so tightly it crumbles, staining her fingers with mud. She drops to her knees on the piece of fake grass lining the edge of the hole.

"Goodbye, Rennie," she whispers and my stony heart cracks open. Loosening her fingers, she lets the remains of her clod trickle down onto the coffin. It's a gentle sound, like the patter of raindrops on a roof, like the soft swish of ballet shoes across the studio floor.

I draw Teddy close and pull him away from the graveside. K should be able to say goodbye to the love of her life in private. K looks up and beckons us to come back, to join her. I hesitate, but she nods in my direction. Dragging my feet, I shuffle to where she's still kneeling. Teddy drops next to her and allows himself to be squeezed in against her side. Their necks follow the same arc as they bow their heads over the grave. These two, they belong together. But where do I fit in?

"Please, Stas," K whispers, reaching her hand to me.

I kneel too, on K's other side. It feels awkward and wrong. This is Mom's space. I should be on the other side of her, not pushed against K like this. Mom and K were always the center, Teddy and I orbiting them like Mercury and Venus. I'm not sure K alone can be the sun.

We stay at the graveside a long time, the weak afternoon sunshine filtering through the near-bare branches of the trees overhead. Behind us, the gravediggers wait impatiently for us to leave. I hear their muffled coughs and shuffling feet.

"We should go." K hauls herself upright and brushes off her hands. "They'll be waiting for us at the wake."

The wake. Argh. I'd forgotten about it. Bad enough to have to sit through the hours of eulogies, then come here and watch my mother be lowered into a hole in the earth, but now we have to go to a party with a bunch of strangers and try to be polite. I don't feel polite. My anger has lessened, but it's still there, swirling in poisonous clouds through my gut, drifting through the other clusters of grief and hurt and uncertainty.

I'll wind up stuck with my aunts too, acting as translator as they try to make sense of the world Mom chose over theirs. I hope Vonnie is there. I haven't spoken to her all week, and it has to be the longest I've ever gone without talking to her. Usually we're on the phone twelve times a day, texting fifteen times between each call.

One of the women in the yoga group K and Mom go to owns a restaurant, and the wake is held there. When we walk in, the single, large room is filled with people. The tables have been pushed to the walls to open up the space. A long row of them holds food and Teddy beelines in that direction as soon as we walk through the door. I wish I could duck so easily under arms and escape.

The owner of the restaurant, a woman called Colleen, grabs K and pushes a glass of wine into her hand. I wish I could have one too. Glancing around, I catch sight of a table groaning with glasses and assorted drinks in the corner near the bathrooms.

"I'm going to find Vonnie," I say. "Are you okay?"

K takes a deep drink from the glass. "As okay as I can be, I guess."

"I'll take care of her, hon." Colleen smiles and nudges K with her through the crowd to where a big group of women stands. The local lesbians. Mom and K's friends. Their community. Yes, they will look after K. They've been sending food on a daily basis. Halmoni has been overwhelmed by the trays of mac and cheese and lasagna showing up like clockwork at dinnertime.

I weave through the crowd, not making eye contact with anyone. I keep the drinks table in sight and work my way toward it. There's no barman or anything tending it, so I'm pretty sure I can sneak a glass of something. If I pour wine into a coffee cup, no one will ever know. Once I've got that, I'll find Vonnie.

I've almost reached the drinks table when someone steps in front of me, blocking my path. I try to duck around, but whoever it is doesn't budge.

"Oh!" A woman exclaims. "You're Irena's daughter, aren't you?"

I nod, raising my eyes slowly to look into a face that's oddly familiar, but I can't place.

"I'm so sorry for your loss." The woman has dark hair twisted into a loose knot behind her head. She's slender and has the unmistakable posture of a dancer.

Instinctively I straighten up, trying to look taller and slimmer. The dress I put on this morning feels too tight, like an over-stuffed sausage casing—even sucking in my gut doesn't help

"Thanks," I say gruffly, eyeing the table that was my destination. Until I've had a drink, something to blunt the raw edges, I can't handle anyone's sympathy.

"She was such a beautiful dancer," the woman goes on. "Such a terrific teacher. I could never compete with her. She worked on a whole different plane." A trace of wistfulness creeps into her voice and I sneak another peek at her, struggling to figure out who she might be.

She keeps talking, but I'm not listening. Not until another woman joins us, cutting her off mid-stream.

"Jules? Is that you?"

The first woman—Jules, apparently—swings around to look at the new arrival, another slender, poised woman. "Sandra. Isn't it sad?"

The blonde nods. "Terribly. She was so respected. Look around, Jules. I don't suppose there's a school in town offering classes today. Every teacher worth her salt is here."

Everything clicks into place with a snap I'm surprised isn't audible. Jules. Julianna. The dance teacher who was undercutting Mom's prices so much she was afraid of losing business. And this Sandra must be another teacher. I haven't seen her before, but now I know who Jules is, I recognize her from photographs on recital programs and advertisements in school newsletters.

While the two teachers talk, I study them. Julianna—Jules—is younger than Mom and shorter. She has a gentle, friendly face and an infectious smile. Her voice is bubbly and enthusiastic, even here. I imagine her students love her. They probably regard her as an older sister and aren't afraid to come to her with problems unrelated to dance.

No wonder Mom felt threatened by her. Even with her favorite students, Mom maintained a professional distance. When she taught me, I wasn't allowed to call her Mom in class. I had to refer to her as Madame, the same as all the other students. Jules didn't only undercut Mom's prices, she undermined everything about her teaching.

She and Sandra have moved closer together now, heads side by side as they share what appears to be some delicious morsel of gossip. I can't hear them over the voices filling the room and I wish I could. It might be juicy. It might be a clue to who killed her.

My stomach turns to ice.

Whoever killed her might be here now, could be standing in this very room.

My eyes flick back to Julianna. Could it have been her? Maybe her financial gamble didn't pay off the way she'd hoped and her reduced prices have her scraping for cash to pay the bills. Maybe she thought if she got rid of the best teacher in town, she'd pick up the extra pupils she needs to keep afloat.

By that logic the killer could be any of the teachers in the room. Any one of them could have benefitted from Mom's death.

But what about the money? I'm certain the two things—Mom's murder and the cash—are linked. I just haven't figured out how.

Blackmail? Did Jules pay Mom to keep her prices prohibitively high so parents would send their kids to her school instead?

It makes no sense. If Mom was being paid to keep students away, she wouldn't have hidden the money. She would have spent it. She'd have had to.

"Excuse me." I have to get away from here. Being so close to Jules, knowing Mom was worried about her makes me uncomfortable. I need that drink more than ever now.

My mind won't stop racing, though. Was the money Mom's after all? Was *she* the extortionist? Maybe she planned to offer the wad of cash to Jules so she *wouldn't* lower her prices.

That doesn't make sense either. The bundle of cash is more than twice what most people make in a year. If Mom planned to blackmail someone with it, it can't have been over their price differences. It would have to have been over something more significant.

But what?

Reaching for a coffee cup, I set it up on a saucer. I throw a quick glance around to make sure no one is looking before I grab a wine bottle and fill the cup. It's red wine and a few droplets splash over the rim and stain the white tablecloth. I brush at one of the spreading red marks, but it only makes the stain bigger. Oops.

Turning, I almost crash right into someone standing behind me.

"Aren't you a little young to drink?" My uncle doesn't sound angry, but amused. His eyebrows quirk upwards as he nods at the cup and saucer in my hands.

"Not today," I tell him, taking a huge slug. "Today I'm definitely old enough to drink."

I'm not lying. I feel eighty, at least.

Ropati smiles and gives me a conspiratorial wink. "I won't tell."

"What are you doing here?" I take another, more ladylike sip of wine. It's pretty terrible, but I can already feel it loosening my limbs.

"Paying my respects." Ropati looks down at the floor. "Irena was a wonderful woman. She made Tusi very happy for a time."

"Yeah, and then she made him real miserable too." The bitterness in my tone surprises me.

"True."

Silence falls between us. I suck up more wine, liking the way it warms my belly and makes my shoulders loosen from the place they've been wedged near my ears.

"Have…" I gulp more wine. "Have you seen him?" I can't look at him.

"Tusi?"

I nod, wishing I could take the question back all of a sudden. I don't want to know. I don't need to.

"I have." Ropati doesn't say anything more.

I struggle to raise my eyes to his, hoping I won't find anything there I won't like. They're clear though. Shiny, the surface impenetrable. Not at all like Dad's eyes. Dad lets every thought and emotion show in his.

I swallow hard. "Did… Did… Did he do it?"

"No." There is such certainty in the way Ropati says this, I feel a rush of relief. Dad didn't kill her. I don't have to hate him forever. He'll get out of jail soon and I can have my father back. If I can't live with Mama K, at least I'll have Dad.

"Thank you," I say, my face splitting into a smile. "Do you know when he'll get out?"

Ropati shakes his head. "Idiot cops think they have something on him. But don't you worry, Anastasia. I've hired an excellent criminal lawyer for him. He will not be going to jail for life. And we will be suing the incompetent police force in this city for holding him without evidence for so long."

Maybe it's the wine, or maybe it's the pure relief I'm feeling, but my legs are suddenly wobbly. If I don't sit down soon, I'll fall over.

"Are you okay?" The glamorous woman I saw with Ropati earlier grabs hold of my arm.

"Um... Yeah." She's so tall. I have to look up to see her face with its gorgeous, high cheekbones and slanted almond eyes. I have no idea where this woman is from. Her features are far too exotic to be from any single ethnicity.

"Anastasia, meet my wife, Jarboe. Jar, this is my niece, the one I was telling you about."

Jarboe. Even the name is a mystery. "Nice to meet you," I manage. I wasn't aware Ropati was married. Nana used to cluck and tut about how he was married to his job and would never meet a woman. Guess she was wrong.

"Oh, you too, honey. We've been so worried about you." Jarboe's voice is high and sweet with a hint of an accent lurking in the vowels. What kind of accent, I can't be sure. Not Russian, anyway. Not Samoan, either, no question about that. Samoan girls don't have tiny round butts like hers.

Over Jarboe's shoulder I finally catch sight of Vonnie. She's standing on the far side of the room, scanning the crowd, obviously looking for me.

"Excuse me." I set the near-empty cup down on the table and glance between Ropati and Jarboe. "I saw my friend."

"We'll talk again soon," Ropati promises. "Before we head back to the city."

I nod, not even sure what city he's talking about. I've never paid a lot of attention to Ropati and his life. Apart from the odd holiday he showed up for and Nana's funeral, I can count on one hand the number of times I've met him. I'm just grateful he confirmed my dad's innocence. That gives me one less thing to worry about.

Chapter Nineteen

I push through the crowd, standing on tiptoes every few moments to check Vonnie is still standing where I'm aiming. She sees me and waves, shoving her own way through the bodies as she pushes to reach me.

"Stas!" She hugs me so tightly my bones might snap. "Oh, Stas. I'm so sorry about your mom."

"Thanks." I mean, what else do you say? I've been struggling to work it out all week. It's not a compliment, but is there another polite way to respond?

"Are you okay? I went to your house the other day and the police chased me away. It's creepy."

"We've been staying with Halmoni." I hug her back. I can't believe I've let so much time pass without talking to her. My cell's been dead for days because the charger was back at our house and I didn't think to pick it up when I went back for clothes and things.

"You are going home, right?"

I shrug. "I don't know. I'm not sure any of us can live there now. Mom… Mom died there."

She pales. "I know. But not in the house, right? They said it was in the studio."

They? Who's they? "Yeah. But it's still so close. And the blood…"

Vonnie swallows hard. "You saw it?"

"I had to identify the body."

Vonnie's arms tighten around me again. "Oh, Stas."

Now the tears are threatening. I fight them, wrapping my own arms around Vonnie and squeezing tight as I force the image of my mother's lifeless body from my mind.

"Anything exciting happening at school?" I have

to change the subject. I can't think about this anymore. The room is too loud, too hot, too close.

I let Vonnie go and head toward the doors. There might be more air there, away from all these people. I catch sight of Teddy with the group of lesbians. He has a club sandwich in one hand, a pickle in the other. He's fine. While I watch, one of the ladies pops her last bite of brownie into his mouth.

The door is open a crack, letting cold air dribble into the room. I drag a couple of chairs into the draft and gesture for Vonnie to sit.

"So? School?"

She fiddles with the braid lying across her shoulder. Strands are already springing loose to curl around her face.

"Well... You know that guy from the party? Your guy, I mean?"

"Zane?" My spine snaps straight.

Vonnie leans forward like an over-eager puppy. "Yeah. Him. You'll never guess what he did."

"What?" I'm breathless for some reason, my heartbeat so strong and loud I'm sure Vonnie can hear it from her seat across from me.

"He got suspended. For fighting."

"What?" I say again. Zane never said anything when I saw him the other day. But... Maybe that's why I saw him the other day. In never occurred to me to ask why he was wandering the streets in the middle of a school day. Time's meant nothing to me since...

"He got into a huge fight with Jeremy Goldstein." Vonnie's practically bouncing in her chair. "I have no idea what it was about. Anyway, Zane creamed him."

"Good," I say flatly. I've hated Jeremy Goldstein since kindergarten. He used to tease me about having two moms back then, and still takes any opportunity to rip into me about it. He deserves anything he gets. "Anything else?"

Vonnie screws up her face. "Nah. Same old, same old. You haven't missed anything."

A part of me is glad. Another part of me can't believe I've been away from school almost a whole week and nothing has happened. The world has ticked on without me.

I'm about to ask Vonnie something more, but my aunts sidle over and stand hovering awkwardly above us.

"It was lovely, what you said," I tell Zoya after introducing her and Galina to Vonnie. They both stumble over her name.

Vonnie giggles. "I love it when you speak Russian," she says. "You sound so different."

"I do?" I've never considered it. While I often resisted speaking it, I've heard Russian alongside English for as long as I've been conscious. Mom thought it was important for me to be brought up with both languages. She thought it helped with learning other languages later on. I wouldn't know. So far the only other language I've tried to learn is French, and I've only started that this year, so I don't know yet whether knowing Russian helps. So far all that's happened is whenever I can't find the right word in French, the Russian one pops out. Which isn't much help.

"Your voice is deeper, or something," Vonnie says.

"Yeah?" Maybe it is. Russian is so guttural, it's quite possible I deepen my voice to make the sounds. It's not something I've ever thought about.

"You should have said something," Galina breaks in. "Irena would have wanted her daughter to speak."

I duck my head. "I know. I just couldn't." Tears blur my vision again. When is this going to get easier?

Will it ever get easier?

"Poor child." Zoya reaches over to pet me and I pull away. "Losing your mother at such a young age. And with no family around to help."

I grit my teeth. "I have family."

"What are they saying?" Vonnie grips my arm.

I shake my head. It's not worth going into. "I'll fill you in later. Family crap."

"I might go." Vonnie casts her eyes around the room. It's not exactly her scene. Vonnie's always the center of any party, but this isn't that kind of party and there's no place for her to shine. "Call me tonight, okay?"

"Sure."

She hugs me again, tighter even if it's possible, then darts out the door, washing the room in cold, fresh air for a second.

"Don't worry," Galina says as I turn back from the doorway. "We will take care of everything."

I bet they will.

Ropati and Jarboe drift in our direction. Ropati's ear is pressed to his cellphone and he's talking into it rapidly. Jarboe catches sight of me and smiles, hurrying over to join us. And I really wanted to find Mama K. I haven't seen her since we arrived and I need to know if she's all right. I should also check on Teddy. If he's not stopped, he'll eat crap all afternoon and spend the whole night throwing up.

Ropati slides his phone into his pocket and joins us.

"Anastasia. How lovely to see you again. And who are these beauties?" He flicks his eyes between Zoya and Galina.

"These are my aunts." I introduce them to Ropati and Jarboe, steeling myself for another conversation where I'll be interpreter.

"Ah. Lovely to meet you." Jarboe shakes hands with both of them. Zoya and Galina look a little awed to be touched by someone so glamorous. Or maybe it's disgust at being touched by someone so dark-skinned. I don't know or care much.

"Ropati is my uncle," I explain. "My father's brother."

Zoya's expression darkens and she mutters "*ubiytsa*" under her breath, the Russian word for killer.

"What did she say?" Ropati's mellow tone sharpens as if he knows already.

"Killer," I admit. "She called Dad a killer."

"Can you explain to her that my brother did not kill your mother? Saying he did is libelous, and I will not allow it."

I tell the aunts Dad didn't do it, but neither of them believe me. It's in the way they roll their eyes at one another, the way they set their jaws against Ropati. They're definitely sisters. Like this, they could almost be twins.

Ropati pulls out his phone again and frowns at the screen. "We should go, love," he says to Jarboe, settling a hand in the small of her back. "I still need to speak to the social worker."

Those two words send a shiver rattling up my spine. Nothing good can come from a social worker. Especially where I'm concerned.

"Social worker?" I manage to keep the tremble out of my voice. I can't keep the panic from my face, though, and Galina picks up on it instantly.

"What, *Lyubov*? What did he say?"

"Yes. Your father would like me to take care of you until this mess blows over. I've been talking to the social workers about assuming your custody." Ropati taps the phone impatiently before depositing it back into his pocket. "I'm hoping to have all the paperwork signed within the next few days so you can come home with us."

Zoya shakes me. "What is it, Anastasia? What did he say?"

"He wants me to go home with him. To live. Until Dad gets out of jail."

Zoya and Galina stare at each other for the briefest of seconds, before exploding into a tirade of Russian. They screech and swear, gesticulating wildly at Ropati and Jarboe who can only stand there, open mouthed, watching them. The whole room turns to look at them, conversations winking out as people become aware of the disturbance and move closer to find out what's going on.

I wish I could disappear. I want the floor to open up beneath me, to swallow me whole. I want to be anywhere except here.

Mama K appears. She slips an arm around me and pulls me close. "What's going on?"

I shrug, helpless to explain this. "They don't appear to like the idea of me living with Ropati..."

K freezes, her arm suddenly too tight and too heavy across my shoulders. Her breath smells of wine. "Why would you live with Ropati?"

"Apparently Dad wants me to."

Mama K's face darkens with blood. "Over my dead body," she spits.

She turns on him too, adding her own voice to the cacophony filling the room.

"Isn't it enough?" she screams. "Your brother killed my Rennie. Isn't that enough? You want to take my daughter now too? Why don't you kill me the way he killed her?" She bares her throat, daring him to slice it open.

My heart sprints off like a greyhound. My head

pounds with it. I can't take this. I don't want to be fought over like some kind of possession. Why doesn't anyone ask me what *I* want? It's *my* life. How dare they argue over me like this. And how did K get from Dad being a suspect to him killing Mom? How can she be sure? Did the cops tell her something they haven't shared with me? Something *she* hasn't shared with me? The relief and calm that rushed through me when Ropati assured me Dad was innocent is gone. Fear and panic thread through my gut. Could Dad have killed her?

I don't know what to believe anymore. I don't even know what I want to believe.

I take a step backward, away from the noise and the confusion. Away from the hands grabbing at me. Away from the anger and hurt. Away. Away.

As soon as I feel the cold air blowing through the crack in the door, I turn and push my way through, breathing heavily in the cold, untainted outside air. Then, just like I did the other day, I run.

Chapter Twenty

I run. My feet, in the uncomfortable heels I decided to wear this morning, pound the sidewalk. I wobble and turn my ankle, almost falling into the gutter. I manage to right myself and keep going, limping a little now. A block later, I turn my other ankle and decide to abandon the shoes. Stupid heels. I kick them off, not caring where they land. I never want to see them again. Even if I didn't lose them on the street, I'll never wear them again. I'll never wear this dress again either. I knew it when I put it on this morning so I picked something I never liked anyway. I should have worn the stupid orange bridesmaid dress. After how little I've eaten this week, I bet it would fit perfectly.

In just my stockings, I keep going, turning corners and following roads as if I know where I'm going. Which I don't. I have nowhere to go. Nowhere to call home. My heart aches. I used to have so many places I could call home. My own house, with Mama K and Mom, Dad's apartment, Nana's place. None of them are home anymore. The closest I can come is Halmoni's house, and there isn't even room for me. Only a couch to sleep on.

And back there, they're fighting over who gets to give me a home.

I'm homesick. Aching for a place to go of my own. Yet no such place exists. Or maybe it's not a place I'm looking for, but a time. The time before all this happened. That makes my situation even more impossible. No matter how hard I wish, I won't get what I really want. My home will be with whoever 'wins' this battle. And no matter who it is, I'll wind up a loser.

Will my new home be in Siberia with my aunts? I can't imagine it. I don't want to imagine it. I can't live in

Russia. Yes, I speak the language, but I couldn't go to school in Russian. I can't read or write it. Mom never got as far as teaching me more than the alphabet. And I'm rusty as hell because I've never used it.

So with Ropati and his wife? He said Dad didn't do it. How can he be sure? Was he there when Mom died? Was he with Dad? Can he prove Dad didn't or is it wishful thinking on his part? Something god told him? How can I go and live with him if Dad *did* do it? I couldn't betray Mom, even if I have only a tiny bit of doubt over his innocence.

And Mama K. How could I leave her? Especially now her heart is broken and she needs my help with Teddy. She's my mother, and she's the one I want to stay with, blood or no blood. How can the law be so foolish as to deny her that right?

I turn another corner and realize I've arrived at Zane's house. My face burns. Seriously? I keep forcing myself on him. He's going to think I'm some kind of stalker or something. I won't go in. I can't. He has his own life to lead, his own problems. He got suspended from school. His parents are getting divorced. His ballet teacher was murdered.

My mother was murdered.

The realization axes my legs and I fall to the ground. The grass beneath my knees is cool and smells green and pure. I let myself collapse into it. There's something so simple about this, so pure. I lie face down and close my eyes against the rapidly fading sunlight. Dampness sinks through the fabric of my dress, but I don't care. I let blades of grass tickle my nose and dance against my closed eyelids. Here, like this, I could almost believe it was spring.

"Stas?" Zane's voice startles me into rolling over. I look up and find his face looming over me like a weird moon.

"I thought it was you." Zane throws himself down beside me. "What are you doing here?"

He's been running or something. He's dressed in sweats and a tank top stained with sweat around the arm-holes.

I shrug. I have no idea why I'm here. I have no clue why this is where my feet brought me. It feels right, though. Perhaps this is my new safe place, my oasis of calm. At least I know no one will find me here.

"It's a beautiful day, huh?" He leans back on his elbows and turns his face up to what's left of the sun.

"Yeah." I look up at the fading expanse of blue spreading above us and wonder again how such cruelty can exist in such a beautiful place.

Zane elbows me in the ribs. "Talk to me. What's going on? You're all dressed up, you have no shoes on, and you're hanging out in front of my house. What gives?"

I close my eyes and swallow against the lump in my throat. It never goes away. It's always there, solid and impenetrable. Maybe I have throat cancer or something. I'm sitting here thinking I'm about to cry over my dead mother, when in fact deadly cells are gathering against my larynx.

"The funeral was today." I sit up and rub at the damp front of my dress, brushing away blades of grass and dry leaves.

"Oh." Zane remains silent for a moment, then looks at me, his eyes peeling back layers of skin to expose everything underneath. "How was it?"

There's something about the very simple way he asks this that breaks me. The tears I've held back for so long burst through and I'm sobbing. This isn't any ordinary crying either. It's like a tsunami rolling through me, shaking my body with such force I can't stay upright. I collapse into the ground again, pressing my burning face into the cool grass once more. My tears are so hot and so bitter, I'm surprised the lawn doesn't shrivel beneath me. I expect a hiss as each droplet hits the ground and scorches holes into the earth. I hear nothing except the unearthly sound of my own grief.

Zane doesn't speak to me. For a long time he doesn't touch me either. He lets me cry, not even looking at me as I howl out my fury at the universe. At Mom for being in the wrong place at the wrong time. At Dad for possibly being the person who did it. At my aunts for turning up and throwing my world into chaos. At Ropati and his righteousness. At Mama K for not having the strength to fight for me. At the unexplained package of money for being there and being ... unexplained. At myself for not going to the studio with Mom. Doing a few stretches with her wouldn't have killed me.

Something touches me and I jerk upright. Zane's next to me now, a hand resting lightly on my shoulder. I'm so close to him. Even through the curtain of tears still blurring my eyes, I realize his eyes aren't a single shade of dark blue. There are endless hues in there, ranging from the navy, near-black rim on his irises, to the pale sky blue flecks in the part near his pupil. He probably hasn't shaved in a couple of days and his chin is coated with fine, patchy stubble. I want to run my fingers across it to feel if it's rough or smooth.

"Cry it out," he says in a voice so low and gentle it slices another piece off my already brutalized heart.

I can't have any tears left. I've cried so much, my tanks must be empty. Yet more flow. I wipe helplessly at them, and at my streaming nose. I must look so attractive right now, with tears and snot all over my face.

Zane takes my other shoulder and draws me

closer to him. My head drops to his chest and I'm too exhausted to pull away. He smells of sweat, but under it is something sweeter, something spicy like cinnamon or fruitcake. It's the scent that clung to the collar of his jacket. I want to breathe it in forever.

With his strong arms holding me and the intoxicating aroma filling my nostrils, my crying slows and finally stops. I'm drained. It takes every ounce of strength I possess to wipe the last moisture from my face with my sleeve. I cringe at the shiny line of snot that has appeared on my dress. Who cares? I was going to chuck it out anyway.

"C'mon." Zane helps me to my feet and leads me away from the little patch of grass. The sun has moved. It sits low in the sky now, not quite ready to dip below the horizon, but on its way. How long have we been here?

Zane looks around, like he's checking to see if anyone is looking our way. Then he grabs my arm and leads me across the front lawn and to a path leading around the side of the house.

"Where..." I begin, but Zane hushes me with a finger to his lips.

I follow him along the side of the house, down a short flight of stairs into a small back yard. It's dim back there, the sun long gone. Zane walks up to a door, his shoulders tense and hunched toward his ears. He gives it a small push, and when it swings inward, he breathes what sounds like a sigh of relief. As I follow him through it, I notice a small wad of folded cardboard wedged in the hinges, not enough to keep the door open wide, but enough to keep it from fully closing.

"Is this okay?" I run my thumb under my eyes. I bet I look like a deranged panda.

"Sure." He doesn't look at me as he says it, though, just beckons for me to follow him.

The light is dim here too. A swinging bulb over a flight of stairs in front of me illuminates only a tiny circle around itself. I have no idea if the space I'm walking into is large or small. I stay close to Zane, terrified someone or something might lurk in the darkness. What am I even doing here? I don't really know this guy at all. Maybe he's lured me down here to do unspeakable things to me. Maybe he's going to kill me.

A sick feeling rises in my throat. I don't like this dark, creepy house. I hate the silence.

"Through here." We've reached the bottom of the stairs and Zane pushes open another door. It's completely dark in there and there's no way I'm following him into that gaping mouth of blackness. I'm about to flee back the way we came when I notice Zane fumbling around the doorframe for a switch. He finds it and the room lights up and buttery electric brightness spills through the doorway to illuminate the basement I'm standing in.

A washer and dryer crouch against the wall on my left and a red plastic basket overflowing with clothes sits on top of the washer. It's so normal, it settles my heartbeat. This isn't some weird dungeon torture chamber. My imagination is running rampant and I need to rein it in. Just because Mom was murdered doesn't mean that's my fate too. Uncertainty about what happened and why is making me crazy. These thoughts are too far out there to really be mine. I can't look at everyone around me as a killer, no matter how much I want to.

I step through the doorway and find myself in a large room. It may once have been used as a rumpus room or man cave, but now it's a bedroom. And more. A tiny kitchen alcove sits at one end; the microwave's green light flashes cheerfully as it announces the time. A small square table surrounded by four chairs is tucked into a corner.

Zane closes the door carefully behind us before walking over to another area where a pair of worn, mismatched couches surround a battered coffee table. A TV perches on something resembling a filing cabinet. My guts make a leap for my throat. A filing cabinet. I have to fight the urge to throw the drawers open and search their undersides. I have to calm down. Not every cabinet is going to hold the same kind of secrets Mom's did.

"Sit." Zane gestures at the couches and goes to the cabinets, rummaging around until he pulls out a small box. "I'll make some tea."

Tea. A boy who offers tea can't be bad. Tea is for kindly British nannies, for Korean grandmothers and new-age hippies. I can't be afraid of a boy who makes tea.

I sit myself on the very edge of the green couch, chuckling to myself. How could I have thought Zane might be dangerous? That's even more ludicrous than thinking Dad might have killed Mom. I think I might be losing my mind.

Chapter Twenty-One

While Zane glides around the kitchen nook, I let myself really look at the tiny apartment—that's what this is, really. If there were windows, it would be a nice place to spend time. As it is, it isn't horrible, but the low ceiling and lack of natural light give it a cave-like atmosphere.

"How do you ever wake up in the morning?" I ask when Zane comes over with the pair of steaming mugs. "Without windows, I mean."

He gives a twisted smile. "Three alarm clocks."

I return the smile even though I still feel jagged and broken inside from sobbing. I wonder if the pain will ever go away. I'm not sure I can live with this raw wound festering in my soul. I run my eyes across the other side of the room, catching sight of Zane's bed partly concealed behind a Chinese screen. A square of wooden floor has been laid to one side, and a barre is screwed to the wall along with a narrow mirror. A graying towel is tossed carelessly across the barre.

"Practice area?" I gesture to the tiny space.

He glances that way and nods. "Not great, but the best I could do. I wasn't sure I'd find a place to dance when I got here. Thought I should at least try to keep in shape if nothing else."

I nod and let myself look away from the pathetic studio. Zane shouldn't have to practice in a space so tight. He needs room to leap and soar. I only saw him dance once, but it was enough to show me how powerful he is. That tiny square of parquet would barely contain one of his battements.

I sip my tea. It's strong and hot and tastes bitter. Zane never asked if I wanted milk, and I didn't tell him I only drink black tea with a lot of milk and sugar.

Somehow though, this tea feels right for the moment. So I take another scalding mouthful, letting it burn its way down my throat to explode into my belly in a ball of heat.

A door slamming upstairs surprises me so much I jump. A small wave of tea splashes out of my mug and onto my hand. I lick at the reddening splotch as Zane leaps to his feet, an apprehensive look clouding his features as he leaps for the door and switches the light off.

"Are you going to get in trouble for having me in your room?" I ask in an almost whisper.

"No." He doesn't sound convinced. "She won't care."

But I think she will. Why else would he have us sitting here in the dark? I barely breathe, not wanting to give myself away.

I hear the door at the top of the stairs open. Someone clatters down the staircase in hard-soled shoes. The footsteps are louder than gunfire.

There is a slamming of doors and the sound of a dial spinning. The dryer turns on, filling the space with a low rumble. Should I go out there and introduce myself before whoever it is finds out I'm here? I don't move. I stay where I am, listening to the person rattle around the laundry room before clomping his or her way back up the stairs. When the door at the top closes with a click, Zane breathes again and flicks the lights back on.

But now he's angry and I can't understand why. He throws himself back onto the couch next to me with a furious puff of breath. He yanks up his tea with such force, he too creates a tidal wave that splashes over the rim.

"What is it?" I ask after the silence has stretched on too long.

He shakes his head and gives a short, bitter laugh.

"It's stupid. I mean, I have no idea how she'd feel about you being here. But she could have at least looked in. She could have said hello."

There is such hurt in his voice. I don't get it. Isn't he relieved she didn't come in and blow up about him entertaining girls? He switched the light off, so how would she have even known he was here?

Zane leaps to his feet again and starts walking tight, angry circles around the floor behind the couch. "I'm so tired of being ignored," he admits finally. "She never speaks to me. She never even acknowledges I'm here."

"Is that so bad?" I ask. I'd love a space like this all to myself, no parents or guardians lurking over me. No one to tell me what time to go to bed, what to eat and whether I'm allowed to go places.

I almost double over when I realize that's exactly the position I am in now. Well, the no parent part. Somehow I imagine anywhere I wind up I'll have guardians lurking over me constantly, watching my every move.

Zane goes on, speaking almost to himself. "I thought I wanted to be here. I do want to be here. I can't be at home. I can't keep being the rope in the middle of the tug-of-war. But I'm not sure how much longer I can handle being invisible."

Zane's voice breaks as he finishes. He falls back into the couch cushions, breath coming in strangled gasps.

It takes a few minutes before he straightens up. "Sorry. I shouldn't be bitching to you about my shitty little problems. You have enough to deal with right now."

He's right, but somehow knowing I'm not alone in my frustration over life is comforting. And he's been there for me when I needed someone. The least I can do is be there for him.

"Hey," I say, trying to keep my voice light. "I ruined your shirt crying on your shoulder. Feel free to ruin mine."

He smiles. A real smile now, dimples forming in both cheeks. God, he's gorgeous. "Thanks," he mutters.

Our eyes remain locked on each other. His smile fades, replaced with an expression I can only describe as hungry. He slides toward me and, as if a magnet pulls me, I drift toward him. We meet in the middle of the green couch. We fall into a hollow in the center of the cushion, our bodies colliding gently. His arms fall around me and mine mirror the motion. His heart thumps heavily against my chest as he lowers his face toward mine.

He's going to kiss me.

The thought sends silvery thrills up and down my spine. Hair rises on my arms and on the back of my neck. I turn my face up to meet him and when our lips touch, I swear a spark shoots into the room.

The kiss is gentle to begin with. His lips are warm and soft, slightly chapped from the cold outside. I explore them with my own. His tongue runs across my mouth and its heat is enough to make me gasp. He takes this opportunity to deepen the kiss and I allow him in. He tastes the way he smells and I let my tongue tangle with his as I try to absorb as much of his sweet, spiciness as possible.

He pulls away too soon, but keeps me in his embrace. He runs his eyes over every inch of my face like he's memorizing it. "You're beautiful," he murmurs, running his fingers over the freckles scattered across the bridge of my nose.

"So are you." I kiss him this time, shocked by the strength of the need I have coursing through me. Without any help from me, my body presses closer to him. I'm almost straddling him now, my mouth moving against his as if I want to devour him. His hands rove across my back, pulling me even closer. He's so strong. So solid. I shiver with the need to touch more of him. I cradle his neck with one hand, his skin and the sheen of sweat beading across it making me wild.

I've never felt this way about a kiss. I've never experienced this ache in my belly that spreads warmly to everything below it. I've never wanted my own body to become a part of someone else's. Yet now, that's how I feel. And it's exhilarating and terrifying in equal measure.

I pull away this time. Breathless, I put a few inches between us. Zane's face is flushed as he looks at me. His mouth looks red and swollen. Did I do that?

"Maybe you should go home," he says. "I'm not sure I'll be able to stop if you stay."

I don't have a home.

"Would that be such a bad thing?" I get up and cross to the Chinese screen. A tall, willowy woman with a fan stands against a backdrop of those pointy Chinese mountains. I slide behind her, listening to Zane groan from where he's still sitting on the couch.

I pull the ugly blue dress over my head and fling it over the screen.

"Stas, please…" Zane sounds like he's in agony.

"C'mere," I growl. I have no idea what I'm doing. This isn't me. It's more like Vonnie. I can't seem to help myself, though. It's like some other woman has invaded my body. Some bolder woman. Some woman with a body she wants to show off. I run my hands over my stomach and hips, not feeling the lumps and bumps I usually do but just warm, soft flesh. Warm, soft flesh longing to touch Zane's warm, harder stuff.

"No, Stas." Zane sounds firmer now. And closer.

The dress drops down off the screen and drifts to the floor next to me. "Get dressed, okay? I can't do this."

He can't do this.

The words are like a slap across my face. He can't do this. He kissed me. The most volcanic kiss of my life. And he can't do this? Didn't he feel the electricity crackling between us? Didn't he feel the sparks?

I grab the dress and pull it savagely over my head before stepping back out from behind the screen. The zip sticks halfway up my back, so I leave it there, feeling myself bulging over the top of it. Zane stands a foot away, head bowed. No wonder he doesn't want to do this. I probably revolt him. Yet ... he kissed me first.

He looks up when I breach the space between us. "I don't think this is a great idea," he chokes out. "Not now. We're both a little too fucked up to know what we're doing."

"I know what I'm doing." I search around for my shoes, then remember throwing them away on the street. Great. Now I'll have to walk back to Halmoni's on these shredded feet.

Zane grabs my wrist and pulls me close to him, his eyes clinging to mine. "I don't think you do. I don't think you can. Your world has changed in a huge way. But let's not rush into something just because we're both hurting right now. I like you. I want to spend time with you. But not like this."

He's probably right. With those sincere blue eyes glued to mine, I can't help wondering if he's right. Our kissing was explosive, but was it because there's real passion blazing between us, or because we both need to lose ourselves in something other than the shitty reality of our lives?

"I like you too." My voice is tiny.

He smiles again, those dimples so deep I want to

stick a finger into them. "Good. I'm glad." He grabs his sweatshirt off the back of a chair and throws it on. "C'mon. I'll take you home."

I follow him out the door. Where the hell can he take me that will feel remotely like home?

Chapter Twenty-Two

It's completely dark by the time Zane pulls up in front of Halmoni's house. Through the brightly lit windows I can see figures moving about. Too many figures to be only my family. Has the wake moved here now? I groan. I don't want to go in there. I don't want to talk to anyone or try to be polite. I want to lock myself into my room to curl up under the covers with my memories of how Zane felt and tasted. But I don't have a room here. Maybe Teddy will let me share his.

"It'll be okay," Zane murmurs, his hand stroking the back of my head.

I lean into his caress. It feels so good. I want to purr like a kitten or something. "I wish I didn't have to go."

"Me too. But I guess we can't always do what we want, right?"

I lean over and kiss him lightly. "Thank you," I say. It's not half what I want to say. It doesn't even skim the surface.

Zane grabs a pen from the jumble of stuff crammed into the space under his car's radio. Grabbing my hand, he scrawls something across my wrist. "My number," he says. "Call me any time, okay? Any time. I mean it."

I nod.

"In fact, call me tonight. Before you go to sleep."

I'll have to borrow K's charger. I nod again, unable to trust my voice not to break if I try to shape words. Then, because I'll cry (again) if I stay there any longer, I push open the car door and step out onto the street. The sidewalk is cold against my now bare feet. My stockings are in tatters around my ankles. Turning, I wave to Zane, but he doesn't leave. He sits there at the curb, watching me until I'm on the porch, my hand on the knob. Only then does he honk the horn once and peel out.

I stare after him until his taillights disappear around the corner before letting myself into the house, taking a deep breath to steel myself for what might be waiting for me behind those doors.

Voices spill from the living room and I head in that direction. Peeking around the doorframe, I try to assess the scene. Mama K is sprawled on the couch with her arms wrapped around Teddy. He is strangely still, as if accepting that right now, K needs him to be there for her to hold onto. Halmoni stands by the window with a bowl of something she's offering to Zoya. Galina is nearby too, her back to me as she stares out the window that only throws back her reflection. Ropati and Jarboe sit in the two chairs flanking the coffee table. Both hold teacups they sip from. A couple of the lesbian ladies are there too, hovering around K like bees around a flower.

I don't want to go in there.

Teddy glances up and sees me. "Stas!" he cries, wriggling his way out of Mama K's embrace to bounce over to me. "Mama K! Stas is back."

She looks up with watery, unfocused eyes. "Stas?"

I take Teddy's hand and let him lead me back to the couch. "I'm here."

She hugs me tightly. "I wasn't sure you'd come home…"

I can't say anything. This isn't home. But it is. Here, in her arms, this is home. But this room? These people? They aren't home. Except Teddy.

"I can't leave you," I whisper.

Her entire body convulses with the sob that racks her. "You may have to," she chokes. "Your father…" she spits the word out like it hurts her to say it. "Your father has declared me an unfit guardian. He won't allow me to apply for temporary foster care."

My head whirls. I'll wake up soon. I have to. I pinch my thigh so hard I'm sure a bruise will bloom there. This isn't happening.

"He's in jail!" I blurt out. "How does he get any say in this?"

Ropati stands, setting his teacup down carefully before striding across to where we sit. "He's innocent until proven guilty. Until that time, he has his rights. And he is your father and sole remaining legal guardian, so his word is law."

I scowl up at my uncle. I hate his low, reasonable voice. I hate he's right. I hate thinking I might be wrong. I hate thinking he might have killed Mom. Because I'm beginning to wonder now. Something about the way Ropati keeps insisting on his innocence makes me suspect maybe he isn't. And thinking that makes my stomach hurt. I wish I could see him. If I could look into his face, his eyes, then I'd know for sure.

"So what now?" I throw my hands up in despair. "What happens now?"

Mama K pulls me close again. "Shh... Stas," she murmurs. "We wait until we read your mother's will."

Mom had a will? I stare at Mama K. "Have you read it?"

She shakes her head. "It's with her lawyer. On Monday we can go and see him. I'm sure she will have provided for you and Teddy."

My stomach freezes into a glacier. When did she write the will? And has it been updated recently? I'm sure she has provided for me, but in what way, I can't be sure. What will I do if Mom's entrusted me to her sisters?

I glance over at Zoya and Galina who look lost

and drained. They pick at the bowl of nuts Halmoni set on the low table by the windows. They have no idea what is going on. They came to bury their sister and to fulfill whatever obligation they feel they have to her. They didn't expect to walk into a custody battle.

And that's what this is. It's the same kind of tug of war Zane came here to escape. But rather than being stuck between two people, I'm being yanked three ways. I can only hope whatever my mother has in her will trumps anything else. But I don't know for sure and it has my stomach tied into a series of elaborate, tangled knots.

Unable to keep thinking about this, I turn my thoughts to Zane. I run my tongue across my lower lip, tasting him there. Being with him was so much easier. In his arms I could forget all this. There, I was wanted. He saw me. Really saw me. Not as something to take from someone else, but as someone whole and real and worth spending time with. I ache for my phone. I want all these people to leave so I can curl up on my couch and call him.

Halmoni comes back into the room from the kitchen. I hadn't even noticed her leave.

"Time to go," she says, clapping her hands so loudly Jarboe jumps. "Family need rest. Difficult day."

Ropati and Jarboe rise first. They stand over the couch where Teddy and I are squished in with Mama K. Neither of us are ready to leave her alone right now. She's so obviously fragile. And how couldn't she be? Today she buried the woman she devoted her life to. She should be broken. Teddy and I just need to be there to hold the parts of her together until she can mend.

"We will be at the lawyer's on Monday," Ropati says.

I close my eyes. Really? Even there? Why does this whole thing have to be such a circus? I've avoided newspapers, but I'm certain my mother's murder has been front-page news all week. Can't we even hear my mother's will read in private?

Mama K sighs and nods. "Thank you for coming," she manages through gritted teeth. Why does she bother being polite? I wouldn't if I were in her position.

The tension in the room drops after Ropati and Jarboe have left. A little. I get up wearily and cross to the windows where Zoya and Galina are conversing in whispers.

"Do you need a ride back to the hotel?" I ask them in Russian. "We need some time alone now."

The pair of them flap like a pair of seagulls as they gather up their belongings. "No, no. We are fine. We can take a taxi," says Zoya

"I don't mind driving you." I hope Halmoni won't mind me driving her car. Ours is still parked in the driveway back at our house. I should go get it tomorrow. If Mama K is ever ready to leave the house, she'll want the car.

Galina shakes her head. "If you can call the taxi, we will wait outside."

"If you're sure…" I push through to the kitchen and call the taxi company's number I can remember from their obnoxious jingles on the radio. "Call three eight, then a whole bunch of fours," I sing under my breath as I dial.

****

The house feels empty and too quiet once everyone is gone. Halmoni rattles around, trying to feed us from the piles of food the lesbian ladies have left. I nibble on the crusty edge of a lasagna, but it's tasteless and sticks in my throat. I wash it down with a big glass of water and push the pan aside. Teddy shovels in a few big mouthfuls, but then he too gives up and lets his fork drop to his plate.

Mama K doesn't even try to eat. She sits with a glass of whisky in front of her, sipping from it occasionally. Halmoni tuts at her each time she goes to the cupboard over the stove to refill it.

"I'm going to bed," K says finally, her words a little slurred.

I watch her go. It's only eight, but I can understand her wanting today to be over. If things had gone as planned, she and Mom would be going to bed in a cabin on the beach in Hawaii. As it is, she's heading up to sleep in her childhood bedroom with only her son for company.

Teddy goes up soon afterward, leaving me alone with Halmoni. Because I can't think of anything else to do, I fill the sink and wash the dishes I find scattered around the house. Halmoni joins me, dishtowel in hand to dry and put them away. We don't speak. We don't need to. There is no real bond between us, just our mutual love of K, our need to protect her. It's not much, but it's enough.

"Thank you," Halmoni says when we're done. "You good girl. You look after Keyung-Seok."

"I'll try," I say. It's the best I can offer.

Once Halmoni disappears upstairs, I shut off the lights in the kitchen and head for my couch. I'm exhausted, but I won't sleep. I can't bear the thought of spending another night lying in the darkness, staring up at the unfamiliar ceiling. I make up the bed automatically then go around the room switching off lamps until the room is dark except for the green-shaded lamp sitting behind my couch. Filtered through the green material, the light is muted and murky. It's like being in a dark swamp or something. Furniture looms in hulking shadows around the perimeter.

I pull my phone out from under the couch and switch it on. No messages. No missed calls. I've been away from it all day and ... nothing. I shouldn't be surprised. I was with everyone who might call me today. I can't help being a little disappointed. I have friends at school. Not a ton—I've never needed a ton of friends. I have Vonnie. I get why they haven't called. What can you say to someone whose mother has been murdered?

Zane's number burns across my wrist. I glance down at it and copy the numbers into my phone. Add contact. Zane ... I can't remember his last name. I know I saw it when I sought out his address, but so focused on getting what I needed, I can no longer remember. It started with T... I struggle to remember. Tanner? Taylor? No, that's not right. I wrestle with it a moment longer then give up and save his number under just Zane. How many Zanes do I know anyway?

I long to press the button and call him right now. But I don't. I climb off the couch and head upstairs, tiptoeing down the hallway to Mama K's room. I should check on her. Make sure she's okay. Make sure Teddy is. I push open the door carefully, wincing as the hinge squeaks loudly. No one stirs. Still tiptoeing, I creep into the room. The curtains aren't drawn so a wash of moonlight bathes the room in cool, white light. Mama K is curled up on the bed, her body curved into a C around Teddy who is sprawled on his back. They're both sound asleep and look peaceful. No nightmares have invaded their night yet.

Confident my people are safe, I creep back out of the room and head to the bathroom for a shower, stopping only long enough to grab the phone charger plugged into the wall outside Mama K's room. Once I'm clean and in my pjs, then I'll call Zane.

Chapter Twenty-Three

Monday rolls around either too quickly or too slowly. I can't tell which. Some moments I feel like Sunday crawls along at a snail's pace and I wish I could speed time up so we could get to the lawyer's office. I need to find out my fate. Others, I want time to stop all together, or at least slow down enough for me to enjoy what might be the last day with the family I've known and lived with for almost as long as I can remember.

Of course, time can't be stopped or sped up and Monday shows up as it does every week. We're not due at the lawyer's office until eleven, but I'm up before six and have drained most of a pot of coffee before anyone else emerges from their bedrooms.

"What's going to happen today?" Teddy asks me when he sits down at the table next to me.

I keep my voice low. "We're going to hear the lawyer read Mom's will," I explain. "It will tell us what she wanted for her things and her money and stuff."

"Is it about you?" He looks up at me with those beautiful brown eyes, so much like Mama K's he could have stolen them from her head.

I swallow hard, not wanting to let my worries affect him. He's safe. Mama K is his mom. No one can take him away from her. "Maybe," I say. "Because Mom was my birth mother. The same way Mama K is your birth mother."

"But Mama K is your mom too."

It should be so simple. I wish it was. "Yeah… But it's not exactly the same thing."

Teddy nods and pours himself a huge bowl of cereal. I'm grateful he doesn't press me further. I don't have the answers he wants. Does anyone?

The lawyer's office is downtown in one of the tall buildings lining the square across from the railway station. We have to be signed in and walk through a metal detector before we're allowed to approach the elevators that will take us to the eleventh floor. Mama K stares at her reflection in the mirrored walls as we ride up. She brushes her hair back with her hand and pinches her cheeks to give them more color. She put on make-up this morning, but it isn't enough to hide the dark circles under her bloodshot eyes.

Ropati is already seated in the waiting area when we step off the elevator. He rises from an oversized leather couch when he sees us.

"Good morning," he says with a smile that's too big and too filled with white teeth. He reminds me of a wolf. Or maybe a piranha.

Mama K nods at him as she sweeps past to the reception desk. We stand awkwardly around the too-large glass coffee table. Halmoni bends and picks up a magazine out of the artfully designed fan of them lying across its top. She flicks through the pages, yet I'm certain she's not reading anything on them. She drops it back a second later and the sound of it slapping against the glass is enough to make everyone jump.

The elevator doors slide open again and my aunts step out with another woman. They give tense smiles as they join us.

"I'm Barbara," the other woman says, showing almost as many teeth as Ropati. "I'll be acting as interpreter this morning."

I glance at Zoya and Galina and am grateful they've thought to bring someone to translate the proceedings for them. That's not a job I want. Especially if things don't go their way. Not to mention, my Russian probably isn't up to translating something like this.

It feels like a really long time before the lawyer shows up and ushers us into a conference room with a huge wooden table and lots of nice, padded chairs.

"Please, sit," she says, gesturing for us to take our pick of seats.

I wait until everyone else has started seating themselves before picking my own spot, between Teddy and Mama K. When K reaches for the glass of water in front of her on the table, her hand shakes so much I'm sure she'll spill it before she gets any to her mouth. I don't even attempt to drink from my own glass, knowing my own hand will shake just as much. My stomach churns with a mixture of fear and nerves. I'm glad I didn't eat breakfast this morning. I'd be puking into the wastebasket by now if I had.

The room grows still as the lawyer opens the document she has lying in front of her on the table.

"You know," she says, looking at all of us through her stylish thick-rimmed glasses. "I've never done this before."

"What?" Ropati, who is sitting on her left, gives her a scathing look.

"A will reading," she goes on. "It doesn't usually happen like this. Only in the movies. But given the circumstances, and the wide range of people involved, it seemed better to get you all together for this."

Ropati seems to relax a little. At least, he leans back in his seat and the crease between his eyes goes from a canyon to a crevasse. A low murmur comes from the far end of the table as the aunts listen intently to their interpreter. I hope she's good. The last thing we need is her screwing up some important detail.

The lawyer begins. I try to focus on her words, but they are all about trusts and estates and other stuff I don't understand or care about much. I *should* listen because this is Mom's stuff we're talking about—her money, her business—none of it feels like it has anything to do with me.

So I drift, letting myself remember the two-hour long conversation Zane and I had on the phone last night. I picture his blue eyes and his dimples and hope I can slip out to see him after school today. I don't want him to have to go back to that cold, unwelcoming house alone. It's so unfair his aunt should treat him that way. It's not exactly neglect because he has everything he could possibly need in his little apartment. Just not love. Or companionship. Even friendship. I wish I knew why she treated him so coldly. Maybe then he could change things and make the house a place he can call home.

Mama K pokes my arm sharply and I sit up, disorientated for a second. I blink down the long, polished table and fix my eyes on the lawyer. She's looking right at me. Uh oh. What did I miss?

"Would you like me to repeat that, Anastasia?" the lawyer asks.

"Uh... Yes, please." I know my face is red. How could I have drifted off for so long? This is important. This is my life.

The lawyer keeps her eyes on me a moment longer, checking to make sure I'm paying attention this time. She lowers them to the paper again. "I'll summarize," the lawyer says. "What it says here is, in the event of anything happening to Irena before her daughter is of age, she grants custody of Anastasia to the child's father, Tusi Nonu."

She keeps talking, but I hear nothing more. She's giving me to Dad. Dad. I can't think. I can't live with Dad. Even if they clear him of all the charges, I'm not sure I'll ever be able to look at him without suspicion. Not unless someone else is rotting behind bars for doing this to my mother. No way. No fucking way.

Mama K makes a noise beside me and I'm back in the lawyer's office. I turn and find her looking at me with a stricken look on her face. "No," she says. "No. No. No."

Ropati leans forward, a smug, self-satisfied smile on his face. "Given the present state of affairs, my wife and I will assume responsibility for Anastasia. I'm confident my brother will be cleared of all charges, and he will assume his rightful role as her guardian."

"No," Mama K repeats. "You can't. Irena wanted Stas to be with me. I'm her mother."

I'm proud of her for standing up to Ropati. Mama K doesn't have Ropati's way with words or his legal knowledge, yet she stands up to him.

Ropati gives her a smile that makes him look even more like a predator. "You are not her mother. Her mother's dead and her will makes her wishes very clear. Under the circumstances, I believe Tusi would prefer his daughter came with me at this time. He's had concerns about the environment she has been living in for a long time, and at this point, I believe it's best we remove her from that environment."

What environment? My home? What's wrong with my home? Dad wasn't thrilled about Mom and K, but this is ridiculous. They've been together twelve years. It's not like this 'environment' is new. The only new thing is my Dad's fucked up thinking about it. I blame that pastor and his velvet tongue.

At the other end of the table, the aunts and Barbara speak in low voices. I can't catch much of it, except for catching my own name several times, along with Mom's.

Barbara stands up. "My clients object to Mr. Nonu's proposal. If Tusi Nonu is unable to take up the role of caretaker, as he clearly cannot do at this time, Zoya and Galina Varushkin would like to be given the same consideration as Mr. Nonu. Their relationship to Anastasia is the same as his."

The lawyer clears her throat. "This is not a custody hearing. I am merely reading Ms. Varushkin's wishes. Should any of you wish to contest the will, the proper channels will need to be followed."

More murmuring. From somewhere in the room, a cell-phone beeps. Ropati glances quickly around the room then pulls the phone out, staring down at it intently. He punches in numbers savagely. Pushing back his chair, he goes to the windows and paces back and forth, muttering into it. How rude.

Mama K closes her eyes and rubs at her forehead as if she has a headache. I bet she does. I do. How could Mom leave me to Dad?

Actually, I think I know. This will was probably written a long time ago. Certainly before Nana died and Dad's views on the world shifted. When Mom wrote this, she and Dad were probably still friendly enough. They might even have still been married. Even if they weren't, it could have been written long before Mom and K got serious enough to consider marriage. Before they had the option of marriage, even. Before Dad decided Mom and Mama K were evil and likely to corrupt my morals. Of course she would have chosen him. He's my father.

But I haven't.

I won't.

Fury tangles with despair somewhere near my mid-section. The combination makes me nauseous.

I shove my chair back with such force it topples over and crashes to the floor. "This is bullshit," I yell, not to anyone in particular. "I'm not taking this."

I storm out, slamming the door so hard behind me

the echo reverberates across the entire floor of the office building.

Chapter Twenty-Four

I don't want to wait for the elevator, so I find the stairs. Running down them, I focus on nothing but the sound of my footsteps pounding the concrete. It's a long way down, and I'm breathless by the time I hit the ground floor. The building foyer is as crowded as it was when we came in, and I'm grateful for the people. They can cover me. Ropati and Mama K and the aunts will be looking for me. Probably even the lawyer too.

Too bad. Let them look.

I join the throng of people heading for the exits, pushing my way through toward the doors. I slide around a tall, elegant woman in a too-tight skirt and heels and find myself pressed against the security desk. Turning, I squeeze along it, my belly pressed against the heavy wood. Something flickers on the other side and my eye is caught by a small television set perched on the corner of the low counter.

I freeze.

My father's face stares back at me from the screen.

It's a picture I know well, the picture that has graced every program or press release about the Company for the last five years or so. Across the picture, bisecting the top of his head, white lettering reads: Dancer charged.

The newsreader starts speaking, but the volume's so low and the room so noisy I can't catch any of the words. I lean forward, practically folding myself over the desk's frame as I strain to hear the newsreader's calm, reasonable voice.

"...evidence discovered in the Varushkin murder case. Police have charged Ms. Varushkin's estranged husband with her murder after finding what has been described as 'a manifesto of hatred' amongst the suspect's belongings. Ms. Varushkin..."

My heart stops beating. My fingers cling to the edge of the desk. I can't tear my eyes away from the screen, even as the image changes and the newsreader moves on to another story. I stagger sideways.

"Whoa. Are you okay?" A man in a beautifully tailored suit sets me back on my feet.

"What?" I blink up at him, surprised I can see him through the lettering emblazoned across my retinas.

"You almost fell. Are you all right?"

I nod, my head clearing a little. "Sorry. Crowded in here."

He nods. "Lunchtime."

And then he's gone, moving easily through the people. I sneak another look at the screen, but my father is no longer there, replaced by footage of soldiers crawling through the wreckage of some once-beautiful town.

Dad did it.

He did it.

Dad killed Mom.

I take a deep breath and unclench my fingers from around the desk. I have to get out of here. I have to see Dad. I have to know if this is true. The words are imprinted on my soul, but they don't feel right. They don't feel like the truth.

The plots of a million cop shows spin through my head. Someone's framed him. I have no idea who or why, but it can't be true. It can't possibly be true.

I find myself outside the building, blinking in the midday sun as I try to orient myself, try to figure out where to go next, what to do now. The sunshine feels wrong. Days have passed since we walked into the building, months. The season should have changed. Everything else in my life has. All in the one morning.

The Central Police Station isn't far from where I'm standing, indecisive on the corner of the street. I have no idea if Dad is being held there, but I can at least go down and ask. Even if he isn't in their jail, they'll be able to help me get to wherever he actually is. Maybe.

It takes me only ten minutes to reach the station. It's less intimidating than it was the day I came here with McMillan and... What was the other cop's name? Allen? I can't remember. I march past the sketchy-looking people lined up on the bench and approach the woman behind the desk.

"Is Detective McMillan available?" I ask, surprised to find my voice shaking.

The cop yawns as she looks my way. "What is it regarding?"

I swallow hard. Do I need to tell her? "The Varushkin murder," I manage, almost strangling on the word murder. My mom's name and murder should never go together.

She picks up a phone from her desk and jabs a couple of digits. When she hangs up, she yawns again and points to the bench. "He'll be up shortly."

Eyeing the bench with suspicion, I take a seat on the very edge. Next to me, a middle-aged woman wearing what looks like underwear slumps against the wall. It's not even good underwear. Most of the breast closest to me spills out over the cup. I glance away, only to find myself looking at a grubby-looking guy who makes gestures at himself, accompanying them with exaggerated eyebrow waggles and some lewd tongue work.

Shivering in disgust, I look at the floor. It's the only safe place. I wish I could take a shower. Just being in this room makes my skin feel layered in filth.

"Anastasia?" McMillan stands in the doorway, looking at me. "C'mon. Let's go to my office."

He throws a sharp glare at the gesticulating guy as he ushers me through.

I follow him through a maze of corridors and cubicles, catching snatches of conversations here and there as we go.

"What can I do for you?" McMillan closes the office door behind us and sinks into the seat behind his desk. Across the room, the other desk is empty.

"I need to see my dad," I say. There's no point beating around the bush. I don't want to have to stay in this place any longer than necessary. It gives me the creeps.

McMillan sighs. "You need to see your dad... Well, he isn't here."

I figured.

McMillan goes on. "This is where we process the criminals, so our jail is only a holding pen, so to speak. Your father's out at Quincy."

I figured as much. "How do I get in to see him?"

"He will need to have listed you as a visitor. Have you spoken to Quincy at all?"

I shake my head. I haven't thought about where Dad might be or how to contact him. I've been too caught up with how or why he might have killed my mother.

"In that case, you will need to speak to his lawyer. Do you know who that is?"

I shake my head again. Ropati? No. That would be a conflict of interest, wouldn't it? I bet Ropati has some powerful lawyer friends, though. Those Armani suits he wears aren't cheap. He'll know who Dad's lawyer is. Probably hired them himself.

"Is there another way?" I don't want anything to do with Ropati.

But I do need to see my father.

McMillan shakes his head. "I'm afraid not."

My skin turns cold and my head spins. I'm glad I'm sitting down or I'd be crumbling into a heap on the ugly industrial gray carpet. "Are you sure?" The words come out as a whisper.

"Yeah. I wish I could tell you something else. If you're not on his list, you can petition him to be put on it, but at the end of the day, it's his decision. If he doesn't want to see you, or in this case it's more likely he doesn't want you to see him, he has the right to refuse you."

"Why wouldn't he want to see me?" I hate how weak and shaky and scared I sound.

McMillan gets up and rounds his desk. He moves beside me and holds a box of tissues toward me. "Because he's ashamed of what he's done, maybe? Or because he was caught?"

I grab a tissue and wipe at my stupid, watery eyes. I don't want to cry over this. I just want to look my father in the eye and listen to him tell me the truth. It's not too much to ask, is it?

"Can I get you a ride home?" McMillan asks, his voice more gentle than I would have thought possible.

I ignore what he asked. "Do you think he did it?"

McMillan sighs heavily and perches himself on the edge of his desk so his eyes are closer to level with mine. "It's an ongoing investigation, Anastasia. I can't discuss it. Even with you."

But he nods.

It's a tiny gesture, possibly even an involuntary one; it tells me everything.

I stand up. "Thanks for seeing me. I'll go now."

"I'm sorry, Anastasia," he says as I bolt for the door.

****

Once I'm outside the police station, I run. Why am I always running? I've never been someone who flees from her problems, but at the moment, it's all I seem to do. It's the only thing I *can* do. I don't believe it. I can't believe it. There's no way Dad did it. I don't care what the cops believe or what they found. Until Dad tells me himself, until I see his guilt painted in neon letters across his face, I won't believe it.

I can't think about it.

Yet I can't stop.

I need to go somewhere. Home? No. I can't go back to Halmoni's. I can't face Mama K. She'll believe it. It might not be easy, but she needs someone to blame for this. She needs the closure. Will she hate me now? Will she be able to look at my brown, Samoan face again? Probably not. Every glimpse of me will be a reminder. Did the cops call her or did Ropati explain after he took the call in the lawyer's office. Now I understand why he took it, why it was important enough to interrupt something as serious as the reading of my mother's will. Will he challenge it? He seemed so certain of Dad's innocence. I wonder if he still is now, or if the so-called evidence is enough to convince him otherwise.

I pull out my phone and turn it back on. Seventeen missed calls and I don't know how many texts. All from Mama K. I ignore them all and dial Vonnie's number. I'll go to her house, hang out there for a while. Until I feel strong enough to face Mama K. The phone rings and rings, finally clicking over to voicemail. I thumb the phone off without leaving a message. Vonnie never listens to them.

I keep running, turning down side streets and crossing thoroughfares at random. I punch Vonnie's number again and listen to the electronic buzz until it clicks off and a robotic voice asks me to leave a message.

She hasn't even personalized her voicemail. Where is she?

I slow to a walk and scroll through the rest of the numbers on my phone. Who else can I call? Where else can I go? I glance at the names of various acquaintances as they roll by. But that's all they are—acquaintances. And I couldn't burden them with my company the way I feel right now. It should be depressing, but I've never needed other friends. Vonnie has always been enough. Where the fuck is Vonnie?

I call her again, knowing this time she's not going to pick up. Maybe she's grounded again and her mom took her phone. I should just go over there. Even if she is grounded, I'm pretty sure her folks will let me in.

Chapter Twenty-Five

I jump off the bus at the corner of Vonnie's street. Glancing at my watch, I'm surprised to see it's only just after 3:30. It feels like hours since I ran out of the lawyer's office. No wonder Vonnie didn't answer her phone. She was probably still in class. I'm exhausted, my feet heavy and clumsy as I stumble down the street toward her house. It's Monday, so I know Vonnie doesn't have any activities after school. It's the only day she doesn't.

I climb the porch steps and knock on the front door. I ring the bell too, just in case. I lean against the door, listening for footsteps.

Nothing.

I ring the bell again, listening to it chime in the hallway I know almost as well as my own.

Still nothing. It doesn't make sense. Vonnie has to be home. I need her.

I go a little nuts then, pounding on the door and jabbing at the doorbell over and over again.

"Hey!" someone calls from the street. "Hey, you! What are you doing up there?"

I turn and find a man standing on the sidewalk with a small dog running circles around his feet.

"Oh. It's you," he says and I recognize him as Vonnie's neighbor, Mr. Jacobs. "They went away."

"Who?" I ask stupidly.

"The Youngs. Evie's father had a stroke."

"Oh…" I can't believe Vonnie didn't tell me. Or maybe I can. I never called her when Mom died. It never even crossed my mind.

"Thanks, Mr. Jacobs." I force myself to smile as I climb down from Vonnie's porch. Now where do I go?

I walk back up to the corner of the street and look around. If I turn left, I can jump on the next bus and go back to Halmoni's. If I turn right, I could go home. To my own house, if I can even call that place home anymore. I can't imagine it feeling homely without Mom.

My feet carry me in that direction without my brain playing any part in the decision. It's like I'm on autopilot. But instead of turning right at the next set of lights, I cross and keep going straight ahead. When I realize my mistake, I stop and start turning to go back. But something stops me. After a moment's hesitation, I keep walking, making turns seemingly at random until I find myself standing at the corner of the little cul-de-sac where Zane lives.

My face heats up when I realize where I've come. Zane's going to think I'm some kind of crazy stalker if I don't watch out, continually showing up on his doorstep uninvited. I should go.

My phone buzzes in my pocket again and I pull it out to see another text from Mama K. I erase it without reading it. I can't deal with her right now. I can't face her, knowing it was my father who killed her wife. I can't...

The honk of a horn behind me makes me jump. I whirl around and find a familiar blue car pulling up at the curb beside me.

Zane leans out the window. "Stas?"

My already burning face blazes hotter. I've been snapped. "Zane."

I must look a wreck because he doesn't even say hello, just, "What is it, Stas?"

He leans across and opens the passenger-side door, gesturing for me to get in. I hesitate a moment, unsure if I'm doing the right thing.

"C'mon, Stas. I won't bite."

And that's what breaks me again. His kindness. His concern.

I collapse into the car, tears stinging my eyes as I pull the door closed behind me. Zane reaches across and brushes away the single tear that has escaped to roll across my cheek.

Zane's arms come around me, pulling me close, the gearstick digging painfully into my thigh. "What happened?"

He's asking about the lawyer. Was it only this morning? It was a lifetime ago. Another century. Does what was said in that room even matter now?

It does, but somehow it doesn't to me. My fears about my future have been washed away by this other, bigger, more important truth.

But it's not the truth. It can't be.

I pull away from him and buckle my seatbelt in a daze. I should cry, but there's nothing left in me to cry. Besides, why should I cry for him? He killed her. That's what they're telling me. He killed her.

A whimpering sound startles me out of my thoughts. I look around, searching for the source of the sound before realizing it's me.

"Let's go for a drive." Zane pulls away from the curb and turns in the driveway across the street. "Are you okay?"

I shake my head. I'll never be okay. How can I be?

I can't think like this anymore. I'm going to go nuts. I'll throw myself out of the moving vehicle. Or I'll start laughing and not be able to stop. Or crying. Or screaming. I don't want to do any of those things so I reach out and flick the radio on, spinning the volume knob until the car throbs with drums and bass. Zane reaches out to turn it down, but I swat his hand away.

The song ends and three high-pitched beeps pierce the car. I wince and reach for the knob, turning it down as the newsreader comes on, announcing it's five o'clock.

Five o'clock? Where did the day go?

"…evidence discovered in the Varyushkin murder case. Police have charged Ms. Varyushkin's estranged husband with her murder after finding what has been described as a "manifesto of hatred" amongst the suspect's belongings. Ms. Varyushkin…"

Zane's hand snaps out and silences the radio. I'm grateful. The same words the TV newsreader read. I can't listen to them anymore. He did it. He really did it. He wrote about it.

"My dad killed her," I say, my voice shaky and uncertain. Maybe if I say the words they'll feel real.

"Are you sure? Cops can make mistakes."

They can, can't they? I watched the whole of *Making A Murderer*. I've seen those films about the West Memphis Three. People are always getting wrongly accused of crimes. I gesture at the radio. What the hell is a "manifesto of hatred" anyway? Dad's diary? Did Dad even write a diary? Probably. He certainly always had a notebook around. Something to doodle in when he wasn't dancing. If his feet weren't moving, his hands usually were. That's probably it. The cops found his diary and mistook some random scrawl that might have been the beginning of a new piece for something it was never intended to be.

Zane breathes out a gust of air. "Do you think he did it?"

I open my mouth to say no, but something stops me. The stack of money flashes in front of me. It can't have been Dad's. He was always so worried about money, always on the verge of losing the theater or his apartment or both. If he had that kind of cash lying around, he wouldn't have been concerned about those things.

But what if it was?

"I… I hope not," I manage to whisper and it's the best I can do.

Zane opens his mouth and closes it again. His uncertainty makes him look like a goldfish.

I decide to change the subject and give a sharp, bitter laugh. "And Mom made him my guardian."

"Is that what the lawyer said?"

After everything else, I barely remember the lawyer's office. Now it comes flooding back. "Yeah. That's what was in the will. So now everyone's fighting about that too." I wonder where they all are. Are they all off with their own lawyers preparing to fight Mom's wishes? Or are they at Halmoni's, arguing while she plies them with tea?

I don't care.

I'm not going back there.

I'm not going to Russia with Zoya and Galina.

I'm not going anywhere with Ropati and Jarboe.

I'm not staying with Mama K while all these people fight and make her already shattered life hell. I won't let her go through that. I won't put Teddy through it. I can't face either of them. If the police are right, it's my flesh and blood who took away the woman they loved more than anything else. They shouldn't have to look at my face and be reminded of that person.

"Where am I taking you?" Zane's voice startles me out of my contemplation.

"Can we go back to your place?"

He frowns, his eyebrows tightening over his eyes. "I guess…" He doesn't sound certain. He sounds like he wants to go there even less than I want to go back to

Halmoni's.

"I wish there was somewhere we could go where we didn't have to deal with any of this." I stare out the window at the darkening sky. Surely there must be somewhere we can go while I figure all this out.

"You want to run away?" Zane's stopped at a light now and he looks over at me with such intensity in his gaze it startles me.

"I think I already did," I say.

****

It happens very quickly. At the next lights, Zane turns left. His posture has changed. He seems to have grown and spread inside his skin. He moves with purpose, every gesture sure and graceful. We're running away.

"Don't you need some stuff?" I ask as we join the line of cars pulling onto the highway.

"Got it," he says, jerking his thumb at the backseat. Bags and boxes cram the small space. I can't believe I haven't noticed them. Or maybe not. I haven't exactly been paying attention to my surroundings.

"You were already leaving?" I can't believe he'd leave without saying goodbye.

"Nah. Just getting prepared. I can't stay there." Zane gives an embarrassed shrug. "I hate it. Almost as much as I hate my parents."

"Where should we go?" Suddenly this feels scary. It's too big a decision. I have nothing, not even clean underwear. I have my dress, my shoes, my stockings and whatever is in my purse. I don't even have a coat since I left it hanging in the lawyer's office when I ran out. "I don't have much money…"

It's a lie. I know where to find more money than either of us have ever held before. If I'm willing to go there, and I'm not sure I am.

Zane shrugs. "I have some. Not a lot either, but enough for now. I can get a job once we get where we want to go."

He's so calm about this. Like he's planned it out. Maybe he has. I bet he never planned on having me come along.

"We'll be fine, Stas," he promises. "I have plenty of food and stuff back there. Where would you like to go? Is there anywhere you've always dreamed about? Some place you'd like to go back to? If you could go anywhere, where would it be?"

I rack my brain. Where would I go? The ocean? The mountains? Another city? I remember the vacations we've taken. I don't want to go back to any of those places. They're Mom places. I need to go somewhere new, somewhere without memories of her. Like I've thought before, the place I most want to go isn't a location, it's a point in time.

We're driving across town and I love that we're putting distance between everything I once held dear and where we are now. Yet I can't help feeling like a coward. I've never considered myself truly brave, but I've never run from anything before. Or at least, never run so far. Or so permanently.

My phone vibrates in my pocket. Fuck. I forgot to turn it off after that last text. I pull it out, and ignoring Mama K's name flashing on the screen, very deliberately thumb the power switch on the top of the phone. I wind down the window and toss it out.

For a moment I panic. I'm cut off from the world. No one knows where I am. I half want to snatch it back so I can send a text to Mama K, to let her know I'm all right. She'll be worried and I hate to worry her, but I can't deal with her right now. If she hates me for what Dad did... I shake the thought away. If it's true, Dad did it. Not me. My only crime is having his genetic code. That and running away.

My logic doesn't convince me. My heart beats another truth.

"Any ideas?" Zane turns my way again, flicking his eyes back to the road ahead every few seconds.

I shake my head. We need somewhere Zane can dance. A talent like his shouldn't be restricted to a square of floor in a basement. He needs space to spread his wings and soar like I've seen him do before. Classes may not be in our reach right now, but space surely can't be too hard to find.

We drive across an overpass and I look down at the buildings below. They're small and shabby with cramped trash-filled alleys between them. I look further over and see the apartment building Dad lived in. What has happened to his place? Is it still the same as it was when he left that day? Breakfast dishes piled in the sink, now-rotted food stinking up every room? Or is Ropati staying there? What happens to the home of a murderer? Is that where they found the alleged "manifesto"?

"Turn left," I say suddenly as an off-ramp approaches.

Zane manages to make the turn and slows as we glide back down into the city.

"You had an idea?"

I nod and give Zane directions.

Chapter Twenty-Six

The theater is dark and abandoned-looking when we pull up outside. The magnificent awning is unlit and no sound creeps from the doors. The poster boxes announcing the next show are empty except for a few stray thumbtacks. A scrap of the same crime tape that surrounded Mom's studio clings to the door. I guess the cops searched the theater too. Maybe they found the "manifesto" here. In that case, it could have been anyone's. Another dancer, an audience member, one of the janitors... I shake my head. They don't arrest people without evidence. There has to have been something tying Dad to whatever it was they found. Hell, he might even have claimed it as his own.

"What is this place?" Zane asks as we try the front doors and find them locked.

"I'll show you." I dart back down the stairs, gesturing for Zane to follow. We head around the back and I try the stage door. Locked too. No biggie. I know where Dad keeps a spare key. He's always coming down here and forgetting to bring one. I walk to the electricity meter box at the corner and spin the dials on the combination lock. 11-11-76. Mom's birthday. Dad never forgot it.

The thought sends a fresh wave of pain through my gut. He never forgot her birthday, yet... Don't think about it. Don't think.

I pull the spare key from its hiding place, lock the meter box again, and rejoin Zane. We let ourselves in, freezing when the door squeals as it opens.

There are no lights on inside so the only illumination comes from the exit signs marking the ways out of the building. It's a weird, green light, but enough to find our way up the stairs to the backstage area. I flick a switch in the hallway, lighting up the long corridor lined with dressing rooms.

"A theater?" Zane whispers.

I nod. "Cool, huh? Showers, running water, heat, light..."

"No one's using it?"

I shrug. I'm not sure, but it feels empty. Here and there items are tossed carelessly to the floor—a wig, pieces of costumes, CDs—evidence the place has been searched by the police. Dad was choreographing a new show. Rehearsals will have stopped because without Dad, there is no Nonu Dance Company. There may be another show booked in while Dad's is still a work in progress, but the lack of any advertising posters out front makes it seem unlikely.

"Feels pretty empty, doesn't it?" I wander in and out of a few dressing rooms, but there's no sign of the place being used. A few stray bobby-pins litter a counter here and there, and a broken tube of lipstick sits against a mirror, drying out in the air.

"Cool..." Zane looks around appreciatively. "Show me the stage?"

We pick our way through the darkened backstage area. Once I find the lightbox, I flick a few of the switches, bathing the stage in colored beams. Zane laughs and runs through the bright pools, his skin turning pink, then green, then yellow. He stops and stands in the very center of the stage and looks out at the darkened sea of seats in the auditorium. His posture changes, becomes more regal and he bows at the imaginary crowd.

Then he starts to dance.

He's in jeans and sneakers, but even so, his strength and grace are apparent. He starts slow to warm up, making beautiful shapes with his body. I ache to join him, but at the same time, I love watching him move. I round the back of the stage, never taking my eyes off him, and fumble with the stereo. I have no idea what music to play. Dad's i-Pod is there, full of whatever he loves to move to. There's bound to be something there for Zane. I scroll through until I find some jazz. It's not ballet music, but it's not the experimental, weird stuff Dad often chooses. It's not tribal drumming or eerie Tibetan chants.

Zane starts when the first blast of brass issues through the speakers. He grins and turns to me, beckoning.

I shake my head. I don't dance. Not anymore. I don't. No, I don't.

Zane shuffles toward me, his hips swinging in enticing arcs. He takes my hands and swings me into him, forcing me to move my feet with his or get stomped on. Without my allowing it in, the music invades my veins and I find myself melting into it. I fall into step with Zane, letting him lead me through the steps he's pulling out of the air.

It doesn't take long until we've fallen into a rhythm with each other. We don't speak in words, yet our bodies move together in perfect synchronicity. I've never had such an easy rapport with a partner. He rests his hands on my waist and lifts me. I don't hesitate. There's no quick intake of air as I steel myself to be dropped. Zane won't drop me. I trust him the way I trust Dad as a dancer. Yet I've never danced with him before. I don't count the drunken swaying we did at that party as dancing, even if it was the moment I knew I wanted to know more about him.

The music stops with us face to face, barely an inch between us. We both breathe hard, our panting too loud in the now-silent theater.

"Wow…" Zane leans in and kisses me softly on

the lips. "And you said you didn't dance."

My face heats up. "I don't," I say.

He pulls me close, nestling his hips against me, his arms around my waist. "Let's try that theory out again, huh?"

The next song starts and we dance that one too. And the next. We don't stop until we're exhausted and sweating, our breath coming in harsh brays as we struggle to haul in enough oxygen to stay upright. We collapse on the stage and lie head to head, fingers entwined as we let the floor's chill soak through our skin.

"Theory proved," Zane says after our breathing has steadied and the sweat cools on our skin. "Hate to tell you, but you're a dancer. Like it or not."

I roll over so I can look at him, my body so close to his now I feel the rise and fall of his chest as he breathes. "I'm not. I dance, but I'm not a dancer." There's a distinction there. How to articulate it, I have no idea. But with Zane, I don't need to articulate. He seems to understand me without words. Perhaps he can read the electric pulse of my muscles under my skin.

"Do you feel better now?" Zane rolls onto his side so we're facing each other.

I consider this for a moment. While we were dancing, I wasn't aware of anything except Zane and the music and the way my body responded to those two things. Without them, my mind comes rushing back and with it, the hollow, empty feeling in the pit of my stomach.

"I was," I say. "But the music stopped."

"Easy to fix." Zane starts to get up, but I stop him, pulling him closer and pressing my lips to his. I need him close. I don't need to dance to lose myself. I just need him.

****

We kiss. It's sweet, but it goes on too long and I begin to feel exposed. His hands creep over my hips and waist and don't recoil at the thick layer of flab resting there. As soon as I realize what he's caressing, I pull away and tug my dress down as if it can mask the flaws his fingers already discovered.

I scramble to my feet and hurry across to the i-Pod to find something to break the silence. I feel his eyes follow me across the room. It's like he's seeing through my clothes, through my skin and reading the secrets nestled in my soul.

"So…" Zane murmurs as he sits up and gazes around the dimly lit space. "We can stay here?"

"Why not?" I follow his eyes around the room. "We're not wasting gas. And no one would look for us here."

Only Dad.

And he's not going to be looking for me anywhere.

I fight the thought away. Don't think about him. Just don't. But it's hard when I'm in this space that's so completely his. I'm glad Zane and I have started making some new memories here. Maybe we can make enough to chase away the old ones.

"We should get ourselves set up," I say. "Bring the stuff in from the car, anyway."

Zane nods. "After that, I might go park it somewhere else. If anyone comes looking for us, the car's going to give us away."

"Good idea…" Although I know it's not entirely true. For anyone looking for him, maybe it is, but not for me.

Zane pulls his shirt over his head. "Let's go then."

It takes only two trips to bring everything inside the theater. Well, everything Zane had in the car. All I have is the clothes on my back and the wallet in my pocket. Thankfully Mom made sure I always had a fifty tucked into a hidden pocket of my wallet for emergencies. Mom's a smart woman. Mom was a smart woman. Tears spring to my eyes once again. Will I ever be able to use the word "was" without crying? Mom shouldn't be a "was." She's still so present in my heart and mind, I can't bring myself to think of her in the past tense.

I can't keep thinking like this. I'll climb the walls. I glance around, searching for a way to change the subject, to redirect my focus.

"Are you hungry?" I eye the cartons of food, realizing I'm starving. I haven't eaten at all today.

Zane grins. "I guess I could eat..."

We each snatch up a box of food and sprint up the stairs toward the dressing rooms. At the end of the hallway is a kitchen area, just a stove and a sink. What more do we need? A tiny refrigerator sits in the corridor outside, its only contents a single souring carton of milk.

"Blerg." I hold my nose as I tip it down the sink.

I poke through the food, wondering vaguely why Zane's so prepared for this, why the back of his car was filled with cans and non-perishable foods. I'm so overwhelmed and exhausted, the thoughts are fleeting. Maybe his family are in one of those survivalist cults and he's been brought up to be prepared for the apocalypse. Maybe he's a Boy Scout. It occurs to me I barely know this person I've run away with. This person I've thrown myself at like some kind of desperate harlot. My cheeks heat up and I turn to the stove to avoid his cool, blue-eyed gaze.

"Soup okay?" I ask, fumbling through a drawer in search of a can-opener.

After we finish our supper of Ritz crackers and

canned tomato soup, we grab pillows, a sleeping bag and a blanket from Zane's belongings and roam the building trying to decide the best place to sleep. Zane suggests the stage, but it makes me feel too exposed. Plus, if anyone does come to use the theater, we don't want to be caught out in the open. Better to lurk behind closed doors.

"How about here," I say, pulling open the door to one of the practice rooms on the level above the theater. A mattress lies in the center of the floor under a trapeze.

Zane grins. "Looks like someone knew we were coming." He flops down on the mattress, letting himself relax enough that he bounces a couple of times before sinking into it. "Your dad did circus stuff too?"

I lie myself next to him and look up at the trapeze. "A little, sometimes. He likes to use a bunch of techniques in his choreography. Some of the Company came from circus, though. There's this one dancer, Maggie, and she does the most incredible stuff on these long ribbons that hang down from the ceiling."

I picture the last show of Dad's I saw, the colored lights splashing across the thick, white cloth falling from the ceiling. It was a spectacular show, one critics from both coasts raved about in national newspapers and magazines. I remember Mom sitting at the table one morning, reading a review out loud, pride in her voice. She may have divorced the man, but she never stopped cheering him on in his career. She remained forever his biggest fan.

And he killed her.

I roll over onto my side and curl up around the aching hole in my gut. How could he do such a thing? A temporary madness? Does he regret it now? Does it keep him awake at night? The pain of knowing he killed someone as beautiful as my mother. When he killed her, was he insane? I don't think so. I don't get it. I can't accept he did it.

But if he didn't, who did?

Zane shifts on the mattress and drapes the unzipped sleeping bag across my bent back. "Shhh…" he murmurs, brushing hair back off my face. "Don't, Stas. We'll be okay. I'll make sure we're okay."

I hadn't realized I was making a sound. Turning, I let myself look deep into Zane's eyes. They calm me the way being near water calms me. "Yeah," I manage. "We'll be okay."

I fall asleep in his arms with his breath, still smelling of soup and crackers, tickling my neck.

Chapter Twenty-Seven

Sunlight sneaks through the narrow windows and falls across the mattress in shards. I yawn and blink in the early morning glow. Next to me, Zane sprawls on his back with one hand flung over his eyes. Overnight, a trace of dark beard has sprung up on his chin. I wonder if he has a razor in his bags. I bet he does. On second thought, it might be better if he grows a beard as a disguise.

Mama K must be beside herself by now. I've never stayed out all night before. I've missed curfew a few times, but I've never not come home. I guess by now she's figured out I'm not going back. She's smart enough to know why too. Every reason why. She probably understands better than I do why I'm staying away. At least, I hope she does. Because I miss her. I miss Teddy. I even miss Halmoni, in a way. I wish I was at home, listening to the too-loud roar of Mom's blender as she whips up her morning poison instead of here, listening to the muffled roar of the city and Zane's soft snores.

As if I've disturbed him with my thoughts, Zane rolls over.

"Mornin'." He blinks sleepily at me, a lazy grin crossing his face.

I'm suddenly aware I've slept in my clothes. My hair is probably matted to my head and sticking up in crazy whorls. I bet my breath stinks too. "Good morning."

Zane yawns. "There are showers here, right?"

I nod. "In a couple of the dressing rooms."

"Good. I reek." He sniffs at his armpits and makes a face. We danced last night. Danced until sweat dripped off us. I bet I reek too. Unfortunately I don't have any fresh clothes to change into.

Zane must read my mind. "You can borrow some of my clothes if you want. That dress doesn't exactly look comfortable."

"Thanks," I say. His clothes aren't going to fit me. Anything that slides easily over those narrow hips will be lucky to make it halfway up my thigh. Maybe he has a muumuu tucked away in there. Or a tablecloth. That'd do the trick just as well.

We don't shower right away, though. As soon as we're awake enough to do anything, Zane moves to the barre and starts stretching. I watch for several moments before my feet drag me across to join him. I cringe when I catch my reflection in the mirror. It's even worse than I thought.

I forget everything once my blood starts warming up and flowing through me. I focus on the exquisite pain in my muscles as I stretch them further than they want to go. Then, once we're stretched and warm, I focus on keeping up with the combinations of steps Zane puts together as we cross the floor. Without music, the only sound in the room is our breathing, the slap of our feet against the floor and the pounding of my heart in my ears.

We're sweaty again when we're done. I lean against one of the windows, looking out at the street below. Nobody walks the narrow strip of sidewalk. No cars venture down the dead-end street. This is the perfect hideout. Which is funny, because less than a block away, the city bustles along without us.

"Think I could give it a go?" Zane points at the trapeze dangling above the mattress we slept on.

"Sure. If you can get up there."

Zane studies the apparatus for a moment. He jumps onto the mattress, lining himself up beneath the bar before leaping upward.

His fingers barely brush the bar, sending it swinging. "Fuck…"

He tries again. This time he bends his knees deeper before launching into the spring and manages to catch the bar. Curling his fingers around it, he swings back and forth a couple of times, experimenting.

"It's tough on the shoulders," he comments before giving his legs a single swing and rolling up over the bar so his hips lean against it, his arms straight to hold him up.

"Well, show us some tricks then," I tease. I can't take my eyes off the bulging muscles in his shoulders or the thick, ropy ones in his forearms. No wonder I feel so safe in his embrace. No wonder I trusted him to lift me.

"Not sure I have any in me." Zane struggles to change position and gives up, letting go of the bar and allowing himself to tumble to the mattress below.

He sits up and rubs at his back. "Ow. Is it just me, or is this the most uncomfortable mattress you've ever slept on?"

"What?" It didn't seem so uncomfortable to me. Maybe I was too exhausted to notice. Or maybe I just have better padding.

"Feels like it's filled with rocks or something." He crawls to his feet, still rubbing at his back. I cross to the mattress and flop down on the side I slept on — the side Zane initially lay on yesterday, before moving over to make room for me—and find it as soft and comfortable as I remembered it being. I roll over to where Zane slept and understand why he's complaining.

A section of the mattress is as hard and lumpy as a quarry floor.

"What's in there?" I ask, running my hand across the large, square patch.

Zane shrugs. "Let's take a look."

Taking a corner each, we manage to flip the mattress. The other side looks exactly the same. We run our hands across the surface and discover the same lumpy section can be felt from this side too.

"Look," I run my fingers across the shiny pink fabric, feeling the tiny ripple of a seam. "It's been cut open here."

Zane leans over and peers at the place my fingers have found. "Wanna go in?"

"Of course!" Excitement has my heart pounding in my chest. It's probably nothing. This is a mattress, probably a second hand one at that. Something someone dragged in after they moved house or finally saved up enough to buy a new bed. Whatever's hidden inside is someone else's long-forgotten treasure, someone else's secret.

Using his nails, Zane manages to snag the fine, delicate stitching and tear a line through it. Once he's started, it's easy to pop the remaining stitches and they tear free with a series of tiny ripping sounds.

"Do the honors," Zane says once there's a big enough split in the seam for an inserted hand.

I look up at him. "Are you sure?"

He nods and gestures for me to dive in.

My hand shakes as I pull the fabric aside and push through the thin layer of quilting underneath it. Then my fingers brush something unexpected. Not metal springs. Not cotton stuffing.

Plastic.

Crinkly plastic.

I feel around until I find the edge of the object and lift it up. It's heavier than I expected. As heavy as…

I drop what I'm holding and tear at the fabric, opening up the hole so it's wide enough for me to lift the whole package through.

"Whoa!" Zane jerks backward as I dump the plastic-wrapped bundle of money onto the disemboweled mattress. "Is that…"

I claw at the plastic, tearing it enough to see the same neat stacks of hundred dollar bills I found in my mother's office.

"What? Where?" Zane can't form a sentence.

Neither can I.

I can only sit back on my heels and stare. This can't be a coincidence. The two packages have to be connected. But how? Dad? He would be the obvious choice, but is it too obvious?

"I think we need to call the police," I choke out.

"No!" Zane's voice is too loud and holds a note of panic. "You can't."

Oh, yeah. I tossed my phone. "You don't have a phone with you either?"

He shakes his head. "Locked it in the car."

I clamber to my feet, leaving the cash lying across the center of the mattress. "There's one in the box office. And in Dad's office."

"Stas…" Zane's voice stops me before I reach the door. It's not panicked now, but low and soothing, almost hypnotic. "If you call the cops, we can't stay here. They'll send us home."

Crap. I hadn't thought of that. Of course they will. "But … what do we…" I gesture at the money.

"Put it back?" It isn't exactly a question.

I bite hard on my lip. It would be easier, wouldn't it? Just put it back and pretend I never saw it. The same way I did in Mom's office.

"Zane," I say quietly, dropping down to sit across from him on the edge of the mattress. "Can I tell you something?"

"Sure. Of course."

I swallow hard and look down at the crumpled skirt lying across my knees. "I found another one of these in my mom's office. I think... I think... I think this might be why she was killed."

Zane stares at me. "Another of these." He gestures at the still-wrapped bundle of banknotes sitting between us.

"Yeah. It was taped to the bottom of a drawer in her filing cabinet."

"Do you think it's hers?"

I shake my head. It can't be hers. If she had this kind of money... It can't be hers.

But it can't be Dad's either, can it?

"So, it's your father's?" Zane asks the question I've just asked myself.

"I don't know." My voice cracks. This is all too confusing. Too frightening. One package of money like this would have been enough to get murdered over. Now I have two. And who knows? There might be more stashed in other nooks and crevasses.

Zane leaps to his feet and starts pacing around the room. "Okay," he says after he's done a couple of laps. "Let's see if we can figure this out."

"Figure what out?" My brain is firing in so many directions at once, I have no idea what I'm thinking.

"The money. Who killed your mom. The whole thing."

"Okay, Detective Zane." My mouth twitches like I want to smile, yet I've never felt less like smiling. "Can we put the money back first?" I don't want to look at it any longer.

We return the bundle of cash to its place in the mattress and stitch it back into place with a needle and thread from the costume room off the side of the stage. I feel better when it's tucked back into place and our sleeping bag and blankets are covering the mattress once more.

Not great, though. Knowing about all that cash makes my skin crawl. I feel dirty from touching it. While I'm desperately curious about whose it is and where it came from, a part of me is terrified to know. It's too much to be from anything legal. Drugs? Human trafficking? Or is my dad secretly a hit man?

I watch too many movies.

"I need a shower," I say, running my hands across my arms. It's probably my imagination, but I'm sure I feel a layer of grit against my skin.

"Meet you in the kitchen?" Zane passes me a towel from the carton of linen he pushed against the wall last night.

"Sure." I take the towel and breathe in the fresh scents of laundry detergent, fabric softener, and sunshine drifting from it. This towel smells like home. Like summer. Like a simpler, easier, and less confusing life. I bury my nose in the towel and let myself fall into the optimism those aromas bring.

We will figure this out.

We will discover who killed Mom.

We will.

Chapter Twenty-Eight

"Crackers?" I ask, holding up a box of saltines. Zane's carton of supplies will keep us fed, but there isn't much variety. Canned soup, crackers, and granola bars. Luckily I like soup, crackers, and granola bars.

"Sure." Zane gives the soup on the burner a final stir before dividing it into two bowls.

I sit down at the table and crumble a couple of crackers across the surface of my soup. Pea and ham today. The white cracker crumbs sit on the green liquid like a flock of doves on a lawn.

"Zane?" I swirl my spoon through the crumbs, drowning the doves in the quaggy mess.

"Mm?" He looks up, pulling the spoon from his mouth.

I study him, wanting to reach over and wipe the thin trickle of soup from his chin. "What's the story with all this?" I gesture at the neatly packed carton of boxes and cans. It's weird he has all this at the ready. Not to mention he showed up at just the time I needed him and his supplies. I even found a pair of old sweats that fit me well enough. And a couple of t-shirts.

He looks down at the table. "I guess I just like to be prepared," he says with an embarrassed shrug.

"Prepared for what? Nuclear winter?" It's a lot of food. Not to mention the sleeping bags, pillows, towels, soap, laundry detergent and other things he had stashed in the back of his car.

He laughs, but it's a nervous chuckle more than a real laugh. "Maybe?" He glances up at me as if asking if that's enough.

I take another mouthful of soup, not taking my eyes off him. I'm avoiding what we came here to talk about and he knows it. Thankfully he seems to understand I need a little more time before I can deal with it.

He sighs. "Look, I told you how it was with my parents, right?"

I nod. "Sort of."

"It was bad," he says, dropping his spoon and pushing the food away as if he no longer has any appetite for it. "Really bad. My dad started showing up randomly at school and dragging me back to his apartment. So I started keeping a couple of changes of clothes in my car. It kind of grew from there. I guess I got pretty obsessed with being ready for whatever happened."

"I get it." And I do. I understand the need to be able to control something when everything around you is spiraling out of it. For Zane, making sure he had everything he needed to survive gave him a sense of being on top of what sounds like a terrible situation. I just wish I knew where I could get that kind of comfort. Without having to run away. Because right now, it seems like the only thing I can do.

He pulls the soup back toward him and starts eating.

When he's scraped the bowl clean, he looks across at me. My own soup has barely been touched.

"So … are you ready to talk about this?" His blue eyes are so full of concern and kindness when he looks at me, it makes the ever-present lump in my throat swell all over again.

I hesitate, then give a reluctant nod. I don't want to talk about it, but I know we should. There has to be an explanation for all this. One where Dad didn't murder Mom over someone else's money. And maybe talking about it with someone not so intimately connected with the crime will offer me a different perspective.

"Okay." Zane gets up and rinses his bowl before turning it upside-down on the draining board next to the sink. On the wall next to the doorway is a whiteboard, a few colored markers hanging from strings beneath it. A calendar grid is sketched across it with half of last month's dates crossed out. I recognize some of the names in the squares and realize this must have been a cleaning roster or something. The handwriting in the little boxes is cramped and slants backward, some of it blurred and almost illegible. Dad's writing. Dad's hand wiping out what came before it because he's a lefty and always smudges his work.

The myriad streams of problems I need to solve flood in again. I wipe savagely at my eyes, not wanting to cry this time. I've cried so much recently my skin feels like a well-used sponge.

Zane pulls the dish cloth off the oven door handle and wipes the board clean. "So what do we have?"

I shrug. A dead body and two unexplained stacks of money? An unsubstantiated manifesto of hatred? Not a lot to go on. Even on TV detectives usually have a few more pieces of evidence.

"Think, Stas." Zane gives me an encouraging smile. "Did your Mom fight with anyone?"

"Just me…" I swallow hard. How could I have fought with her over such stupid things? Eating right and skinny jeans?

"Okay, so no fights. What about disagreements? Any kind of conflict?"

"I already answered these questions," I say. "You don't think the police didn't go over this? I don't know who killed her. I wish I did. I wish I could understand all this."

"We'll get there, Stas."

But we won't. In my own head I've already

exhausted every lead.

Julianna? No motive. If anything, Mom had a good reason to kill her, not the other way around.

Dad? I can't believe Dad would kill her. He had no reason to do it. If it was a hate crime like the cops say, why now? Why didn't he do it years ago, back when Mom and K first moved in together? Nothing about this theory makes sense.

My mind spins outward. Who else might have a grudge against Mom? A big enough grudge to kill her?

Dad's pastor? He certainly had a lot of hatred to spew about homosexuals. But murder? He's a man of God and isn't one of God's commandments thou shalt not kill?

Could it have been one of Mom's students? She was strict, and she told everyone the truth about their ability and talent, maybe sometimes not as diplomatically as she could. I've seen more than one girl run out of the studio in tears. But really? Killing someone over a badly timed critique?

The pieces just won't click. Whenever I think I'm starting to grasp at something plausible, the money creeps back into my thoughts and douses any hope I might have had at figuring this out.

Who do I know with money? I can't think of anyone. The closest I can come is the guy who held the party where I met Zane. And I never even met him.

Ropati? Dad's brother certainly has money. Don't people with money always want more? So if Dad had money, wouldn't it make sense that Ropati might want it? But... How does that lead to my mother being murdered? Unless...

"Zane..." I say slowly. "I remember something. Dad was at my house the night before Mom died. I ran into him on the driveway when I was putting the garbage out. He said he needed to talk to Mom, but he wasn't coming from inside the house. And I know Mom *was* inside the house because K was giving her a facial. Do you think…"

My head spins. He was coming from the studio. Oh, god. He did put the money there. It was his. That's the only explanation. Unless he was in the studio to collect the money. But how would he have known it was there if he didn't put it there?

A whimper escapes my lips. They were right. Dad did kill her. She must have found it, or caught him coming to collect it, or…

"You think he did do it?" Zane's voice is low and almost sounds awed. His eyes are wide.

I can't speak. The truth sits on me like a lump of lead. Everything points to it being Dad. The money. His presence at the house that night. Even without the so-called "manifesto of hate" things don't look good for my father.

"Who else could have?" I give a helpless shrug. I hate thinking like this. I hate the truth.

"You're really sure there's no one else you can think of?" Zane stares into my face concernedly. He wants there to be another option.

"No." The word sounds bleak and stark as it falls from my lips.

Zane steps toward me and engulfs me in a hug. "At least they've already got him in jail, then. And you're already on your way to dealing with it. All things considered, I'd say you're doing pretty great."

I sink into his embrace. His words aren't true, but they're nice to hear. I'm not dealing with anything. I've run away, put everything I'm supposed to be doing or working through into some metaphorical too-hard basket while I play house in this abandoned theater.

"Can we dance?" I ask quietly, surprising myself with how much I want to do just that, how much I need it. I can't believe I've denied this part of me for so long. No wonder I've been bad-tempered.

"Of course." Zane releases me from the hug, but takes my hand, squeezing it softly as we make our way down the unlit corridor to the theater and the stage.

****

Once we reach the theater I let go of his hand and hurry to the lighting desk. I flick some switches and fiddle with faders until the stage is bathed in cool, blue light. I don't want brightness right now. I don't want Zane to see me and all my flaws. I just want to dance.

Zane finds the i-Pod and starts dialing through the tracks, stopping occasionally to play a snatch of this or that before moving on.

"Here," I step behind him and take the gadget from his hand. A moment later the first note vibrates through the speaker.

"What…" Zane begins. I stop him talking with a finger across his lips.

I move to the center of the stage before the drumming starts. When it does, I start dancing, my body finding the shape and rhythm of the music without any thought. Muscle memory is an amazing thing. I danced to this piece once, yet my body remembers exactly what it is supposed to do with every phrase and every change in rhythm or key.

Yet it isn't the same dance I did while Dad showered the last time I was here. The steps might be similar, but the stories I'm telling are darker and more anguished now. The problems I danced out that day seem so petty and insignificant now.

I'm so deep in my own world, I don't notice Zane joining me onstage until he reaches for me and takes my hand. A shock of recognition pulses through me, so strong I almost recoil from his touch. Dad did this too. Dad leaped in and made this dance not just mine, but ours.

I chase the thought away and force myself to clasp Zane's hand in my own. This is my dance. Mine. Not Dad's. And if I want to invite Zane into it, it's my choice.

Instead of yielding to Zane, letting him take over and lead the rest of the way, I force him to follow me. This is my music. It's my heritage. If he wants to share it with me—and I hope he does—he needs to do it my way.

Zane appears to understand my unspoken rule and falls in beside me, mirroring my steps. Only when I'm ready to get closer do I move near enough for him to touch me. And I want him to touch me. I take a step forward and rest my hands on his chest, elbows bent, one leg raised behind me in an arabesque. His hands move toward me and gently, cautiously, cup my waist. I don't object, and his fingers tighten around me as I lower my leg and spin around so my back presses against his front.

We stand like that for a beat or two. His chest rises and falls against my spine and his breath blows through my hair. As the music changes, I slide my arm up, snaking it around the back of his neck as I rise up onto my toes. I don't have pointe shoes so I can only go to demi-pointe, but in my head I'm there.

One quick turn and I'm facing him again, my other arm rising to his neck. We're so close now. Even on my toes I have to look up to see his eyes. They rest on mine, dark blue like the ocean and easily as deep. I try to read the layers of sadness, but find myself sinking. I draw away before I drown, resting my chin on his shoulder and looking beyond him across the twilight-blue stage.

The music stops and Zane doesn't pull away. His

arms slide around my waist and we stay there for a long time, chests heaving with exertion. Once I can breathe without panting, I raise my head from his shoulder and look back at those intensely blue eyes. They're glued to me, and before I have a chance to speak, Zane lowers his mouth to mine.

The music starts again. Something different this time. I can't say what. I barely hear it through the erratic heartbeat pulsing through my ears as we kiss. And kiss. And kiss.

The music changes again, and we keep kissing. His lips are soft and warm, his tongue gentle as it probes my lips and teases my own. My legs turn to rubber and I pull Zane down to the floor with me, our lips never losing contact even as we tumble in a heap of tangled limbs.

He draws me to him, wrapping his arms around me and pulling me into his chest. I throw a leg over him to keep balanced and he groans. My hands find the bottom of his shirt and I delve under it, discovering hot, slightly damp skin. He moans as I run my fingers across the ridges of muscle on his belly and trace the fine line of hair vanishing below his belt buckle.

He kisses me harder, his tongue tangling with mine as his hands clutch my thighs, pressing me further against him. I can feel his need, hard against me, and reach for his belt buckle.

He pulls away and looks right at me, his lips red and swollen from the pressure of mine. He raises an eyebrow questioningly.

I ignore the question and kiss him again, my lips crushing his with bruising force. This time he doesn't pull away. He doesn't say it's the wrong time. Instead he peels his t-shirt off me, raising it slowly over my head and casting it aside. Once it's gone, he trails soft, soft, kisses across my neck and shoulders and down my sides. I tug his shirt up and over his head, mirroring his actions as I kiss my way across his collarbone and down his chest. A light dusting of dark hair circles his nipples, but otherwise he's smooth and hard as a statue. The colored lights create weird shadows across his skin and I kiss these too, tracing them between the muscles in his stomach and the tiny ones laddering his ribs.

He groans and I know I'm taking too long to get where I'm needed. I continue downward until I reach his belt, kissing a line along the skin above it. He moans again and tangles his fingers in my hair. I unbuckle his belt and pull down his fly, surprised at the size and shape of what's beneath. It presses insistently at the soft fabric of his boxers, begging me to free it. I'm happy to oblige and pull at Zane's jeans. He stops me, rising to his knees to pull me toward him. His hands creep around my back and a moment later my bra slides down my arms. My breasts drop from the cups and hang loosely from my chest. I glance down at them, hating their fleshiness, the way they hang there, heavy and pendulous. Zane slides the bra from my shoulders and sits back on his heels to look at me.

"You're so beautiful," he murmurs, reaching for my breasts and catching one in each hand. He holds their weight, testing them, one in each palm. "God, you're beautiful."

I flush. I'm not beautiful. I'm short and heavy and round in all the wrong places. My hair is frizzy and unmanageable. My skin is too dark or too light. Nothing about me is beautiful. Yet with Zane looking at me like this, I begin to wonder if I might be wrong about that.

Chapter Twenty-Nine

We don't leave the theater for three days. We eat granola bars, crackers, and canned soup from Zane's stash of supplies. I attempt a box of mac and cheese. Without milk, it's sticky and barely edible. Crackers don't make such a bad dinner if you're hungry.

And I have been hungry. With nothing else to do, Zane and I dance. We get up in the morning and stretch using the barre in one of the practice rooms until we're warmed up enough to do more. After showering and eating, we move to the theater to use the stage and the lights, choreographing elaborate routines. With only two of us, it's hard to get a sense of how epic our imagined ballets might be, but we're always the stars and our *pas de deux* take center stage.

I've never met another person who speaks my language like Zane does. Neither of us talk while music plays, relying on our bodies to convey what we need to say or express or feel. My preference has been for angry music with driving beats and loud, crashing climaxes. I use the violence of the sound to rail against everything I can't cope with, all the confusing, painful emotions filling my brain and my blood.

Zane follows, never questioning my motives or trying to lead me away from my frenzies.

When he chooses, the tunes are always simpler and more melodic. As a dancer he has such poise, such beautiful line. I love that he's unafraid to move slowly, letting himself unfold into a piece rather than leaping into it and tearing it apart. It's an unusual trait in a male dancer. Most of them want to show off their athleticism with elaborate jumps and turns.

Zane's jumps are as good as any dancer's, even

Dad's, but he doesn't use them to prove his masculinity. He doesn't need to. His quiet self-confidence radiates from him, even in the moments he's most vulnerable, the moments he allows himself to sink into the darkness lurking beneath the composed surface he presents to the world.

Cocooned in this place, it's easy to forget everything going on outside these walls. Here there is no confusion. Our bodies don't lie.

"Do you miss it?" I ask while we lie on the silent stage, staring up at the lights and waiting for our breathing to steady again.

"What?"

"Home. Your own bed. Do you miss it?" I roll to look at him, watching his face harden at the thought.

"I have no home," he growls and stalks away to the side of the stage.

I cringe. I have such a knack for saying the wrong thing. But with Zane, it's hard to know what might set him off.

I get up and brush dust away from the back of my clothes. Well, Zane's clothes. As I suspected, his jeans didn't come close to fitting me, but his sweats are surprisingly comfortable. Apart from being a little snug across the butt.

"You have such a great ass," Zane smiles as he rejoins me, running his hand across the fabric stretched tight across it. How he shakes off his moods so quickly is a mystery. I'm glad he can, though. Being stuck in here with a brooding storm cloud wouldn't be fun.

"My ass is big enough to have its own congressman," I mutter.

He laughs out loud. "Why are you so down on your body? You're gorgeous."

What if Mom was wrong about how cow-like I

am? Maybe she was holding me up against her own whacked out idea of beauty, an ideal drilled into her by generations of anorexic Russian ballerinas. "Mom was always riding me about my weight."

"What about your dad?"

I think back, trying to remember if Dad ever said anything negative about my weight. If he did, I can't remember it. But Dad was related to Nana, and Nana's butt was even bigger than mine. You could have used that thing as a shelf. Samoans tend to be fat. Probably because our metabolisms are designed for an island diet of fish and coconuts. Maybe if I lived in Samoa I'd be svelte.

"You're changing the subject," I say, trying to steer the conversation away from me, and back onto him. I'm so tired of me. "Don't you miss anything about home?"

He looks thoughtful for a moment, his forehead creasing as he squints into the lights beaming down onto the stage. "Maybe my cat," he says with a shrug. "Not enough to go back, though. Are you getting homesick?"

Am I? I was homesick long before we ran here. My homesickness began when I discovered Mom was dead. Because without Mom, there is no home.

But what about Mama K?

No. She doesn't want me. She's better off without me and my stupid brown face, my crazy Polynesian hair.

"I guess I am kind of homesick," I admit. "It's stupid because I don't have a home anymore either. Mom's gone and Mama K won't ever go back to the house. Not now." Even if she did want me there, I add in my head.

Zane raises his eyebrows. "Really? You don't think she'll want to hold on to all the memories there? That's why Mom's fighting so hard to hold onto our house. She wants to keep the happy times close. But

Dad's never going to let her keep it."

I study the tension in his face and the way his mouth has gone crooked with the tightness in his jaw. He says he hates his parents, but his face tells a different story. He wants desperately to go home. Just to a home that no longer exists anywhere except in his memories. "What do you want?"

He shrugs and gives me a smile that looks hopeless rather than happy. He shifts his feet awkwardly, like there's something bothering him. Like he has something to say, but it isn't sure how to get it out.

"What?" I ask, trying to prompt him.

He glances down at his feet for a second, then decides to plunge onward and looks back at me. "I thought of something that might work for you. No guarantees, but have you thought about becoming an emancipated minor?"

"A what?"

He leans back against one of the struts leading to the lighting rig above us. "An emancipated minor. Do you know what that means?"

Something sparks at the back of my brain and I struggle to bring the idea into focus. "Isn't... Like when kids divorce their parents?"

"Not quite that simple, but kind of, yeah. It could be an option for you. Better than Siberia, anyway."

"You think?" I shiver. It's not cold in here, but just the word "Siberia" sends chills through me. I wouldn't survive an hour there. "What would I have to do?"

"It's not simple, you know? Most of the time the only kids they emancipate are getting married or joining the army. Or really rich kids, like movie stars. They'll let them be emancipated if it looks like their parents might steal all the money they make. For anyone else, it's a lot more complicated." He runs his hand through his hair in the gesture I now recognize means he's agitated or uncomfortable.

"Wanna get married?" I grin to let him know I'm kidding.

He grins back, shaking his head slowly. "I love you, Stas, but no…"

The easy way he says he loves me sends warmth flooding through me. I can get through this. I can do whatever I need to do. Just as long as he keeps loving me.

"So…" I move close to him, wrapping my arms around his waist and pressing myself against his chest. "Who do I need to see to get emancipated? Do you know?" The word tastes strange on my tongue. I don't think I've ever said *emancipated* before today. It makes me think of slavery and barely remembered history lessons.

"I looked into it last year, so I know a little. I didn't go through with it in the end, but I've done some research."

I nod. His parents' divorce must have been bad. Worse than he's let on, anyway.

"I thought about suggesting it to you earlier, but I wasn't sure you'd want to hear it… I mean … with your mom and all. And the way you talked about K. But, y'know…" Zane's hand rakes compulsively through his hair. It looks like a tractor's passed through it.

"And?" There has to be more.

"Well, you could think about it. Talk to your lawyer. You'll need to get a job, prove you can take care of yourself. And—"

Zane's head snaps up and he cocks his head toward the front of the theater. "Did you hear that?"

"Hear what?" I whisper it even though I haven't heard a thing.

"Shh…"

And then I do hear it. A hollow banging, muffled by the closed auditorium doors. "Who…"

Every muscle in Zane's body stiffens. I can almost feel electricity thrumming off him as he drops into a crouch and moves toward the front of the stage. His intensity is frightening and I find myself tagging along behind him, half-hiding in his shadow.

We jump off the stage and into the darkened theater. Still dazzled by the brightness, I struggle to see as we make our way up the aisle. I grip Zane's hand and let him guide me.

The banging grows louder as we approach the doors.

"Someone wants to get in," Zane says. "Any idea who?"

I shake my head. It could be anyone. A gang looking for something to steal? Mama K searching for me? Ropati? Zane's aunt? One of the Company? No, they'd know where to find the key. Ropati probably does too, at least by now.

A flock of tiny birds flaps through my belly. Any way I look at it, I'm caught. Our escape from the real world has been too brief. I close the space between myself and Zane, draping myself over him like a blanket.

"Open up!" A voice barks through the door. "Police!"

Breath catches in my throat. Police! Peeling myself away from Zane, my heartbeat accelerates to uncomfortable speed.

"Back door!" Zane hisses, grabbing my hand and dragging me back into the auditorium. I stumble over my own feet as I try to keep up with him, almost falling, but managing to right myself before landing face down in the dusty red carpet of the aisle. Was it only minutes ago I felt graceful?

As we duck behind the stage, I hear a crash. The cops have managed to break down the door. Crap! I force myself to run faster despite the ache in my chest that's not only from exertion. Panic threads through my veins, fluttering like a hummingbird at my throat. I can't get caught. I can't. I can't.

We reach the back staircase and fly down it in the dark. How did the cops find us? The theater can't have been the first place anyone would have thought to look for us. Or for me. Does anyone even care Zane has run away? Somehow I doubt it. If what he's said is true. If what I saw at his house is the way things always are. No. These cops are after me.

"Ready?" Zane stops by the back door and I can hear the harsh pant of his breathing, feel the gusts of air puffing against the side of my face. The only light down here comes from the exit sign at the top of the stairs. The greenish cast makes Zane's skin the color of chartreuse. But even in the dimness the tense lines etched around his mouth and the fear storming through his eyes are visible.

I nod. Zane kisses me, his lips a warm surprise on mine for a second. Then they're gone and he flings the door open, letting in a blast of surprisingly chilly air.

I blink at the sudden brightness as we burst through.

"Stop right there." A policeman crouches in the mouth of the alleyway in front of us, gun drawn.

I scream. A gun! I back away from the black eye, but there's nowhere to go. A brick wall blocks off the far end of the alley. Zane looks stricken as he turns and realizes there is no other way out. The door we came through has already whispered closed behind us and without the key, we can't get back inside. The policeman walks cautiously toward us, muttering things into a radio he must have concealed beneath his collar. Moments later, a second policeman sprints into the alleyway and stops a few feet behind the first.

"It's just a couple of kids," he says in disbelief.

The other cop shakes his head. "They could be on drugs. Be cautious, okay? You never know what you're walking into in these trespassing cases."

Trespassing? Us? A brittle laugh catches in my throat. Is it trespassing if you have the key? If you have permission to be in a place?

"Shhh." Zane doesn't look at me as he issues this warning. "Don't tell them anything."

He walks forward, his hands raised to shoulder height, surrendering himself to the police.

I only hesitate a second before I follow him.

Chapter Thirty

Neither Zane nor I protest or kick up any kind of fight as the police cuff us and deposit us in the back of a police car.

"Don't say anything," Zane warns under his breath. "We'll straighten this out."

I nod, too scared to open my mouth anyway. I'm certain if I do, I'll cry. Or scream. Either is likely. I stare at the metal grille blocking the backseat from the front. Their radio crackles and spits, but I can't make out many words through the static. Is Ropati waiting for me? The aunts? Mama K? What will they do to me for running off? What will they do to Zane?

I flick my eyes in his direction. He's sitting upright, his spine as straight as while he's dancing. His jaw clenches so tight a tiny muscle twitches, like a fish trying to escape. He must feel the weight of my gaze because he turns to me and gives a ghastly approximation of a smile. Fear seethes off him in waves so cold I can't help but shiver. What will his aunt do to him? Send him home? Beat him?

I set my own jaw. No way. I'll shoulder the blame for the whole thing. It wasn't Zane's idea to run away. It was mine. He shouldn't be punished for my crimes. I dragged him along with me.

I lean forward, pressing my mouth to the grille. "It wasn't Zane's fault," I manage. "Please, let him go. It was me."

"Stas!" Zane turns on me, genuine fear in his eyes. "Keep quiet."

Neither of the cops seem to have noticed I spoke, so I slump back in my seat, obeying Zane. There will be time to sort this out. At the police station, I promise myself. I won't let Zane go to jail.

We're bundled out of the cop car still in our handcuffs. They're not removed until we're inside the building, locked into a small room containing a table and four chairs. It's too familiar. It's not the same room I was questioned about Mom in, but it might as well be.

"Wait here," one of the cops says gruffly.

I hear the lock slide home behind him when he leaves. Where the heck does he think we might go? There are no other doors in this room. No windows. Just the table and chairs sitting right in the very center. Zane glances up at the ceiling and I follow his eyes. In the corner by the door, a security camera glares down at us.

Zane sits in one of the chairs, his posture as erect here as it was in the car. I follow his lead and sit too, taking the chair next to his. The other two chairs sit across from us, mocking us with their emptiness.

It feels like a long time before the door swings open to admit two people, a woman and a man.

"You two are in big trouble," the woman says without any preamble. She's middle-aged, not fat, but soft around the middle. Her shirt's buttons strain to stay closed over her large breasts. "Trespassing is a serious charge."

"I wasn't trespassing," I spit. This whole thing feels way too dramatic. The locked room, the two cops. We're just a couple of kids hiding out from the world for a while. "I have a key."

She throws me a scathing look, like she's heard that one a thousand times before. Maybe she has.

"Name?" She looks bored as she tosses a pen at the other cop, a tall, dark-haired man who looks like he might be from India or Pakistan.

"Anastasia Nonu," I say. I expect some reaction, some kind of recognition. Surely Mama K has reported me missing by now. Or if she hasn't, one of my other "guardians" will have. "Daughter of the building owner."

"And you?" She nods toward Zane.

"Zane Talbolt."

Again, not a flicker. Either this lady is really good at concealing her emotions, or the names really mean nothing to her.

"Age?" She looks at me.

"Sixteen."

She glances at the man who is scribbling this information onto a yellow pad. "A minor."

"You?" She juts her chin in Zane's direction.

"Seventeen," he says almost too quickly.

"Both minors. We're going to have to contact your parents or guardians."

This time I can't choke back the bray of laughter shooting up my throat. "Good luck with that," I say, surprised at the poison coating the words.

"Excuse me?" The man cop speaks for the first time.

"I said, good luck with that." I can't look at Zane.

"What do you mean?" He cocks his head to one side and regards me thoughtfully with eyes the color of coffee beans.

"I mean, good luck finding a parent or guardian." My voice startles me. I'm being rude. And to the police. This isn't me. I don't talk like this. But then, as if I have no control over my tongue, I keep going. "My mom's dead, okay? Murdered. And according to you guys, my dad did it, so you have him locked up. As far as guardians go, there are so many people fighting to take me away from my other mom, you can take your pick."

There's a stunned silence for a moment. My words hang heavily in the air.

Zane remains silent. He doesn't explain about his

parents and his aunt. He stares at the ground, muscle still jumping crazily in his jaw. I can't help thinking about the conversation we were having when the cops busted in on us. How different would this scene be if we were both emancipated? Would we be in more trouble or less? I wish I knew more about it.

The woman cop nudges her partner. "Check it out, okay? Anastasia Nonu and Zane Talbolt. I bet someone's lookin' for them."

The guy leaves the room after sliding the paper and pen over to his partner.

"Look," I say, desperate suddenly to clear the whole thing up. I want to go home. I want to see Teddy and Mama K. I don't want to be here anymore. I don't even care if Mama K doesn't want to see me, if she hates me. "I know we probably shouldn't have been in the theater. It's my dad's place, though. I know where the key is. We didn't break in. We just needed some time out for a couple of days."

The woman nods. "There was no evidence of breaking and entering," she admits. "Neighbors saw lights in the back and because the place has been shut down, they reported it."

"Shut down?" I guess I already knew that. The fact the company hasn't been in to rehearse or do class should have told me. The lack of posters out front. The loose piece of police tape flapping in the door. Who wants to go to a show in a place owned by a suspected murderer?

How fast did it happen? Or were things already turning sour for Dad before all this happened? The questions race maddening circles through my head like a cat chasing its own tail. It's never ending. Where does the money fit into all this?

The cop sits down, easing her bulky frame into

one of the chairs across from us. "That theater's part of an ongoing investigation. Your being there may have destroyed key evidence."

It crosses my mind to mention the money. I imagine that's pretty key evidence. Of what I'm not entirely sure. Something holds me back and I bite my tongue to keep the words from spilling across my lips.

Zane reaches over and takes my hand. I'm so grateful for his touch, I squeeze back, trying to communicate how much it means that he's here with me, that he chose to spend this time with me. The warmth of his skin is enough to remind me of what we were doing on the stage mere hours ago and my body flushes with heat. I want to be back there. It was hiding, but sometimes you need to hide.

The door to the room opens and the other cop slips back inside. I wince when the lock falls behind him again, reminding me I'm trapped in here.

"Her story checks out," he says, swinging himself back into the seat across from mine. "There's a lot of people worried about you, missy. Mom's the ballet teacher who was killed over in Richmond, and Dad owns the theater, like she said. Property's in trust with a Ropati Nonu."

"And the other one?" The female cop jerks her head in Zane's direction.

Zane sucks in a breath and straightens up, seeming to freeze in his chair. When I glance at his face, his eyes are wild. Not on the surface—if you didn't know him, he'd look perfectly calm. But I've been with him for three days non-stop and can see the caged-animal intensity boiling beneath the glassy exterior. I wonder what he's afraid of. Maybe if they call his aunt, she won't come and he'll be forced to give one of his parents' numbers. And they might force him to come home.

The cop tosses Zane a pointed glare. "Mom in Rosemont reported him missing about six weeks ago. Looks like he's a runaway."

Runaway? I turn to Zane. He didn't tell his mom he was coming to live with his aunt? Wouldn't she have called when Zane showed up on her doorstep? "But…"

Zane shakes his head in my direction, cutting off my questions.

"Your mom's on her way," the cop adds with a smirk in Zane's direction. "Might be a while."

Zane crumples, sinking into the chair like someone let the air out of him.

"So, who do we call about you?" The woman glares at me under her eyebrows like she's not at all pleased we were telling the truth.

"Mama K?" I ask in a small voice. I don't know anymore. A month ago it would have been automatic to give her name. Now, I have no idea who my next of kin might be. Teddy, probably. "Kyung-Seok Lim. I can give you her number."

The male cop slides the pad over to me and I scribble down Mama K's cell number. I just hope she has it turned on for once.

"Won't be long," He rips off the slip of paper and, without being told to, leaves the room once more.

I breathe a sigh of relief. It's going to be okay. At least this part will be. We're not going to be arrested and imprisoned. Once Mama K is called, she'll come get me, and we'll deal with whatever comes next.

I turn to Zane, mouth full of questions, but I don't get to ask even the first one.

A loud pounding comes at the door. The cop jumps, her pen trailing a thick, dark line across the page she was writing on.

"Who…"

Before she can get the words out, the door swings open and in marches Ropati.

Chapter Thirty-One

My mouth drops open. What is he doing here? How... And then I remember the other cop saying something about Ropati and the theater. I guess he's looking after that and all Dad's things. Assets. That's what the lawyer called them, wasn't it? They must have called him to ask if he wanted to press charges against me and Zane. Crap.

And now he's here.

Fuck.

"Stas, honey?" Ropati strides into the room. "Let's go, sweetheart."

Sweetheart? Honey? Who does this guy think he is? What kind of sick game is he playing? I don't know him and I'm nobody's honey.

"Excuse me..." The cop stands up behind the table and faces Ropati. "And who...?"

"I'm Ropati Nonu," Ropati towers over her, making her look tiny. "I'm this child's lawyer and her legal guardian. Unless you're charging her with a crime, which I'd strongly suggest you don't, she's free to leave with me."

The cop gobbles like a turkey, but can't form any words. I don't blame her. With Ropati standing over me like that, I doubt I'd be able to speak either. I'm not even sure I can manage to form a word or two now. He's my guardian? Did that happen while I was hiding out with Zane? Or is he lying? Wishful thinking? How can I live with this man? The brother of the man who killed my mother. It will kill me. It will kill Mama K. It might even kill my Russian aunts too. They didn't want me to stay with my mother's lover, but letting me go with the brother of her murderer?

I shake my head. I'm back in the nightmare I fled the lawyer's office to escape, yet this time it's worse. This time I'm stuck with my uncle. Who's also my lawyer, according to him. There's no way I'm getting out of this. I pinch my arm hard. It's a bad dream. I'll wake up and be back in the theater, curled up in my sleeping bag with Zane's arm draped across me.

Fat chance.

I blink hard as tears threaten to spill from my eyes. They catch the harsh fluorescent light and momentarily blind me. I force them back. Crying isn't going to do me any good.

"Zane?" I look toward him, desperate for him to be freed too. I can't leave him here. I don't understand what's going on, but I'm not going without him.

"Not our problem, honey. He can get his own lawyer if he needs it. Now, come along." Ropati crosses the room and pulls out my chair as easily as if I weren't sitting on it. He drags me to my feet in a single motion. His fingers bite into my shoulder and I swallow a gasp. Before I have a chance to say anything to Zane, even to look at him, I'm propelled across the room toward the door.

"Zane!" I call. "I'll… I'll…" I stop. I don't know what I'll do. I don't know what I can do. I have no idea where Ropati is taking me. To Dad's apartment? The no-doubt fancy hotel he's staying in? Across the country to where he lives? "I'll call you," I finish lamely. "I'm sorry."

The last thing I see as I'm hauled out the door is his face and the agonized, forced smile that crosses it as he watches me go. I wonder if he remembers, too late like I did, I threw my phone away. The phone with his number saved in it. I glance down at my arm, but of course the digits he scribbled there have long since washed away.

Ropati keeps his hand firmly on my arm as we march through the police station. At the main entrance, he signs several pieces of paper and I'm given back my change and bobby pins, the only things I had on me when we were brought in. In fact, pretty much the only things I had with me when I ran away. Other than the long-gone phone. Will Ropati at least let me get some of my things before he takes me home with him? I tried washing my underwear in the sink at the theater, but it still feels grungy after so many days.

"Car's outside," Ropati says crisply, the first time he's spoken since we left the tiny questioning room.

The cold is like a slap when we step into the frosty dusk. I shiver and wrap my arms around myself. What has happened to the weather? It's barely fall yet. It shouldn't be this cold. I stuff my hands into the pockets of Zane's sweats, but it does little to alleviate the numbness creeping into my fingers. My breath puffs into the falling night in clouds.

"Stas!" Someone calls my name and I whirl around to see who it is. Ropati's hand grabs onto me more firmly, grinding into the meat of my shoulder as he hurries me across the floodlit parking lot.

"Stas!" I manage to turn my head enough to catch sight of Mama K jogging across the lot toward us, a mixture of relief and terror painted across her delicate features.

"Mama K!" I jerk my shoulder, desperate to wrench free of Ropati. "Mama!"

"You're coming with me, young lady." Ropati's voice is tight and hard as volcanic rock. When I glance up at him, his face matches. Fear freezes my belly. This isn't right. Something is seriously wrong here.

"No," I shout, digging my heels into the ground and refusing to take another step. He keeps towing me, my feet skidding along in the mixture of mud and rainwater coating the ground.

We reach the car and he has to stop. He doesn't let me go, though, not even when he has to dig into his coat pockets for his keys.

"Mama K!" I call, searching the parking lot for her, but not seeing her. Has she given up on me so easily? She came for me. That means she doesn't hate me the way I thought she might. If she hated me she would have told the cops to leave me there.

Or she would have let Ropati take me.

My heart sinks as I scan the lot again, more slowly this time. No one moves. What is going on? Where did she go? Did she show up to make sure I went with Ropati? I was really and truly gone from her life forever?

No.

I heard the panic in her voice as she called my name, saw the fear in her face when she saw who I was with.

"Anastasia Nonu!" Ropati's voice tugs me back into the present. "Get in the car." He holds the door open for me with one hand and tries to manhandle me into the passenger seat with the other. I know only one thing. I'm not getting into his car. If I do, who knows where he'll take me?

I brace my shoulder against the rim of the door, pressing against it hard enough the metal cuts into my skin. It hurts, but I don't care. As long as I keep myself wedged like this, Ropati won't get me into the vehicle. I need him to let me go for a second or two, so I can run for it.

I fix my eyes on the police station's entrance. That's my best bet. Run in there and tell the police I'm being kidnapped. I wonder if it will work. If Ropati is my guardian… I shake my head. He's not. No way could it have been settled so fast. The others would never have let it go so easily. Unless….

An uneasy niggle slithers through my belly. Ropati has money. Could he have paid off the others to give up their fight for custody? Could Mama K be bought off so easily? The aunts I know too little about to be sure, but Mama K wouldn't be easy. She already has everything she needs. Everything except the woman she loved.

The thought doesn't go much further because I catch sight of Zane walking down the police station steps. He pauses on the sidewalk, his face distorted by the streetlight overhead, and looks uncertainly around. He's wearing only his jeans and sweatshirt and looks as cold as I feel. How did he get out of the questioning room? After what the cops said about him being a runaway, I thought he'd be locked away in there until his mom arrived to pick him up. Did he manage to sneak through the door while it was open to let Ropati and me out? Or to let someone else in?

"Zane!" I shout, lunging toward him. A moment too late I realize my mistake and try to wedge myself back into my position by the open car door. Ropati is too quick, though, and takes this opportunity to sweep me up and deposit me into the drivers' seat. He's strong, I'll give him that. With one arm, he pushes me over into the passenger seat as he climbs in next to me, slamming the door closed behind him.

"Buckle up," is all he says as he turns on the engine.

I ignore him and turn around, kneeling on my seat so I can look out the back window to where Zane still stands, his head whipping about as he searches for where my voice came from.

Ropati throws the car into gear and stomps the accelerator so hard the car leaps forward. The momentum sends me flying off the seat, my ribs connecting with the glove compartment with a bruising thud.

"I said, buckle up."

He's at the entrance to the parking lot now and indicates to turn into the street beyond. I glance both ways, finding headlights in both directions. This might be my only chance.

I wait until he slows to let the cars pass, his head turning left and right as he gauges how close they are, where the next clear space might be. While he's focused on that, I hurl myself into the backseat and press down on the door handle there. It's locked and I'm as trapped here as I was in the front.

"Get back up here," Ropati growls. He tries to yank me back into the seat beside him with one hand, but he still has one eye on the traffic, one hand on the wheel, so I elude him easily, sliding across to the other side of the backseat where he can't reach me.

"I know you know about it," Ropati says quietly. "So tell me where he hid it?"

"What?" I freeze, my hand stopping short of trying the handle on this side of the car.

The car swings out into the road and my heart sinks. I scramble to my knees and peer out the back window, desperate for a glimpse of Zane or Mama K or even one of the cops who held us in that little room. Anyone familiar. Anyone who could help me.

I see no one.

The car speeds up and I crumple against the door.

"The money," Ropati hisses as we speed up, following the rows of blinking red taillights heading out of town. "Where did Tusi hide the money?"

It takes every ounce of strength I possess to keep

my face in what I hope is a neutral position. "What money?"

Ropati snorts. "Don't play dumb with me, Anastasia. That money is mine. Your father stole it from me and I need it back. Now tell me where he hid it."

"I have no idea what you're talking about." I take care to keep my voice to a low, bored drawl. Inside, I'm not bored. Here are the answers I've been searching for. It's Ropati's money, not Dad's. But if Dad took it... I'm just as confused as before, this new information as useless as a single jigsaw puzzle piece in a frame that fits a thousand.

"Don't lie to me!" Ropati shouts. "He told me he took it for you. So where is it?"

I glance out the window and suddenly know where we're headed.

And we're almost there. I only need to stall him a minute or two more and I might get another shot at escaping.

"I don't know anything about any money. Dad never had any. I know that much. He certainly never gave me any. Not even enough to buy a new pair of jeans."

Ropati gives a frustrated grunt and hunches back over the steering wheel, gunning the engine as the lights turn orange ahead of us at the turn-off to the theater. He squeaks through, a second before they turn red. I gasp when the red seems to follow us down the narrow cul-de-sac leading to the theater's front entrance, flashing and glowing across the building's darkened facade.

It takes me longer to figure out what I'm seeing than it does Ropati.

"Fuck!" he swears, slamming the brakes on so hard I tumble from the seat and wind up in the footwell, my already bruised shoulder throbbing from another jarring concussion. As Ropati struggles to throw the car into reverse, I remember I never tried the handle on the door next to me. I reach up and press on it, certain it's going to be as unyielding as the others.

The handle gives.

I push all my weight onto it and shoulder the door open. The rush of cold air takes my breath away momentarily, but I ignore it and let myself fall through the now-open door, landing heavily on the frozen cement.

Chapter Thirty-Two

I don't wait to find out if I'm hurt, just scramble to my feet and run, my feet slipping and skidding across the slick pavement, my breath spurting from me in harsh, furious bursts.

"Stas!" Ropati's voice lashes through the night toward me. I ignore it and keep running. The police car parked outside the theater is a few strides away when my feet fly out from under me and I crash into the ground, my chin glancing off the tarmac so hard stars flicker before my eyes. For a moment I'm too dazed to do anything except lie there, the chill soaking through my thin shirt. I have to get up. I have to get away. I stumble to my feet and keep moving, slower now, my chest and chin burning with pain.

"Stas!" Mama K's voice is there and I run toward it, not even questioning how she can be here when I saw her outside the police station only minutes ago. She'll keep me safe. Something warm drips onto my chest. I look down to find crimson plashes of blood staining the ground beneath me.

"Mama?" I manage.

"Shh ... I'm here."

And then she is. Mama K's arms come around me and she's holding me. I smell the mixture of kimchee and apple shampoo I will always associate with her.

"...blood. Stitches."

"Catch..."

And everything goes black.

When I wake up, bright lights shine in my eyes. I blink around, disorientated. Where am I?

Weird fragments of voices wind around me, but I pay them no attention. Only Mama K's, right by my ear.

I relax. Mama K is here. I'm safe. That's all that matters.

"You're at the hospital," she says in a low, gentle voice, answering the question I haven't yet asked. "You're okay."

I struggle to sit up and my head spins. Someone hands me a towel and I stare at it as if I've never seen one before. Mama K takes it from me and presses it gently against my chin. It hurts and I jerk away, but she comes after me.

"C'mon, Stas," she murmurs. "You don't want to bleed all over these nice clean sheets."

I look down at the paper-covered table I'm on. "Yeah, right."

Mama K smiles. "There you are."

"I'm sorry, Mama," I say, ducking my head. She must have been so worried. What the hell was I thinking?

She strokes my hair. "Don't worry about it now, okay?"

The adrenaline I've been running on since the cops banged on the theater door drains away, leaving me exhausted. "Why..." I can't even find the strength to form the words.

"Ropati?" she asks, seemingly able to read my mind.

I nod.

"I don't know." She shakes her head. "That whole family must be some kind of crazy."

She doesn't sound angry or bitter, just sad. I wonder if I'll ever get to a place where I can feel that way. I'll never forgive Dad for what he's done, and after today, I can't help thinking Ropati is just as bad. Maybe even worse. How did such terrible people come from Nana? There wasn't one ounce of evil in her. I never heard her say a bad thing about anyone. Even Mom and

Mama K. I don't think she approved of their relationship, but I never heard her say anything against either of them. Even to Dad. That's part of why I don't get Dad's sudden change of heart toward Mom and K. Nana was always religious and she accepted them. Why couldn't Dad when he suddenly found god?

"Are you okay?" Zane stands at Mama K's shoulder, his face white and pinched. His hands twist against one another. "Stas?"

How did he get here? Wasn't he at the police station? Is everyone here? How long was I out? "I'm okay," I mumble. My chin throbs, as do my ribs where I was thrown into the dashboard. But given I hurled myself out of a moving vehicle, I'm fine.

"I shouldn't have let you go with him," Zane babbles. "I knew he was shifty..."

I reach up and press my finger to his lips. "Don't."

He stops and looks at me for a long moment, his eyes drinking me in as if he's memorizing me.

"Stas?" Mama K repositions the towel on my chin, sending a fresh burn across it. "Who is this boy?"

My face heats up. Of course. She hasn't met Zane. No one has. Not really. Yet I feel closer to him than anyone else on the planet.

"This is Zane," I say through the lump swelling in my throat. "He goes to school with me. He was taking lessons at the studio... Or, he was supposed to... Zane, this is Mama K. This is my mom."

Zane's face reddens. He plows his fingers through his hair before stepping forward to shake Mama K's hand. "Pleased to meet you... Um..." He trails off, clearly unsure what to call her.

"K." Mama K clasps his hand in both of hers. "Call me K. Everyone else does. And thank you, Zane.

Thank you for taking care of Stas for me."

He blushes even deeper now, his face crimson in the harsh light of the overhead fluorescents. "It was pretty mutual, I think." His eyes meet mine again, and for a moment I can imagine we're back in the theater, on the stage where we shared so many intimacies, real and imagined. "We kind of took care of each other."

"Either way..." Mama K begins, but is cut off when a pair of cops push through the little knot of people around me. I recognize these two. McMillan and ... I struggle to remember his partner's name, but it's as elusive as smoke and I give up. I'm getting real sick of talking to the police. At least these two have the decency to look embarrassed. Sheepish, even.

"Firstly," McMillan says, "I want to apologize for everything that has happened this evening."

I don't know what to say to that. How the hell did it even happen? I know Ropati is intimidating, but this is the police department we're talking about. Surely the staff are trained to deal with people like him. He tried to kidnap me in front of Mama K, in front of the police station. He can claim he's my guardian until he's blue in the face, but until I'm holding signed paperwork, I won't believe it.

"Did you get him?" Zane steps toward the cops, his mouth pressed into a tight, angry line. "Did you get that asshole?"

The second cop—what *is* his name?—nods. "We apprehended Mr. Ropati Nonu and he's in custody."

I breathe a little easier. For about a second. Ropati will talk his way out of this. He's a lawyer and that's what lawyers do. Especially good lawyers, and despite my hatred toward him, I know Ropati is a good lawyer. Or at least, he used to be. Nana was always so proud of him.

"I know you're probably eager to get home." McMillan pulls a notebook out of his pocket. "But I need to get a statement from you. About what happened." He turns to Zane, then to Mama K. "And from you."

The last thing I want to do is talk about it. Or even think about it. I'm tired. Sore. Aching. Not to mention hungry. I'd even eat that disgusting mac and cheese I made back at the theater. What does a girl have to do to get some food around here? I glance around, but we're alone in the curtained cubicle.

"I'm not sure how much help I'll be," Zane says with a shrug. "But I can tell you what I saw."

"As soon as I saw Stas with that man I ran inside to tell someone," Mama K adds. "So I didn't see much. I'd been called and asked to come pick her up from the police station, so when I was on my way in and saw her leaving with him, I knew something was wrong."

"As soon as I saw him I knew something was wrong." Zane rubs the back of his neck. "His eyes…" He pauses like he's searching for the words in the air around him. "Evil," he says finally. "Pure evil."

"He wants the money," I say tiredly.

That gets attention. McMillan's head jerks up. "Money?"

I nod. I should have told someone about it as soon as I found it. I don't know why I thought I had to keep it a secret. I guess I believed I was protecting Dad, but I don't even know anymore. "There's a whole bunch of money sewn into a mattress in one of the dressing rooms. And a whole lot more taped under a drawer in the filing cabinet in Mom's office."

The second cop steps forward, clearly very interested in this new information. He opens his mouth to speak, but before anything comes out, another voice cuts him off.

"Time to go." It's a woman's voice. Calm and low, but threaded with a ragged desperation I recognize all too well.

She steps uncertainly into the cubicle and even with the harsh light shining in my face I notice her eyes are the same dark blue as Zane's.

"Have you said your goodbyes?" She wraps an arm around Zane in a way I'm sure is supposed to be comforting. Zane cringes as it tightens across his shoulders, but takes the embrace without moving, his expression pained. "Please, Mom…"

Mom? I stare at him and at the woman who has released him from her embrace still clings to his arm, studying him as if she can read his thoughts. She's a small woman with hair a shade or two lighter than Zane's. This is Zane's mom? She turns slightly and I know it's true. She looks too much like him for it not to be. Either she broke a million speed limits to get here so fast, or it's way later than I think it is.

"It's late, Ed," she says. Or at least that's what it sounds like she says. "We need to get home and these gentlemen want to talk to you first."

She sweeps him up and moves outside the curtains to speak to the policemen crawling around me like cockroaches. I'm too confused and dazed to really care. I must have misheard her. It's so noisy in here, it wouldn't be hard. Voices and footsteps and beeping machinery compete for space in my ears. I'm surprised I can even understand the cops standing over me.

"Can we go home?" I ask Mama K in one of the quiet moments between questions.

"Soon," she says, getting up and poking her own head through the gap in the curtains.

She gets up and moves away to speak to McMillan. I close my eyes for a second, reveling in the relief the cool darkness brings.

When I open them again, they move toward the spot I last saw Zane.

But he isn't there.

His mom isn't there.

I stand up, clinging to the table for balance as I stagger toward the curtain and the shapes moving behind it. "Zane?"

But he's gone.

"Zane?" I repeat stupidly, unable to accept or understand he's left. Left without saying goodbye. Didn't his mother say something about that? But Zane never said...

My stomach hollows out and fresh tears threaten to spring to my eyes. He's gone. His mom has taken him home. Who else are they going to take away from me? I glance skyward. I don't believe in god, but someone out there has it in for me, that's for sure.

"Sorry about the wait." A tall, skinny woman in scrubs and latex gloves strides into the room and probes at the gash on my chin. "I think this will heal fine without stitches. I'll get a nurse to tape it up for you, and you can go home."

I wish she could tell me where that might be.

Chapter Thirty-Three

It's late by the time the police finally let us go. A deputy drives us back to the police station where Mama K's left her car. I want some food, a hot bath, and my own bed.

I'll settle for two out of three.

"Does your head hurt?" Mama K asks after we're buckled in. "Do you feel sick?"

"I'm fine." I cover her hand with mine. Her concern is touching, but it's making me claustrophobic. "I promise I don't have a concussion or anything. I bashed my chin a little. It'll heal."

She smiles, but it's tight and laced with worry. I don't blame her. The cut chin is the wound she can see. The deeper ones are the ones she can't, the ones I can't even bring myself to examine.

How could Zane leave like that? He said he loved me. At least, I think he did. Everything's so jumbled and chaotic, I'm no longer sure what is real and what may have been imagined.

Halmoni meets us at the door of her house and hustles us inside, rattling on in Korean to Mama K.

"Mom, she's fine." Mama K rolls her eyes at me. "Thank, god."

Halmoni eyes me suspiciously and says a few more words in Korean.

I drift away from them as Mama K sighs and starts explaining the whole situation to her mother in a mixture of Korean and English.

I'm exhausted, but I know I'll never sleep. My blood feels like bees buzzing through my veins. My heart is a lump of old, burnt coal, so fragile a single poke will be enough to send it crumbling into powdery ash. I climb the stairs and pop my head into Mama K's room, needing to see Teddy.

"Stas?" He sits up as soon as I get the door open a crack.

"Yeah, it's me..." I step into the room, closing the door behind me again.

Teddy flicks on the lamp by the bed and stares at me with eyes ringed with dark shadows. The poor kid looks like he hasn't slept in a week. Maybe he hasn't. I'm so selfish. How could I have not thought about how my leaving would affect Teddy?

"Where were you, Stas?" he asks. "I thought ... I thought you were ... gone."

I cross the room and sit down by him on the bed. He looks so young and scared. I can't see even a trace of the brash, loud little boy who snuck junk food whenever our moms' backs were turned.

"I'm sorry, Teddy. I couldn't take it. All the fighting. I want to stay here. I want to live with you and Mama K. When that lawyer said I couldn't, well ... I kind of freaked. I had to get away for a while."

"I want you to live with us too."

"Working on it, kiddo..." I reach out and tousle his hair. Amazingly, he lets me this time. For a while.

He grabs my hand and pulls it away from his head. "What are you gonna do?"

I hesitate. I have no idea. Ropati's arrest has changed things, but not enough. He could still talk his way out. My future remains uncertain.

"I can't say yet, Teddy." I look right into his beautiful coffee-bean eyes. "I don't know. But I promise you, I'm going to do everything I can to stay with you guys, okay?"

"Promise?" His face brightens, but it's still guarded. I hate that look. I hate that the openness and trust I thought were a permanent part of him have been snatched away. Dad's knife has cut far deeper than through my mother's flesh. I wonder if he knows how far the collateral damage has spread.

"I promise, Teddy." I switch the light off and pull the heavy quilts back over him. "Go to sleep, okay? I'll see you in the morning."

"'Night," he says, but as I start to get up, he grabs my wrist and pulls me back down beside him. "Stay?"

So I lie down next to him, listening to the deep, even sound of his breaths as he drifts off to sleep. I'll just stay a minute or two, I tell myself. Then I'll go back downstairs. But before I know it, I'm asleep too.

****

When I open my eyes, I'm confused. I don't recognize the swirls in the plaster over my head or the muted light filtering through the floral curtains over the windows. I turn my head and find the bed beside me empty, the quilt tossed back as if someone has just climbed out of it. A very well-loved stuffed whale winks at me with its half-broken plastic eye.

Teddy.

It comes back to me. This is Mama K's room at Halmoni's house. I must have fallen asleep.

I yawn and stretch, feeling a sharp pull of pain along my ribs. My fingers fly up and prod at the tender spot on my chin. I wince when I feel the gauze and tape holding my gashed chin together. That and the stickiness of dried blood. I never got that bath I wanted.

Rolling out of bed, I wince again. My whole body aches. I don't think I've ever felt so stiff. Not even after a long, intense dance class. I guess escaping almost-kidnapping uses different muscles.

Limping a little, I head downstairs. Voices drift from the kitchen along with the tantalizing scents of coffee and bacon. Bacon! My mouth waters and my stomach growls in anticipation. I never got that meal I wanted either. I'm starving. Literally starving, not the *oh, I haven't eaten since breakfast* kind of starving. I understand the way those people in Africa and other places afflicted by famines tear each other to shreds over a few grains of rice. Right now I'd trample a yard full of preschoolers to get to the bacon I can smell.

"Stas." Mama K leaps up from the table and comes to meet me as I shuffle through the door. "How are you feeling, honey?"

"Where did you sleep?" I run a hand across my head and realize my hair must be a total disaster.

"I slept with Mom," Mama K says quietly.

"You need to eat," Halmoni says decisively, getting up and leading me to the table.

That's one direction I won't question. I'm digging into the plateful of bacon, eggs, and toast before Halmoni has even placed it on the table before me. It's not until I'm more than halfway through the mountain of food I realize there isn't a grain of rice or spoonful of kimchee in sight. Halmoni must have missed me or something. Or Mama K cooked breakfast.

Once the gorging is finished and my stomach has stopped screaming at me, I glance around at the familiar faces surrounding the table.

"So…" I begin, unsure I should even bring this up. But it's easier than any of the other questions arcing through my brain. "What's going on with the Russian aunts?"

Mama K sighs. "They're still here. Their lawyer is putting together a case for them. I imagine things have changed somewhat since last night…"

"You mean because Ropati…"

"Shh!" Halmoni gives me a stern look. "Don't

talk about that monster."

Everyone falls silent. *That monster* is very much on all our minds, but I don't want him to be. Because thinking about Ropati makes me think about Dad, and I can't think about Dad. Knowing what he did hurts too much. I wish I could understand. Even having told the police about the money doesn't seem to have made anything clearer.

I can't help thinking about the aunts, though. Staying here, launching a legal battle, it has to be costing them a lot. How can they afford it? Don't they have jobs back in Russia to go to? Families of their own? How long can they stay? It occurs to me I never asked Mom about her family. For me, her story began when she met my dad. Nothing beforehand mattered to me. Until now, when it's too late.

I push my plate away. I'm not hungry anymore. My stomach feels like it's full of rocks. One for each of the people who have hurt me in some way. Mom, Dad, Ropati, Zane... It's a miracle I can even stand up. To prove I can, I haul myself out of my seat and walk into the empty living room. The curtains are still drawn, but I don't pull them open. Instead I duck behind them, hiding in their thick, heavy folds as I stare out at the empty street below.

"Stas?" Mama K joins me at the window, slinging an arm across my shoulders and pulling me close. "Are you going to be okay?"

I look at her. How can I be okay? Real life isn't like this. The bad things in my life are getting called fat in my skinny jeans or being told I can't go to a party. Murder and kidnapping and falling in love with runaways who tell me they love me and then leave without a word are not part of it. I'm living the plot of a soap opera. A really bad soap opera.

I don't say any of this to Mama K, though. She has enough to worry about right now, enough to deal with. It can't be easy for her to be living with her mother again, too scared to go back to the home she made with Mom because she knows the memories will shatter her. The threat of losing people she loves hanging over her. Not to mention her stupid, impulsive daughter constantly running away.

The thought is like a sledgehammer to the knees. I ran away with Zane, not realizing he had already run away. He was already hiding. And it's my fault he was found.

"Will I ever see him again?" I let Mama K slip her arm around me and lean against her shoulder. It makes me feel like a little kid again, despite the fact I'm as tall as K now. My hips are about twice as wide as hers too. She doesn't seem to notice, though. And for once I don't care.

"I don't know, Stas. If you want to see him, I hope you do."

We stand there in silence for a long time. I like that she doesn't talk to me, doesn't try to convince me Zane's a bad person. I'm not sure he is. I'm not even sure he lied to me. He just didn't tell me the truth.

Mama K shifts and I become aware of how long I've been leaning on her. It must be uncomfortable. I straighten up and turn away from the window.

"Would it be okay if I went to Vonnie's?" Suddenly I'm desperate to see my friend. I hope she's back from her grandparents'. It feels like centuries have passed since I spoke to her. Usually we talk or text about a hundred times a day, so in relative terms, maybe it has been. I think about my phone, lying somewhere off the highway. How many messages have piled up on it?

Mama K smiles. "Sure. But maybe take a shower

first?"

I look down at myself. I'm still wearing Zane's too-tight sweats, the knee on one now ripped from my escape from Ropati.

I shiver. Yeah. A shower sounds good. I feel like layers of filth coat my skin and wonder how I've managed to stand myself this long.

Chapter Thirty-Four

Mama K drives me to Vonnie's. I said I'd take the bus, but she refused to consider letting me do that. I guess I wouldn't trust me either.

"I'm glad you're going to see Vonnie," she says as we pull up at a light. "After winter break, it's probably time for you to go back to school."

I shrug. "What's the point? I mean, if I'm going to get pulled out again to go to Siberia or somewhere."

K's lips press together and her eyes narrow. "That isn't going to happen."

"Yeah? How's that going to work?" I don't mean to sound belligerent. It just comes out that way. I agree with her actually. I should go back to school. God knows I want my life to be normal again. And school is normal.

"I'm going to fight this, Stas." Mama K sounds stronger and more determined than I've heard her sound since we got the news about Mom. She sounds like my Mama K again.

"Yeah... Me too."

We don't speak the rest of the way to Vonnie's, but the words fill the car like a viscous cloud.

"Call me when you need a ride home." Mama K's eyes rest heavily on me until I nod my assent.

She stays parked at the curb, watching as I run up the short walk to Vonnie's front door. She doesn't pull away until the door opens and Vonnie pulls me roughly through it. I catch a glimpse of her taillights disappearing up the street as Vonnie kicks the door closed behind us.

"How's your grandfather?" I ask before she has a chance to say a word.

"Fine," she says with an exasperated sigh. "Grandma is such a drama queen. We pretty much got there, were told there's nothing wrong with him, and came home. Total waste of time. She never read the boy who cried wolf story, that's for sure."

I can't help but smile. I bet on the day Vonnie panicked more than her grandmother did. It's only now she knows her grandfather is fine she can afford to be flippant about it.

"Anyway. Forget me. Where have *you* been?" she screeches, hands on hips as she glares at me. "I've called and texted you about a hundred million times! We got back two days ago, and no one knew where you were!"

"Sorry..." I whisper. "I lost my phone."

She raises an eyebrow. It sounds like a lie. My phone has been pretty much super-glued to me since the day I got it. I used to feel naked without it, almost panicked. Yet somehow, I haven't missed it.

"Well, not exactly lost it," I admit. "I chucked it out the car window when Zane and I ran away."

Vonnie's eyes widen and she cocks a head to one side, regarding me curiously. "I think we might need some provisions for this story..."

I can't help but smile as I follow her into the kitchen that smells like coffee and freshly baked brownies. "You're probably right."

A whole pan of brownies and three sodas later, I've told her everything. "So ... what now?" I ask her.

She picks at the last few brownie crumbs littering the dish, pressing down on them until they adhere to her fingertips and she can lick them off. "Give me a minute. There's a lot to process."

"Tell me about it!"

Vonnie licks at her thumb thoughtfully, crushing a particularly large crumb between her front teeth. "Sounds like Zane's idea was a good one."

I stare at her. "What? Running away?"

Vonnie shakes her head and gives a tight little laugh. "Not that part. The emancipated minor part. If you do that, then *you* can decide where you want to live. And if it's with K and Teddy, that's your business. Or you could come and live here if you want to. I'm sure my folks wouldn't mind."

"You might want to ask them before you go offering up their home." But I can't help grinning at her. "Do you think it could work? Zane said it's mainly to protect assets or if you're joining the military or getting married."

"So you and Zane *aren't* going to get married?" Vonnie giggles and waggles her eyebrows.

God, I've missed her. How can I not have realized that? Her presence doesn't fill the gaping hole Zane's left in me, but it helps mask the emptiness.

I waggle my eyebrows back at her. "No. We're not."

"Maybe you guys should think about it." She looks more serious now, her forehead crinkling the way it does when she starts really thinking about things. And this is one thing she really shouldn't be thinking about. I've known Zane all of five minutes. Not to mention I'm sixteen. There's no way I'm marrying anyone.

"Vonnie, he disappeared on me. He didn't even say goodbye. I thought he loved me, but..." I shrug.

"I'm sorry," she says quickly. "Maybe he couldn't get to you to say goodbye?"

I shake my head. He was there. How hard could it have been? "I don't really want to talk about Zane right now."

I don't know how to talk about him. I don't know how to even think about him. The sound of his name tears ragged strips from my soul. I can't picture his soft blue eyes or the way his hair kicked out at the back of his head without a needle puncturing my heart. His smile, the way his incisors crossed slightly over the teeth next to them, the soft, plump fullness of his lips. Each whisper of memory is a razor blade carving slices from my heart. He left without a word. Didn't leave a phone number or address. Nothing. I don't know if I'll ever see him again.

"I get that." Vonnie nods and all of a sudden she looks ten years older than she actually is. "We should talk to my Dad. He probably won't be able to help you—he's a property lawyer—but he'll know someone who can."

I nod. She's right. I've been going about this all wrong. *We've* been going about this all wrong. We should have hired our own lawyer right away and demanded to be heard. I can only hope the process is not too far along for us to be able to get our voices into the mix. For me to be heard. It's my life after all.

"I don't have a whole lot of money..." But I do. Or, I will. I listened to the will being read the other day. I'm not supposed to get my hands on Mom's assets until I'm older, but I'm sure she'd agree to let me use the money to keep from being taken from Mama K and Teddy. If Mom had any inkling that she'd die this way, so soon, I'm sure she would have changed her will to make Mama K my guardian. But no one expects to be murdered. Well, unless you're one of those paranoid kings in a Shakespeare play. Or in the mafia or something. People like my mom don't expect to be murdered. They think they have time to adjust their wills to reflect the changes in their lives. If I know Mom, it was something she already had on her to-do list. She would just have been waiting until the ink dried on her wedding certificate.

A fresh pang of grief passes through me and I have to let my head drop to the tabletop for a second. My throat is thick and heavy, my eyes prickling with tears.

Will this ever get easier? I'm not sure I can deal with being sideswiped by grief like this every five minutes. At the same time, I'm terrified of the pain easing, of forgetting her.

"Shit…" Vonnie runs her hand around the brownie pan one last time before shoving it away from her. "I didn't think about the money." I could kick myself for telling the cops about the money in the theater, in Mom's office. Ropati said Dad stole it for me. If it could help me stay with my family, I'd even try to ignore the fact I'm certain it's stolen. I can't keep obsessing about this. It's going to drive me batshit. Every story I tell myself is more full of holes than the last. I need to see Dad. I need him to explain. I need him to tell me the truth.

But can I even trust him to do that?

I shake my head to try and shake my thoughts loose. Vonnie looks at me expectantly. She asked me something, didn't she? Oh. Her dad. "Let's talk to him," I say. "I can figure out the money stuff later. If I don't have a case, I won't have to pay."

Vonnie gets up, determination painted across her face. "You're right. Let me call Dad and see if he has time for us today."

I watch as she crosses to the phone on the wall by the door, saddened a little that she has to call to make an appointment to see her father. I guess it makes it more legitimate, makes our case more difficult to ignore.

"C'mon," she says a few minutes later. "He can see us at three."

****

Vonnie drives toward the city. In the passenger seat, I slump against the window, staring out at the familiar streets flashing by, the landmarks that have been a constant in my life since I was old enough to recognize them.

The grocery store Mom always went to because she said their produce was fresher, the dry-cleaner we stopped using after they destroyed an entire corps-worth of tutus, the daycare Teddy went to when Mama K still worked in the city as a graphic designer, the narrow street the school bus sometimes sneaks up when it's running late and wants to skip the traffic lights.

I glance up the compact street and recognize the next corner. "Vonnie. Can we stop somewhere on the way? Just for a second?"

She glances in my direction before turning her attention back to the road. "Sure. Where?"

"Turn left down there." I point to the next turnoff. "Then hang a right. It's a little street called Grivas Place."

She opens her mouth as if to ask me something, but closes it again and flicks her indicator to turn left.

We pull up in front of the neatly mown lawn and flagstone path leading to Zane's door. I hesitate before climbing out of the car. Something about this place puzzles me.

"Whose house is this?" Vonnie asks. "Why are we here?"

My fingers itch to open the door without answering, but that wouldn't be fair. "I'm not entirely sure," I say honestly.

Before she can ask me anything else, I push open the door and climb out.

My pulse thuds in my ears as I walk up the path. What am I doing here? This is a stupid idea.

But I don't stop.

When I get to the door, I wipe my hands on the back of my jeans. My hand shakes a little as I reach up to knock.

"Yes?" A woman opens the door a crack and peers

out at me through thick, owlish glasses. She's older than I would have imagined Zane's aunt to be, but what do I know? I barely saw his mother last night, and this aunt might not even be his mother's sister.

"Uh... Hi," I say awkwardly. "I'm a friend of Zane's and I was wondering if he left an address or something? I ... I didn't get a chance to say goodbye."

"Who?" She opens the door a fraction wider. "I'm not sure you have the right house. No Zane here."

"But..."

"I don't know any Zane." She moves as if to close the door in my face and I shove my foot through the crack to keep her from it.

"The basement!" I cry desperately. "The guy who lived in the basement. Zane."

Now it's the woman's turn to look distressed. "No one has lived in the basement since Jenny died." She chokes a little on the last words in this sentence then adds, "My daughter."

I bite down on my tongue. Suddenly it makes sense. The way Zane took me around the back and let me in through the basement. His terror when someone came down the stairs. How he searched through the cupboards for cups and tea. He never lived here. Not really. It was an address he used when he needed one. A place he could come to when he had nowhere else to go.

I feel sick. I kissed him on a dead woman's couch. I drank her tea. And this woman was on the other side of the door, innocently doing laundry while we trespassed. How much more of what he told me was a lie? Were his parents really divorcing? Is his name really Zane? Does he really think I'm beautiful? I feel like I fell in love with a shadow or a watery reflection of a boy. The only thing I know about him for sure is that he's a dancer. That's the one thing he couldn't lie about.

"Are you telling me there's someone living in my basement?" The woman clutches the door with white knuckled fingers, pulling it closer to her.

Crap. I've gone and terrified a vulnerable old woman. "Uh... Must've come to the wrong house. Sorry."

I practically run down the path and throw myself into the seat next to Vonnie before the old woman can even get the door open wide enough to come after me.

"Let's go," I say, but Vonnie is already turning the key.

"What happened?" she asks as she does an illegal U-turn and heads back toward the main drag.

I sigh. I wish I knew. Another puzzle with more missing pieces. I don't recognize my life anymore. It's like one of those weird surrealist paintings where everything is there, but nothing looks the way it's supposed to.

"Nothing," I say finally, because it's easier than trying to explain yet another inexplicable fragment of my existence. "I got the wrong house. Let's go see your dad."

Chapter Thirty-Five

Vonnie's father works in a fancy office building only a block or so away from the lawyer who read Mom's will. I wonder vaguely if this might be the city's "lawyer district," like Dad's theater is in the so-called "crack district." The big difference is everyone around here looks like a lawyer and I've never seen anyone doing crack near the theater.

There's no metal detector in this building, just an overweight security guard yawning behind his desk in the cramped foyer. He shoves a clipboard at us to sign in, but barely looks at the signatures before handing over a pair of stickers with the word 'visitor' printed inside a circle made up of letters spelling the building's name and address.

We take the elevator to the eleventh floor and step out into a reception area dominated by a huge glass-topped desk behind which a striking black woman wearing violet lipstick sits.

She looks up from the computer she's typing on when the elevator doors slide closed behind us. "Can I help you?"

Vonnie steps forward and looks as if she's about to rest her elbows on the desktop, then stops as if afraid to leave a single fingerprint on it. "We're here to see Frank Young."

The woman presses a button and a series of calendars appear on her computer monitor. "Do you have an appointment? Mr. Young has a very full schedule this afternoon."

Vonnie nods and when she speaks her voice is so cold the words are like sharp shards of ice puncturing the over-conditioned air. "Yes. I'm his daughter. Vonnie

Young."

The woman ignores her tone and gestures to a group of plush couches clustered around a coffee table topped with the same thick, highly polished glass as her desk. "Take a seat. I'll let Mr. Young know you're here."

Vonnie tosses her head. "Please do." She sounds like a princess speaking to a servant, and a very lowly servant at that. I can't help admiring her poise. The receptionist would probably have had me in tears before I could give her my name. Not like reducing me to tears is a big job at the moment.

We wait on the couches that aren't nearly as comfortable as they look. There aren't even magazines to read here. Just books with leather covers lined up on a low shelf against the wall. The spines are so straight, I don't dare touch them lest I ruin their decorative alignment.

"Vonnie?" Mr. Young pushes open the frosted glass doors to the left of the reception desk and gestures for us to follow him through. "Hello, Stas."

"Hi, Mr. Young." I feel suddenly shy and tongue-tied, which is ridiculous. I've known Mr. Young since I was five. I've been on camping vacations with him. Yet in his suit and tie, he looks more like a lawyer than I remember ever having seen him before.

He ushers us into his office and closes the door. As he drops into the seat behind his desk, he waves us toward the chairs on the other side of it. "So, what's this all about, then?"

"I need a lawyer," I blurt out. "At least, I think I do."

Mr. Young frowns. "A property lawyer? Is this to do with your mother's estate?"

"Kind of?" I throw Vonnie a desperate glance.

"Dad, I know you're a property lawyer. But we

thought you might know someone who can help Stas."

Mr. Young leans back in his chair. He looks far too relaxed to me. It's my life I'm trusting him with. "Okay. But if you want me to help, I'm going to need to know what the problem is."

"I want to be an emancipated minor."

The words escape my mouth and fall heavily into the air around us. I can almost see them, dropping downward to sink into the thick pile of the carpet beneath my feet.

Mr. Young remains silent and I feel as if the words gain weight with every second he doesn't speak. If there was any way to take them back, I would. I can't look at him. I don't want to see what might be written across his face. If it's hopeless, I'd rather not know.

"Dad?" Vonnie's voice is slightly shrill as she prompts him.

"I'm thinking, Von."

I do look up then, and find Mr. Young' s face creased in thought, his fingers steepled beneath his chin. A tiny spark of hope ignites in my belly. He didn't shut me down as soon as I said the words. That has to be good, right? He's thinking. That means it isn't a completely stupid idea. At least, I hope it does.

"Look, Stas," Mr. Young addresses me, leaning forward and angling his body entirely in my direction, turning his back on Vonnie. "I'm not an expert on the subject, but I don't believe it's easy to become an emancipated minor. You may spend a lot of money on legal fees and still get denied. Is this really something you're prepared for? Isn't there any other solution?"

I shrug. "You tell me ... my dad assigned custody of me to his brother who tried to kidnap me yesterday." Was it only yesterday? I trace the still-tender gash on my chin and realize it must have been. Time has slowed down. It can't possibly have been only twenty-four hours since Zane and I were kissing on the theater stage. It feels like a lifetime or two since then. "And my aunts seem to think because Dad killed Mom..."

"Allegedly," Mr. Young breaks in. "Until your father has had his day in court he's only accused of killing her."

"Whatever, Dad!" Vonnie sounds exasperated.

Mr. Young frowns at her. "It's an important distinction, Vonnie. Go on, Stas."

"So my aunts seem to think they have the right to take me back to Russia with them. And I don't want to go with my uncle or with my aunts because Mama K is still here, and so is my brother, and they're way more my family than Ropati or the aunts ever have been. But for some sick reason, the law says all these strangers have more rights to me than the woman who's brought me up since I was five."

I'm breathless by the time I finish, my cheeks hot. It sounds so simple laid out like that. But it isn't. The money, stolen or not, complicates everything so much I can't even think about it. My guts are tangled in so many knots I feel like seagulls are flapping around inside.

Mr. Young nods slowly, his brow furrowed as he regards me. "What you're saying isn't really that you want to be emancipated, but you want to keep living with your mother and brother."

I nod, grateful he actually understands. "Yes. But it seems Mama K has fewer rights than all these other people."

"Let me make a couple of calls." Mr. Young has already picked up the phone.

****

Vonnie and I fidget while her father makes call after call, his fingers flying across his phone's keypad. I hear him murmuring snippets of my story, but he speaks so quickly and so low I can't follow everything he's saying. It feels like a really long time before he sets the telephone down and turns back to me.

"Stas," he says seriously. "This isn't my area at all, I'm afraid. But a colleague of mine knows a very smart woman who has had some experience in this kind of custody case. I think it would be a good idea for you and your mother to go and talk to her."

"My mother's d...." I start, then realize he's talking about K. "Oh."

He slides a Post-It note across the table. I glance down at the name and telephone number scrawled across it. I squint at the jagged lettering, trying to make sense of what is written. Finally the words come into focus—Frannie Sawyer.

"My friend has briefed her on your situation. She'll be expecting your call." Vonnie's dad smiles at me. "Talk to K first, okay? This isn't something you need to do on your own. Emancipation is a last resort. Especially since you don't really want to separate yourself from your family. The law isn't as rigid and unbending as you probably think it is, especially when it comes to families. It's taken a long time, but the law is starting to recognize good parents come in a variety of different packages."

I pocket the Post-It carefully. "Thank you," I say, the words feeling thin and inadequate for what he has given me here today. He's given me hope. For the first time since the word 'custody' was uttered after Mom's death, I feel like maybe I will get to stay with the people I love most, the people I consider my home.

"You're welcome. I hope you manage to make it work."

"Yeah, me too," Vonnie chips in. I'd almost forgotten she was there.

"Now," Vonnie's dad peers at us both under his thick, bushy eyebrows. "Do you girls have a way to get home?"

Mama K picks me up from Vonnie's.

"It was great to see you," Vonnie says as I climb into the car.

"You too."

"Let me know what she…" Vonnie tilts her head in Mama K's direction.

Mama K says nothing, but gives me a questioning look.

"When we get home," I tell her. I want to be able to call Frannie Sawyer as soon as I've explained the situation to K. The sooner we can get an appointment to see her, the sooner we can get at least this one part of our lives back on track. And once that happens, well, maybe everything else might start falling into place too.

Maybe.

"Hey," Vonnie says as Mama K fumbles with the keys in the ignition. "Are you moving back home soon?"

I'm about to answer, but Mama K gets in ahead of me. "I was thinking about it too. Stas, do you want to go home?"

"Me?" I stare at her. "I thought maybe you wouldn't want to."

"Why wouldn't I want to? It's my home. Our home. All my happy memories are in that house. I thought it might be hard for you. Because you…" She trails off, but I know what she means. Because I found Mom's body. All this time I thought we stayed at Halmoni's because she was too afraid of the memories, but she was protecting me.

"I want to go home," I tell her. I can't say anything more. My throat is thick again and my eyes burn with unshed tears. What's happened to us? K and I have always talked to one another. I've talked more to her than I ever did to Mom, actually. K was always less judgmental, slower to cut me off if she disagreed with what I was saying or asking. How can I have forgotten?

"Thank goodness," K says with a chuckle. "I don't think I could stand staying with my mother much longer."

"Me too," I admit. "Halmoni's awesome, but…"

"It's time to go home," K says with a nod. "It's time to figure out how to make a home without Rennie."

Chapter Thirty-Six

Back at Halmoni's place, I'm barely inside before Mama K turns on me. "Now tell me what's going on?"

"We went to talk to Vonnie's dad," I tell her, automatically heading for the kettle and filling it from the tap. This isn't going to be an easy conversation. Halmoni must have rubbed off on me with her insistence a nice cup of tea makes any difficult situation that little bit easier.

"Why?" Mama K opens a cabinet and pulls out two delicate teacups.

"He's a lawyer."

"We have a lawyer."

The kettle boils and I busy myself with boxes of tea. Green tea with a pinch of jasmine for K, a blend of peppermint, lavender and ginger for me. I pull a lemon from the overflowing fruit bowl on the counter and squeeze a drop of lemon juice into each of our cups.

"*I* don't have a lawyer," I say as I set the two pots onto the table between us. The competing fragrances of the two brews tangle in midair. "And it's my life in question here."

"And Mr. Young is going to represent you?" K turns her teapot in half circles on the table, then pushes it away with a longing glance at the empty coffeepot.

I shake my head. "No. He's a property lawyer. He gave me this lady's number. She's supposed to be good and has handled custody cases like ours before."

"You mean gay custody cases?" Mama K looks steadily at me.

I drop my gaze to the cup in front of me and take my time pouring scalding liquid into it. My face burns. Is that what Mr. Young meant when he said Frannie Sawyer had experience in this kind of case? I thought he'd meant complicated cases or cases in which one parent had been murdered. The 'g' word hadn't ever crossed my mind.

"Maybe?" But she's right. That is what Mr. Young meant.

I dig the Post-It out of my pocket and slide it across to Mama K. She takes it and frowns down at it, tracing the messy lettering with her fingertip.

"Should we call her?" All of a sudden the excitement and urgency I felt in Mr. Young's office has drained away. I sip at my still-too-hot tea in an effort to fill the hollow space opening up inside me again.

"Do you want to?" Mama K pushes the Post-It back to me. "What do you think she will do that our lawyer can't?"

I shrug. I have no idea. I just know I want to have a shot at this. If there's any chance I can stay here without having to emancipate myself, I have to take it. "You don't think we should?"

Mama K sighs and pulls the teapot back toward her, grimacing as she pours some into her cup. She looks exhausted. God, the poor woman. Is it any surprise? Every day she takes a new hit, a new punch to the guts. And it's all my fault. Maybe she realizes how much better off she'd be without me. Maybe that's why she's so reluctant to call this new lawyer.

"Stas," she begins, her voice slow and measured. "I've heard of this woman. I know she's good. But she also has an agenda and a case like ours is going to be a big deal for her. Politically. I can't speak for you, but I feel like our lives have been in the news enough."

Oh.

"I want to go home, Stas," she goes on. "I want to try and pick up the pieces of our lives. I'm not sure parading my private life, a life that doesn't even exist anymore, will do us any good."

"So…" I'm not sure I can speak through the thickness in my throat. "So, you'll let them take me away?"

"No!" Her head snaps up. "No, of course not." She rounds the table and hugs me hard. "You're my daughter, Stas. I don't care what the law says or any piece of paper. I've been your mother since you were five years old. Nothing can change that."

But doesn't she get it? *Everything* has changed that. Saying she's my mother isn't enough. Believing it. It's like Zane telling me he loved me only hours before he left without a word.

My chest aches. Zane. Another one I lost. Is that what my life is going to be from now on? One loss after another until I'm alone somewhere, curled into a ball until the loneliness kills me?

"Don't you get it?" I cry, my voice rising. "Everything has changed. I know you're my mom, but the rest of the world doesn't seem to agree. This lady," I stab at the Post-It with my finger. "This lady might be the only one around here who does."

Mama K's lip quivers. Oh, god. I've made her cry. Good one, Stas. It's not as if I don't understand how emotionally fragile she is right now. Why'd I have to go and start yelling at her?

"I'm sorry," I offer finally. It feels like there are no other words between us anymore, the last twelve years a wasteland we can no longer recognize.

Mama K glances at me and I see the way misery has scored lines around her eyes and mouth. She looks her age now, and she never has before. Their friends used to tease Mom about being a cradle snatcher, even though K is actually only four years younger than her.

"Stas," she says quietly. "You don't need to be

sorry. I just wish it hadn't come to this."

"Me too." And I mean it more than I've meant anything in my life before. I'd give anything to be able to get my life back the way it was. Mom alive and yelling about stupid things like too-tight jeans and peanut butter. Dad dancing and praying. Mama K and Teddy living their lives, cheerful and untouched by the craziness surrounding us now.

"I love you." I mutter the words as I stare down at the tabletop.

Mama K's mouth twitches into a smile that's sadder than her eyes. "I love you too."

Mama K clasps my hand in hers. "You're right. We should talk to this woman. But let's go home first. Let's figure out if we can find a new normal before we do something likely to change everything all over again."

I don't let her go when I nod my agreement. A new normal sounds good. Another seismic change is not something I'm in any hurry for. I've had enough of them for this lifetime.

****

When Mama K said she wanted to go home, I thought she meant she wanted to go home soon. Like this week sometime. I didn't realize she meant today. Now. We finish our tea in near silence, clear the cups and rinse the tea leaves from the pots. Then Mama K tells me to go and pack my things.

"Now?" I stare at her. It's almost dinnertime. Wherever Halmoni has taken Teddy, they'll be back soon. She can't possibly mean we're leaving now.

"Yes," Mama K confirms. "I've already packed Teddy's stuff and my own."

So I head into the living room where my few possessions are in a neat pile on the window seat. Zane's sweatpants and t-shirt are folded neatly on top. I bury my nose in them, hoping to catch even a trace of his scent. But it's gone.

I wish water and laundry detergent were enough to wash my memory clear. It's hopeless, but I hunt through my assorted memories, searching for a clue Zane was lying to me all that time. But there's nothing. The same nothing I find when I hunt for clues pointing to my father wanting to kill Mom. Or even stealing money from his brother.

I guess it's true nothing in life makes sense.

Halmoni and Teddy come home while K and I are loading the car.

"Where are you going?" Teddy asks, his eyes wide, a note of undisguised terror in his voice.

"Home," Mama K tells him. "And you're coming too."

"You can stay," Halmoni says over and over. "You don't have to leave."

"I know," Mama K keeps repeating. "But it's time, Mom. We need to go home."

It's dusk when we pull up outside the house. The police tape has been taken down, but a few tiny scraps of yellow plastic still cling to the trees and fence.

"God…" Mama K breathes, saying exactly what I'm thinking. The house looks dark and imposing, anything but home.

"Guess we have to…" I push open the car door and step out. Teddy follows me, bounding up the path as if he can't wait to get back inside. He stops before climbing the steps, though, looking back as if to make sure we're following him.

My key is heavy and unfamiliar as I put it in the lock. I used to do this every day without thinking. How is it so difficult now?

When the door swings open and I step inside, the

scent of home assaults me. It's stale now, old and tired, but it's still the smell of home.

Teddy dashes in, dropping things as soon as he enters the foyer. His bag by the door, his jacket tossed carelessly toward the coat closet to land on the floor. I flick lights on as I follow him through the downstairs, illuminating rooms that feel both familiar and strange. I recognize everything, yet nothing looks the way I remember it looking.

"It's weird, isn't it?" Mama K has joined me. She looks weak and shaky and I wonder if she might be having second thoughts about coming back.

"Yeah … I keep feeling like something's missing." I wipe my fingers through the fine scrim of dust that has settled across the kitchen table.

"Rennie," K says simply. "That's what's missing."

I can't do anything but nod because she's right. There are Mom-shaped holes in every room.

"C'mon!" K claps her hands, the sound like a gunshot in the quiet house. "Let's put on some music and clean up this place."

It's almost midnight before we've finished. The quick dust, mop, and vacuum we planned on doing turned into a much bigger job and we've moved the furniture, switched the purposes of rooms around and basically re-made the house into something that works for our new family of three. I take a long, hot shower before collapsing onto my bed in the room that used to be Teddy's. He's taken Mom and K's old room while K has moved her things into mine. I like the change, even if I will have to repaint the walls in here soon. Teddy's friezes of cartoon turtles and superheroes still march in a circle near the ceiling. I haven't put up my own posters yet. One part of me wants to make everything look the same as it did, but another thinks maybe I need a change.

Everything else is different, so my room should be too.

I lean over and switch off the lamp. Maybe tomorrow I can figure out what, if anything, needs to adorn my walls. Right now I want to see if I can sleep in a bed that feels wholly familiar in a house that feels anything but.

Chapter Thirty-Seven

A week later I'm starting to feel like our house is a home again. At least some of the time. We keep the curtains closed in the rooms overlooking the studio. None of us have been brave enough to go out there yet. We'll have to some time, but it feels too soon. It will probably always feel too soon. Even now the police tape has come down.

Inside the house we've made our changes and are doing everything we can to fill the hole Mom's absence has left and while it isn't easy, it's possible. Out there it's all Mom, all hole—a giant, sucking void sitting there, waiting to swallow us.

Going back to school makes things easier too. I've missed a lot of classes and catching up is going to be a bitch. But I'm grateful for the workload. If I'm stuffing my head with algebra, history, and physics, I'm not focusing on Mom or Zane or the various relatives circling like vultures.

"How do you concentrate?" Vonnie asks me in the library one lunch hour. "I couldn't focus on math if I didn't know where I'd be living in a month or if my dad was going to jail for life." She doesn't mention Zane and I'm glad.

I shrug. "It's easier to do math. There's only ever one answer."

And it's the truth.

"Have you called that lawyer lady yet?" Vonnie's like a dog with a bone sometimes. Can't she see I don't want to think about this stuff? I want to keep my head down, fill it with facts and figures until there is no room for anything else.

I shake my head.

"Why not?"

"Mama K isn't ready," I tell her. I'm not sure if it's the truth anymore. We haven't talked about it again. We've been ignoring the whole thing. It's getting increasingly difficult, though, especially when the aunts keep popping over to visit. Hearing them speak Russian is like a blow to the chest. Looking at them and finding Mom's features, blurred and distorted in their faces, makes the permanent ache inside me throb with fresh hurt. At least they've stopped talking about how happy I'll be in Toblosk.

Maybe they can see it's not true.

Mom rarely even mentioned Toblosk. Why would she? She left for Moscow when she was still a child. It was no more her home than it is mine. I can't believe anyone would actually send me there. It'd be crazy to disrupt my life like that. I'm more than halfway through high-school and moving to Russia, where I can speak but not read or write, would set me back too far. No. I won't be sent there.

"Hey," Vonnie stands up and jams her books into her backpack. "You never know. If you keep your mouth shut, they might forget about you."

"Fat chance," I say as I pack my own books away. Ropati has been ominously silent ever since K and I told her lawyer we wanted to press charges. He's out on bail, I'm told, but he hasn't tried to see me. I bet he hasn't forgotten about me, though. Not with the police having impounded the two bundles of cash he claims are his and Dad stole from him. What Dad says, I have no idea. He still won't let me visit.

I try to push this conversation out of my head all through afternoon classes, but not even a history quiz is enough to distract me now my worries have been uncovered. We can't keep ignoring this. We should be proactive and face it head on. Otherwise, we're going to have a long way to fall when the rug gets pulled out from under us.

My stomach churns as I walk toward the house, keeping my eyes carefully away from the sign still planted in the middle of the lawn. We have to get rid of that. The stupid ballerina Mom smiling up at her name. I can't get away from it either. The only other way into the house is around the back and walking in the shadow of the studio would be worse than accidentally catching a glimpse of the sign.

As I start up the walk, I catch sight of the small blue car squatting at the curb. Just what I need. The aunts are here. My heart hammers at my ribs. Are they going to take me away this time?

My legs weaken at the thought and I grab hold of the mailbox at the end of the walk to keep upright. I can't go to Russia. No offense to Galina and Zoya, but they can't take Mom's place. I live here. This is my home. Or at least, it was my home. I'm working hard to make it my home again. They can't take that from me.

Or can they?

My legs slowly recover their strength and I gingerly let go of the mailbox. Almost as an afterthought, I open it and peek inside.

A small stack of mail lies jumbled together. I pull it out and flick through the usual assortment of bills and advertising. A plain white envelope catches my eye. Unlike the others with printed address labels or those crinkly cellophane windows, this envelope has the name and address written by hand. The handwriting is small and cramped, the letters tilting backward at such an acute angle they look as if they're about to tumble down on top of each other. I smile at the thought then freeze when I realize the letters across the top spell out my name—

Anastasia Nonu.

I flip the envelope over and find an intricate sketch of a tree, its branches stretching and spreading to the very edges of the paper. The handwriting is as unfamiliar as the drawing style.

At the bottom, I see a name scribbled in a corner: Zane Talbolt, followed by an unfamiliar address in Rosemont.

Not now. I can't read this now. I've been doing fine without thinking about him at all. I can't let him into my head now.

But that isn't true. I can't stop remembering him. I can't stop missing him.

"Fuck you!" I say out loud, a sudden wave of anger surging though me as I stare at the cramped writing crouched beneath the sprawling tree. "I don't need this crap."

I drag my backpack from my shoulder and scrabble through its contents until my fingers close around a pen. I cross out my address and slash the words "return to sender" across the white space beneath it.

I don't want the letter here any longer than it has to be. If it's here, I'll weaken. I'll get curious about what he has to say and I'll open the letter. And if I do, his words will poison me. They'll break me.

I've just managed to glue myself back together. The glue hasn't hardened yet, though, and the fractures are weak enough I know the slightest nudge will be enough to send me back into the pile of shards I was just a few weeks ago.

When I get to the mailbox on the corner, I don't hesitate before dropping the letter inside. It lands without a sound and I feel weight lift off my soul. Maybe this will stop his voice from drifting through my consciousness while I fall asleep at night. Maybe now he'll stop haunting my dreams. Maybe now I can see a dark-haired boy without my heart rising into my throat.

Maybe…

I turn and run back to the house, leaving Zane and his scrawled words behind.

I trudge up the walk, half hoping the aunts will be gone by the time I get there. I can't take anything more today. Zane's letter has brought back those hurts too, lining them up alongside all my other pain. How did I ever consider life fun or happy or carefree? Why did I worry so much about the size of my thighs or a zit on my nose when I could have been enjoying time with the people I loved?

I try to shove those thoughts out of my mind. I fill my head with sunshine, rainbows, the way bacon tastes when it's cooked to the perfect crispiness, the way my body trembles when someone kisses a certain spot on the back of my neck, when Zane kisses that spot, his hands spread across my waist in a way that makes me feel tiny and protected.

Argh! I can't get Zane out of my head.

His face flashes before my eyes at the most peculiar moments. And sometimes, before I open my eyes in the morning, I swear I can feel his breath on my neck, smell the spiciness of his skin drifting by. I miss him. He's part of the aching hollow that has taken up permanent residence in my chest and gut.

I push open the front door and take a deep breath before closing it behind me.

"Stas?" Mama K's voice drifts from the living room.

"Yeah, it's me." I drop my backpack and trudge down the hallway that seems to have become the length of a football field.

"Zoya and Galina are here," she calls and even in

those few words I can hear the tension in her voice. I wonder how long they've been there. Hopefully not too long. Yet even a few minutes is too long when you can't communicate.

I force my shoulders back and stride into the living room with a confidence I don't feel. "*Dobryj dyen,*" I say. "Good afternoon."

The two aunts are perched on the edge of the sofa like a pair of birds. And like birds, they leap up and start twittering around me as soon as I enter the room. I have to resist the urge to swat at them as they peck my cheeks and mutter in Russian about how I'm getting too thin. I can't help smiling at the irony. I don't think the word *iskhudavshiy* is one Mom ever used in relation to me.

"So pretty," Galina says softly. "Such a lovely figure. Your mother was always so thin. She never ate. You're a real woman and men like a woman who enjoys her food."

Maybe in Russia they do. Here a real woman eats salad, dressing on the side, while her man tucks into steak and fries. Maybe I would like living in Russia after all.

It takes a long time for them to sit down and stop fussing over me. Zoya keeps touching my hair as if she can't believe such coarse, wiry stuff could sprout from a human head. I hate it and duck away, wondering how she'd like it if I started running my fingers through the fine cornsilk hair she has in a braid down her back.

"What do you want?" I ask bluntly, sliding out from under Zoya's hand and crossing the room, away from her grasp. "Why are you here?"

That sets off a whole new round of twittering.

"What?" Mama K asks, clearly lost by the rapid-fire Russian spinning through the room.

I shrug. "They haven't told me anything yet."

Both aunts finally sit down again. I drop into an

armchair across from them. "So?" I ask again, taking care to use only the most formal of Russian. I'm not going to pretend we aren't strangers by using the more familiar terms. "What's going on?"

"We wanted to say goodbye," Zoya says finally, her blue eyes brimming with tears. "We must go home. We have been away too long."

"What?" I can't believe what I'm hearing. Goodbye? They're leaving without me? They're giving up on taking me home with them?

"Goodbye?" I ask stupidly.

"Our families need us," Galina adds. "It is a long time to be away from our husbands and children."

My face burns. I didn't even know they had husbands or children. I never bothered to ask. "Of course," I say.

"We wish you would come with us," Galina says. "But your life is here. We can see that now. We can see how much you are loved." She glances at Mama K who gives a cautious, trembling smile.

"You will come and visit?" Zoya asks.

I nod. Maybe I will someday. On my own terms. I'd like to see where Mom came from. Just so long as I can leave and come back here when I'm ready to.

"Thank you," I say gratefully. "*Spasibo.*" The words seem too small to carry the weight of how grateful I am. They have given me my life back. A small piece of it, anyway.

I turn to Mama K, unable to keep the smile away from my mouth. "They're leaving," I tell her. "And they don't want me to come with them."

After many hugs, kisses, photographs, tears, and promises to both write and visit, the aunts leave. The sudden silence is overwhelming and I collapse into the couch cushions. Mama K is about to sit next to me when the phone rings. She sighs and crosses to the bookcase the phone sits on.

"Hello?"

I watch her face as she listens to whoever is on the other end and the relaxed smile that had just appeared on her face slips away.

"What?" I mouth, standing up and moving closer in the hope I might be able to catch some of what is being said.

She shakes her head and brushes me away. Her knuckles are white with clutching the receiver.

"I'll let you know," she says finally and hangs up.

"What?" I ask again, hating the way her hands shake and the agitated look in her eyes.

"Do you still have that lawyer's number?" she asks, her voice trembling.

Chapter Thirty-Eight

Mama K dresses up for our visit to the new lawyer's office. She picks me up outside my school, imposing in her two-inch heels and perfectly fitting suit. Yet her smile when she sees me is broad and genuine even though the corner of her mouth twitches, a sure sign she's nervous.

"Hi," she says, "Are you ready?"

I just look at her. How can I be ready for this? How can anyone?

She smiles again. "It's going to be fine, Stas. I promise."

How can she be so certain after that phone call?

This lawyer's office is smaller and shabbier than the other ones I've been in. It's on the ground floor and the receptionist has an impressive head of orange dreads coiled into a cone at the back of her head.

"Frannie's running a little late," she drawls and points us toward a faded green couch. "Can I get you anything?"

"No thanks," we both murmur.

Mama K sits down. I'm too wired to sit. I pace up and down the narrow strip of linoleum separating the waiting area from the receptionist's desk. I'm so nervous I can feel individual beads of sweat forming along my vertebrae. One by one they trickle down my back, tracing their way across my skin with agonizing slowness before being absorbed into the waistband of my skirt.

After about fifteen minutes, the front door opens and a tall, solid woman bursts in, juggling a briefcase and several files.

"So sorry," she says when she sees us. "I'm Frannie Sawyer. Traffic is a nightmare this afternoon. It's usually less than ten minutes between here and the courthouse, but today…" She breathes out an exasperated gust of air. "Anyway. Come on in. Do you want water? Coffee? I'm running on empty here. Ana, can you bring me some of my tea?"

She's like a tornado and Mama K and I are swept up by her. Before I know I've moved, I'm inside her office, perched on a surprisingly comfortable wooden chair. A stick of incense burns on the windowsill.

Frannie tosses her briefcase in a corner and dumps the files on a desk with stacks of the things piled all over it. Yet when she sits down, there's no hesitation as she reaches for a precarious stack on her left and pulls out a folder, opening it in front of her. "So," she murmurs as she scans the file. "This is an interesting situation."

"Yes," Mama K says tightly. "We want to hear your thoughts. Stas thought perhaps it would be better if she had her own lawyer, given the circumstances."

Frannie looks at me. "How about you tell me what you're thinking."

I take a deep breath. I have no idea what I'm thinking. I'm confused. I've never really understood the idea of a moral dilemma, but here I am, stuck right in the middle of one and none of my options feel great to me.

"I want to be emancipated," I say finally and the words surprise me because they're not true. At the same time, it's the only way I can see getting out of being forced to make a choice I don't believe in.

"What?" Mama K stares at me.

"I want to be an emancipated minor," I say more firmly.

Frannie frowns and looks at me over the thick lenses of her glasses. She straightens them and glances back at the file in front of her. The theatrics of all this are plucking painfully at my already-stretched-thin nerves.

Any minute now, they're going to snap.

"Is emancipation really what you want, Anastasia?" Frannie's words surprise me. I'm here aren't I?

"Yes, ma'am," I say, but my body betrays my words. My head shakes as I say it and my eyes cut toward Mama K. "Well, no ... not really."

Mama K watches me with dark, liquid eyes. I think there may be tears pooling there, but I don't want to see her cry and know I'm the cause of her tears. She's cried enough. More than enough. Especially over me. I don't want to hurt her anymore. I don't want anyone to hurt her ever again. And as far as I can tell, this is the only thing I can do to keep her from being hurt. As long as I'm around, she's going to have to deal with all these crazy people who want their piece of me.

"If you could make the choice yourself, where would you live?" Frannie speaks so quietly I have to strain to hear the words.

I open my mouth, but no words come out. If I tell the truth, what will the consequences be? Will it make things harder for us? For Mama K?

I look at Mama K and find her eyes fixed on me. I stare into them and calm infuses me. It's like a storm has been raging inside me and suddenly the wind has dropped, allowing the clouds and trees and water to cease their frenzied movement and drift.

"I want to live with Mama K," I say, my voice loud and clear and steady in the suddenly too-close room. "I want to live with my Mom."

****

"Thank you for your honesty, Anastasia." Frannie smiles then, and for the first time I see her as being human. Perhaps she has kids at home too. A husband. A wife, even? Maybe I can trust her to do what's right for me after all.

"I've read all the paperwork pertaining to this case," she goes on. "And frankly, I don't believe it would be in your best interests to be emancipated."

My heart plummets to my feet, taking my blood with it. My head spins and I have to reach out and hold onto the chair to keep from falling over. Why do I keep doing this? Every time I even consider trusting someone, they let me down. Every. Single. Time. You'd think I'd learn from my mistakes.

"But," she continues. "I also don't believe it is in your best interests to be taken from the woman you've considered a mother since you were a small child."

"What about Ropati?" I ask, my heart thumping sickly at the base of my throat. "He says…"

"That would be Ropati Nonu?" She peers at me over her glasses again. "Your uncle?"

I nod.

"He's trying to negotiate a plea bargain with you, is he? He'll drop his custody case if you drop the criminal charges? Blackmail. No judge with an ounce of sense in his head would send a child to live with that man. Apart from his own criminal activity, he's the brother of a suspected murderer. Press charges. You have nothing to be afraid of there."

She says it with such certainty, with such disgust in her expression. I like this woman. And I think she might be able to get me what I want.

"Now," she says. "What about the other family? The Russians? It says here they're also trying to get custody?"

Mama K shakes her head. "They went home."

Frannie's head snaps up and she tugs the glasses off her face. "When?"

"About three days ago?" It comes out a question.

"And they said they were dropping their custody claim?"

I nod. "They said they understood my home was here."

Frannie frowns again and scribbles something on a pad of paper next to the still-open file before turning to Mama K. "Do you know if they documented this with their lawyer?"

"No, I'm afraid not." Mama K looks worried again now.

"I can find out." Frannie closes the file and sets it aside. "It would be better if they had, but it sounds like perhaps they left in something of a hurry?"

"It did seem very sudden," Mama K says slowly.

"D'you think Ropati had something to do with the aunts leaving?" I ask, an idea starting to crystallize in my head.

"What?" Mama K doesn't turn to look at me, but I can tell my question has startled her.

I shrug. I've had three nights of lying awake, tossing big questions around in my head. I can't help but wonder. "They left so suddenly. You don't think he paid them off or something?"

Mama K's lips are tight as she hisses, "I wouldn't put it past him."

No. Neither would I. He strikes me as a poor loser. If he doesn't get what he wants, no one can have it. So when the chips came down against him, he took his toughest competition out of the picture. Wouldn't it be nice to have that kind of cash? Enough that throwing it at a problem makes the problem melt away? I'm kind of surprised he hasn't tried throwing any at me yet. Or at Mama K.

"Don't go rushing ahead of me here," Frannie warns. "I will need to get in touch with the Russians' lawyers. Once I've spoken to them, we'll have a much better idea of where we stand."

I nod. As far as I know, this is only a preliminary meeting with Frannie. Yet she's talking like we've already hired her. I like her confidence.

Frannie turns to Mama K again. "Now, Ms. Lim. I have a few questions for you. I hope they won't upset you. It's important I understand a few things about your relationship with Anastasia and Ms. Varushkin."

Mama K swallows hard, then nods.

"You and Ms. Varushkin were about to get married?"

Mama K nods again, her eyes shiny. She reaches up and wipes at the side of one eye.

"Did you have any plans to formalize the custody arrangements for Anastasia and her brother after the wedding?"

"Yes." Mama K ducks her head and swipes at the other eye. "Rennie and I talked about it. I was going to adopt Stas, and Rennie was going to adopt Teddy. Once we were legally married, it would be easier, so we waited."

Frannie's voice drops and becomes more gentle. "Had you filled out any preliminary paperwork to do this?"

Mama K shakes her head.

"Did you write down your intentions anywhere?"

"No." Mama K's voice shakes. "We had so many plans, but they were between us. We talked and talked about these things, but we never thought to write anything down. We never thought anything like this would happen. We planned to adopt each other's children, and then to update our wills to reflect that. That's why Rennie's will…" Mama K stops, her voice stuttering to a halt at a sob strangles her.

I reach over and take her hand, squeezing it gently. I had no idea of any of this. These plans must have been made between them in bed at night or in other pockets of time when they were alone together. I wonder if Teddy had an inkling, if he might have overheard something. He was always home more than me.

"It's fine, Ms. Lim," Frannie says in a soothing voice. "Obviously it would be better if you did have something in writing, but it's not the end of the world. People make plans, and they don't always write them down. You and your partner seem to have planned better than a lot of other clients."

Mama K takes a tissue from the box Frannie nudges in her direction. "So, what do we do?"

"What about my father?" I ask in a voice too small to actually be mine. "He's the one who wanted Ropati to take me. He's the one whose name is in Mom's will."

"That would be Tusi Nonu?" Frannie barely has to glance at the file to access this information. She's good.

I nod at the same time as Mama K says, "Yes."

Frannie scans her notes again, summarizing what she reads under her breath as she does. "He's in jail. Looks like he'll be there until the trial. Evidence points to him being the perp. No plea entered at preliminary trial. Hmm ... odd." She looks back up at us. "As far as I'm concerned, nothing he says holds weight. He could say he wants the Easter Bunny to be your guardian and it still wouldn't mean anything. Murderers don't get to make that call."

My face grows hot. "What happened to innocent until proven guilty?"

Frannie flushes and for the first time seems to lose her poise. "You're right. I shouldn't have said that. I'm sorry."

She seems genuinely sorry. Flustered at making such a mistake.

"He won't let me visit," I say finally. "Is there anything you can do?"

"You want to see him?" Mama K looks stricken.

I can't meet her eye as I nod my head. "I have to," I explain. "I can't believe he'd do it. I won't believe it until I see him."

Frannie scribbles something on a piece of paper. "I'll see what I can do. I'll be in touch in the next day or so. It's obviously important to you, Anastasia."

"Thank you," I say and it's not just for her taking my request seriously, but also for understanding how much I need this. No one else has.

Chapter Thirty-Nine

I'm shell-shocked when we walk out of Frannie's office an hour or so later. The woman is terrifying, in the best possible way. I glance over at Mama K as we make our way to the car and she looks as overwhelmed as I feel.

"Well," I start as I watch her fumble for the car-keys. "She's kind of impressive."

Mama K gives a strange sort of chuckle. "I guess that's one word for it."

Something clutches at my heart. Didn't she like Frannie? She signed the paperwork to hire her, so she must believe she can help us. Or did she do it just for me?

"Didn't you like her?" I ask. My voice sounds weird because my breath is trapped somewhere near the base of my throat.

"Like her?" Mama K stops digging in her purse and looks right at me. "I don't have to like her, do I? She seems very good at her job. That's why I've hired her. If you like her, it's a bonus. She's your lawyer."

"Not ours?"

Mama K's face softens. "Well, yes. To a point. But remember, I have my own lawyer working on this too. Hopefully she and Frannie will get along because the more people we have advocating for us, the better."

We slide into the car. Now I'm not being carried along in Frannie's whirlwind, I'm exhausted. I hadn't realized how keyed up I was about meeting her, or how terrified I'd been about what she might say. Hearing her tell me Ropati wasn't a threat has lifted a huge weight off me. I know what to do now and while it's still scary, the fear is manageable. I can control it.

And knowing she's going to try and get me in to

see Dad is another one. She at least seemed willing to try, unlike Dad's lawyer who is a brick wall and won't give an inch. I bet he hasn't even asked Dad since the first request was made. He just keeps repeating the same "no" over and over again.

****

Frannie works fast. By the time I get home after school the next day, she's left a message on voice mail telling me I can visit Dad the following day. A flock of birds take off in my stomach at the sound of those words. I never thought it would be so soon. I'm not sure I'm ready for it to be so soon. I thought I'd have some time to prepare myself. Although how to do that, I'm not entirely sure.

Mama K is in her studio, working, or at least trying to. Several deadlines have drifted past in the last few weeks and she's scrambling to catch up. I knock on the door and let myself in, a cup of coffee in my hand.

"You're home?" Mama K looks up from the easel, her eyes bleary. "What time is it?"

"Around three-thirty. Here." I hand her the coffee.

"Thanks." She cups her hands around both sides of the mug before taking a sip.

"Frannie called," I say as casually as I can. "Apparently I can visit Dad tomorrow afternoon."

"You really want to see him?" Mama K looks like she can't comprehend this desire.

I nod. "I have to."

She's silent for a long moment before she nods too. "Okay. If it's important to you."

"I can ask Vonnie to drive me," I blurt out. "If you—"

"No." She cuts me off. "I'll take you. I won't see him, but I'll drive you."

"But, Teddy…"

"We'll drop him at Halmoni's on the way."

That's all my arguments gone. "Thank you." She has no idea how much it means to me.

Or maybe she does.

****

Quincy sits alone in the middle of some fields. I've driven past before, but never really noticed it. Several fences surround the hulking brick building, all topped with lethal-looking razor-wire. We have to stop several times on the way in, and each time both Mama K and I have to show our drivers' licenses and endure the guards comparing our features to those in the photos.

We park in a lot that stretches the width of the building. Wire and bars cover every window, making them look like bandaged eyes. To walk through the main entrance, we have to pass through a metal detector and I'm reminded of the building where we heard the will read.

"Are you okay?" I ask Mama K once we're through all the security and sitting on a hard wooden bench in the waiting area.

"Fine," she says through gritted teeth. "It's just like TV, isn't it?"

I giggle. It is. I almost feel like I'm on a set, not in a real place. But then I remember my father is on the other side of all these concrete walls and I don't feel like laughing anymore.

After about fifteen minutes, a guard leads me into a room and tells me to sit on a rickety folding chair facing a window. Mama K should be here. It's so exactly like the movies. Dad's going to be on the other side of the glass. We'll have to talk through it. Sure enough, when I glance around, I notice the telephone handset hanging to the left of the frame.

I sit, staring at the blank window for what feels

like a long time. It isn't real glass, though, is it? I reach out a hand and touch a surface that isn't cold and smooth like glass is. Instead it's the same temperature as the room and faintly sticky. Perspex, or something. I sit back down, wiping my fingers on my skirt in disgust.

And then he's there.

A flicker of movement registers in the corner of my eye, and when I look up, Dad's face fills the window. Not ready for that, I drop my gaze to the orange jumpsuit he wears. Huh. Again, like the movies. Who knew? Dad's muscular forearms bulge beneath the rolled-up sleeves. The fabric is loose and baggy around the rest of him, disguising the incredible shape I know he's in.

It's a long time before I'm ready to raise my eyes to his face. When I do, I focus first on his chin, covered in a scrim of thick stubble. White hair flecks this emerging beard, and for the first time he's showing his age. His head has been shaved, and if anything, the lack of hair makes him better looking.

He gestures for me to pick up the handset, but I'm not prepared yet. I don't think I can speak. I can't even bring myself to look into his eyes, so how can I talk? I reach out and take it, not bringing it to my ear yet, but holding it against my sternum. Dad puts his own handset to his ear, and I wonder if he can hear the way my heart thumps in my chest, its beat far too frantic.

I let my eyes slide up his face until I catch his eyes.

They're bloodshot. Rings beneath them are dark enough to look like bruises. New lines creep from the corners, more bracket his mouth like a pair of commas. He looks old. Worn. Most of all he looks sad. No, not just sad. Tortured. This is the face of a man who hasn't slept in weeks, a man who can't chase some horror from his skull.

My breath catches in my chest and expands painfully there.

He did it.

He killed Mom.

I can't look away now. His gaze doesn't waver. He looks at me. He looks through me. He looks into me. And every way he looks, he's telling me what it is he did.

He killed her.

"Why?" I whisper, still clutching the phone to my chest. "Why? Why? Why?"

Fury burns my veins. How could he do it? Why would he? He's a dancer. A creator. He gives life, not takes it away.

"Why?" I shriek again, the word the only thing I can think or feel or say. "Why?"

He sits there in his ugly orange suit, eyes calm and impassive as they tell me the truth about his guilt.

I hurl the phone at the window, but it just bounces off and dangles uselessly from its cord. It looks pathetic hanging there, so I reach out and pick it up.

"Stas." Dad's voice issues from the handset as I'm about to hang it back up. "Stas."

My hand shakes as I lift it to my ear. With anger or fear, I'm not sure. Probably a mixture of both.

"Dad?"

"Stas. Listen to me. There's something you need to know." There's an urgency to Dad's voice, something I've never heard in it before.

"What?"

"There's money, Stas. I hid some money for you."

"At the theater? Yeah, I know. And at Mom's office. Is that why you killed her?"

Dad winces and recoils like I've hit him. "You don't understand," he says.

"No, I don't. So why don't you explain it." My

confusion appears to have morphed into anger and my voice is way too loud for this space. I bite my lip and try to control the rage racing through my blood like a swarm of fire-ants.

"I hid the money in the ballet school because I knew Ropati would never think to look there," he says in a low choked voice. "No one was ever in the studio in the evenings. But he followed me…"

"Ropati?"

"He's not a good man, Stas."

"Tell me something I don't already know."

Dad's knuckles whiten around the telephone receiver. "The money's dirty, Stas. He's been using the theater to clean it. It was … it was the only way I could keep it open. So I let him. I let him blackmail me. I let him make me a criminal. But I wanted out."

"Ropati says you stole that money."

Dad snorts. "I never stole anything. I never wanted any of his filthy money. I refused to spend my cut and he knew it. Everything fell apart at his end and he wanted it. He came after it. I was saving it for you, and I wasn't letting him get his hands on it. That's why I hid it. That's why he came after me."

"That's why you killed Mom."

The agony on Dad's face twists his features into something unrecognizable.

But he doesn't nod.

He doesn't acknowledge the words I just said.

I can't say anything more. It's like the plot of a movie, not real life. Money laundering. Blackmail. Murder. None of these things should have touched my life.

But they have.

"Did you kill her?" I ask finally. I need to hear him say it out loud, even though his posture, his face, his eyes are all telling me he did. I still need to hear the words.

He remains silent. Unmoving.

I raise my eyes to his and see the depth of pain he's suffering.

"You didn't, did you?" The words come out in a whisper because suddenly there isn't enough air in my lungs to speak. "You didn't kill her?"

He still says nothing, then his lips curl into the smallest smile I've ever seen. It's only for a second, but it's enough. He's told me the truth and it's the truth I knew in my heart. Dad couldn't kill Mom. He couldn't kill anyone. I knew that about him. Yet I let everyone convince me I was wrong. This is why I needed to see him.

A few more of the elusive puzzle pieces fall into place, but the picture they complete isn't one I like or even want to look at anymore. I'm tempted to break the connected pieces apart to try and create a new picture, one more pleasing.

"Two minutes," the guard at the door barks. I'd forgotten he was there. Was he listening to everything Dad said. Does he even care that an innocent man is behind this faux-glass wall? That the real murderer walks free?

"Ropati shouldn't be free," I say. It's wrong that Dad is here, while Ropati tries to manipulate Mama K and me into bending to his will.

Dad shakes his head. "It's my own fault. I let him dominate me. I let him use me. I deserve to be here. I will serve my time. There will be no deals made. I have sinned against God, and I will accept my punishment with grace."

"But it isn't your sin you're being punished for," I protest. The anger is back, but it isn't directed at Dad anymore.

He bows his head and starts to pray. I won't get anything more from him now.

"You don't deserve to be here for life," I say to the window as I hang up the phone. "You don't deserve to pay for his crime."

He looks up as I back away, his dark, dark eyes filled with such sadness I can't bear to look. "Please..." His lips move silently from behind the glass and I understand he's asking for my silence. He genuinely believes he deserves to be here, that his sins are as large as his brother's. I'll never understand his god.

But how can I stay silent when the wrong man is locked away?

I pound on the door I was shown through until the guard comes to let me out. I manage to gather myself together as we walk back through the waiting room to where Mama K sits patiently. I keep myself together as we walk back out to the parking lot. By holding my lips tightly squeezed against each other, I hold myself together until we've left the prison behind us.

Chapter Forty

I'm shaky as we walk across the vast expanse of parking lot to where Mama K left the car. My head whirls with the new knowledge I hold. Dad's innocent of killing Mom, yet he holds enough guilt about it he'll take the sentence without a whimper. And Ropati is letting him. Does Dad feel some weird loyalty to his brother? Some need to protect him?

I don't know what to do.

"He didn't do it." I stand outside the car, hand on the door handle. "He didn't kill Mom."

Mama K gives me a pained look. "I understand it's hard to accept…"

I open my mouth to cut her off, to tell her everything. As I do, her phone rings and she turns away to answer it.

I lean back against the car and close my eyes, letting the breeze lift my hair off my neck. It's cold, but after the close air of the prison, it feels like freedom.

"Can I have the phone?" I ask when she hangs up. "I need to call Frannie."

Mama K eyes the barbed wire and ugly, squat buildings before us. "Can it wait?"

"No."

She knows better than to argue and passes me the phone before climbing into the car.

Frannie answers after the first ring. "Frances Sawyer here."

"Frannie? It's Stas. I need to tell you something."

And I do.

I tell her everything. About Dad and Ropati and everything I know about the money and the theater and their relationship. I tell her about the way Dad looked at me. I tell her I'm certain he didn't kill my mother.

"So who did?" she asks, snapping me back to reality. "Your father isn't getting out until there's proof someone else did it. And your dad hasn't denied it, Stas. That's another big black mark against him. He didn't even deny it to you."

I realize then she's right. I *know* Dad didn't do it. I know it with every inch of me. But Dad didn't tell me that. Not in words anyway. "He didn't say he did either…"

"I'm sorry, Stas." Frannie's voice becomes gentler. "I wish there was something I could do."

"Isn't there a way to get Ropati checked out some more? Dad said he was a bad man. I bet he had something to do with it."

"You're probably right. But it's not as easy as that. There have to be reasons to look into someone in that way, and with your father already in jail for the crime, there isn't a reason. You need evidence that Ropati was involved."

I rack my brain for a memory, something, anything. The money. It all goes back to the damn money. I think back to finding the first package in Mom's office, then the second in the mattress in the theater.

"Frannie!" I cry suddenly. "I think I might have evidence."

And I tell her about the notebook. The one I slipped on in Mom's office after opening the first package of banknotes. The one with the columns of numbers and letters I didn't understand.

"Where is it now?" Frannie asks when I'm through.

I bite my lip. What did I do with it? I remember thinking I'd look at it later, try to decipher the code. But I never did. I never saw the notebook again.

I think back to that night, tracing my steps as I try to remember where I put it.

"I think Zane might have it," I say finally. "I was wearing his jacket that night. I shoved the notebook into the pocket."

Frannie's voice remains calm, patient. "And who is Zane?"

I tell her. I tell her everything.

"Do you know where Zane is now?" Frannie asks when I'm done.

I glance at Mama K who is watching me from inside the car, a concerned frown on her face. "Yes."

I give her the address that's branded across my brain despite my rush to return the letter to Zane unopened. I didn't want to remember it, but even after one glimpse, the numbers and street name are emblazoned across my brain.

"So will Dad get out?" I ask, tears burning in my eyes as I look back at the ugly concrete building where my father still sits, probably unaware the truth has been discovered.

"Probably not right away." Frannie sounds almost apologetic as she says this. "He's an accomplice and he will go to trial for his involvement. It won't be for murder. If his lawyer's worth his salt, your dad will be out in a couple of years. Less if he behaves himself."

"Will you be his lawyer?" Frannie's so good, I bet she'd have him out in less than a year.

She laughs. "He'll have to ask me."

"He will," I say.

"Love your confidence," Frannie says. "Anyway. I'll be in touch about what happens next. You'll be needed for the trial, no doubt. In the meantime, I'll get onto filing some guardianship papers for your mother."

"Thank you," I say, and never have two words

ever felt so inadequate. "Thank you!"

****

"I'm proud of you." Mama K inserts the keys into the ignition, but doesn't start the car. She reaches over and brushes some of my uncontrollable hair behind my ear. It springs back a second later and we both giggle.

"You shouldn't be," I say, grabbing the offending strand of hair and tucking it back into my ponytail. "I haven't exactly dealt with any of this in a great way." I've made everything so unnecessarily complicated, caused everyone so much pain.

Mama K shrugs. "Who has? Who could?"

I say nothing. Mama K is hurting, but she's been so great through all of this. Even with her heart broken, she's managed to hold everything together. I just ran. Every time the pain got too much for me, I ran away. Not the most mature way to deal with a problem. Not by a long shot.

But I came back. And I never ran as far from my problems as Zane did.

There I go, thinking about Zane again.

Like I ever stopped.

I wonder how he is, if he's happy.

I hope he is.

"You're doing a fantastic job, Stas," Mama K says as she pulls into traffic. "You're not sitting back and letting people push you around. You're fighting for what you want. I wish I was more like you."

I stare at her. She wants to be like me? Why would anyone want that? I'm a coward. About the toughest thing I've ever done was throw myself out of Ropati's car, and that was pretty much instinct.

"Don't look at me like I'm nuts." Mama K glances over at me when she's pulled up at the lights. "You're so much like your mother."

That sends a stab of sadness through me. I'm nothing like Mom. "I wish..."

"Stas, you are." Mama K weaves through the traffic, but her attention is on me. I feel it in the weight the air in the vehicle seems to have taken on. "You're so like her. Rennie never let anyone push her around. She always knew what she wanted. The same way you do. And she went after it. Sometimes she went too far, but she never lost sight of the goal. And you're the same. Better, maybe, because you take your time to decide what's right."

My cheeks burn. I feel like I've been let in on something private, something that belongs between Mom and K.

"You're so brave." Mama K smiles over at me. "I'm so glad you're my daughter. I'm so proud you're Teddy's sister. I hope you'll teach him to be like you."

A warmth spreads through me. Maybe she's right. I always thought Mom and I fought because we were so different—maybe it was because we were so alike.

For the first time in a long time I let myself think about Mom. Really think about her. Not just the pain of her not being here, but who she really was. K's right. She was strong. Stubborn, sometimes, but always strong. How could she be anything but? She left home at fourteen to chase an impossible dream. And she never stopped. The dreams changed, but Mom never quit charging after what she wanted. A life outside Russia, Dad, K, a successful ballet school, a tiny ass. She went after all of them with the same laser focus.

"Mom wouldn't have let Zane go," I say finally.

Mama K looks over at me with sad eyes. "There wasn't anything you could have done," she says.

But she's wrong. There is so much I could have done. I was so intent on my own pain, I forgot to consider his.

"I didn't tell him I love him," I murmur. "I should have told him."

I should have told Mom too. It's one of those things we never say enough. The words aren't precious, but when they're bestowed on you, they mean so much. We should use them more often.

"I love you," I tell Mama K.

"I know," she replies. "And I love you."

"I love Zane too."

"I know."

"I think it's too late, though."

Mama K looks over at me again. "It's never too late to tell someone you love them."

"He wrote to me," I say quietly. "I couldn't open the letter. I sent it back."

At the time it made perfect sense. It was the only possible thing I could have done. But it was selfish. It must have taken guts for Zane to write that letter after everything that happened. Getting it back unopened must have broken his heart all over again.

"Do you remember the address?"

I nod.

Mama K pulls into the driveway. "Well, then. You know what to do."

Epilogue

Nine weeks later

The scent of Mama K's chicken stir-fry drifts into the night air as I let Vonnie out the back door.

"Call me later." She heads for the new car her dad gave her for her birthday last week, clicking the button on her keyring that unlocks the doors from a distance. "You can talk me through our calc homework."

"You wish! That stuff might as well be Greek."

She laughs and swings herself into the driver's seat. "Okay. We'll do it together then."

I nod and wave as she peels out of the driveway, her tires laying a streak of rubber on the cement. Mr. Young had no idea what he was doing when he bought her a car. He should have got her a tank.

I wander down to the street, not ready to go back inside yet. The night air is still chilly, but it's not as frigid as it was a few weeks ago. As I cross the lawn, I see pale green blades sprouting amongst the dry, brown stubble. The sign advertising the ballet school is gone. The lawn has a bare patch where it stood. A few blades of green are beginning to poke through. By the end of summer that scar will be gone too.

I wonder if my own will be.

They're beginning to heal, I think. Little by little.

Once I reach the street, I look back at the house with its brightly lit windows. Teddy darts past one with one of his toy planes held above his head. Steam from the kitchen has left the windows fogged with condensation so I can only see Mama K as blurred colors moving around behind the glass. I shiver. I don't want to be out here looking in at my life. I head back toward the warmth of the house, pausing only to check the mailbox. A handful of mail sits inside and I pull it out, glancing down at the assorted bills and junk that make up the mail most days. I shuffle through it as I walk toward the door, smiling when I see the letter addressed to me. I finger the postmark with its now-familiar Russian lettering and look forward to reading my cousin's shaky English as she recounts what has been happening to my family in Tobolsk.

I pause on the steps up to the porch, thinking back on what the notebook Frannie retrieved from Zane's pocket uncovered.

Ropati didn't pay my Russian aunts to leave the country, or to drop their custody suit.

Turns out he couldn't.

His whole wealthy lawyer schtick was a sham. A string of bad investments left him so in debt he hadn't a hope of climbing out from under it. To try, he borrowed money from the only person who'd lend it to him—a shady loan shark. He couldn't meet his obligations there either, and the loan shark set him up to clean dirty money coming in from the various illegal activities his clients and associates were involved in.

Ropati figured Dad's theater would be the perfect business to launder the money through. Who would suspect a struggling dance company? And Dad's own debts were so high, he trusted his brother's business offer, and signed over a percentage of the business. Just not enough of a percentage to give Ropati control. At least Dad was that smart.

When the loan shark disappeared and the money to launder dried up, the only thing Ropati had left was his stake in Dad's theater. He needed to liquidate it, but Dad wouldn't sell. He knew the area was being cleaned up, gentrified. He knew the theater's value was set to explode.

Ropati thought having me would be all the leverage he needed to get Dad to agree to sell—and to hand over the cash he'd received as his cut of the illegal activity. Cash he'd never touched because he was saving it for me. Not to mention whatever inheritance I got from Mom. Ropati had ambitious plans for administering that money too. Plans he made the mistake of committing to paper. Plans that would, no doubt, have left me with nothing.

Yet Dad's still in jail. At least until his next court appearance in a few weeks.

****

The newly painted walls of my room seem too bright. The long, relentless planes of off-white paint scream for color or something to break up their monotonous sameness. The posters from my old room are rolled up in my closet. I pull them out and flick through them.

Nothing there means anything to me anymore. I try to remember who the girl was who liked that rock star enough to have his grinning mug staring down from her wall, who practiced kissing on a now-lipstick-smeared picture of some young movie star whose name I've long forgotten. I can't find her, though. The only picture that means anything to me is an old poster of Mom's. It's mounted on a block of wood and is a simple photograph of a dancer's legs from the knees down. Her feet are turned out in fifth position and her pointe shoes are worn to rags. Above these a pair of mis-matched legwarmers are pulled over her muscular calves, a red one reaching her knee, the other one, white and fraying, barely covering her to mid-calf.

This one I hang, centering it on the wall above my desk.

I sit back on my bed and study it. I've been

avoiding dance or anything that might remind me of it, certain the pain will be more than I can bear. The studio has been locked and silent, a fence erected between it and the house so we no longer have to look at it as we enter the house. Mama K says one day she'll sell the business and some other teacher can teach in there. She's just not ready yet.

I don't know if she'll ever be ready.

I don't know if I will be.

I'd die if I heard the sound of piano music drifting across the fence along with the soft thump of dancers' feet hitting the floor.

Yet an hour later, once the house has fallen silent around me, I slip out the back door and head for the gate in the high, wooden fence. It opens easily and without a sound. I only hesitate a second before ducking through, closing it carefully behind me. My feet take me up the familiar path to the studio door without a pause and punch in the code for the lock without a second thought, as if I'd done this yesterday, not months ago.

I do pause once I'm inside. The place is cool and the scent of the ultra-strong disinfectant the cleaning company used fills my nose. I long for the familiar smells of rosin and sweaty bodies, the faint hint of my mother's perfume telling me where she is.

"She's not here," I whisper to myself. "You don't have to like it, but you have to get used to it."

But she *is* here.

I walk into the main studio and switch on a light. Just one. It casts a warm glow across a patch of floor by the barre. I step into it and rest my hand on the smooth, familiar wood. In my head my mother's voice admonishes me to take off my shoes and I kick them aside, tugging off my socks to let my toes curl against the floor.

Without even thinking I pull myself up straighter and push my heels together, raising the arm that isn't resting on the barre into position. I've dropped into the first *plié* before I'm even aware I've done it. After feeling the familiar pull in my muscles, I focus and drop into a second.

Before long I've finished an entire barre and my body is loose and warm. In my head, my mother urges me to the center of the floor for the next set of exercises and I obey. The familiar routine is comforting. I don't even miss the music because every note is etched into my brain. I know every beat so intimately I find myself counting them.

When I've finished the center exercises I'm as limber as I'm going to get. I haven't danced since Zane and I were dragged from Dad's theater and it feels like it. Everything is tight and stiff. I'll be sore tomorrow. I don't care, though. I cross to the stereo in the cabinet and shuffle through the jumble of CDs in the case next to it until I find something I can dance to.

The first notes fall from the speakers and my body aches to move to them. I hold back though, waiting for the perfect moment to dive into the music.

There.

My mother's voice disappears and I let the melody take me, whirling me this way and that, pushing me forward and pulling me back until I'm too breathless and sweaty to do anything but collapse to the floor.

I lie there, listening to my heartbeat thudding in my ears as the last notes fade away. I wait until it's slowed and my breathing has evened out before I stand and stretch some more against the barre. If I stretch I may be able to walk tomorrow.

But I don't want just to walk. I want to dance.

That's right. I want to dance.

I catch sight of myself in the mirror, red-faced and sweaty, my hair a halo of frizz around my head. I'm still only 5'2". My thighs are still thick and heavy. My stomach isn't completely flat. And yes, I have a booty hanging out behind me. And it's never going to be as small and tight as Mom's, even if I starve myself.

Maybe this isn't Mom's image of a dancer, but I can't fight it any longer. Dancing is in my blood and I'm never happier than while I'm moving to music. I don't have to be a prima ballerina. I don't even have to dance in front of an audience. I just have to dance.

I leave the stereo on when I leave the room. I'll be back tomorrow. And every day after that too.

****

I sneak into the studio every night, waiting until everyone is asleep before I make my silent mission across the back yard. I look forward to it. It's my time with Mom. I'm sure she's there, watching me, correcting me. Some nights her voice is so loud in my head I turn and am surprised when I don't see her there. But she is there. I feel her pressing on my spine when I let it sag and pushing my leg higher when I arabesque. She urges me to practice each series of steps until their sequence is tattooed into my muscle memory.

I'm dancing better than I have in years.

I'm practicing harder than I ever have.

I love this more than I was ever willing to admit.

And never do I hear her voice telling me I'm too big to dance.

I realize I never did. *I* was the one who decided I was too heavy to dance. I was the one who hated the reflection the mirrors threw back at me each time I stood at the barre. I felt the humiliation when the boy I was partnered with puffed and groaned when he lifted me. Mom obviously didn't help with her remarks about my body and clothes, but she never said I shouldn't dance.

"I'm sorry," I say to the spirit I feel in the air around me. "I should have come and danced with you that night."

I stand in front of the mirror and stare at my reflection until I go cross-eyed. My features blur into one another and parts of me disappear into those blank spaces that appear when you let your eyes slide like that. Something tightens against my scalp and my eyes snap back into focus. I look up at my head, but there's nothing there. Except I know how my mother's hand feels over my hair. I know how she shows her forgiveness.

"Thank you," I whisper as I step back into the center of the floor, my pointe shoes tapping as I rise onto my toes.

****

The night before Dad is due in court again, I arrive in the studio and find the door slightly ajar. I shiver. Did I forget to lock it behind me last time? Or has someone else been here? I have wondered. Mom's presence is so strong, I'm surprised Mama K hasn't figured it out. But maybe she has. Maybe she has her own times for coming here to speak to Mom, to feel Mom's spirit whispering across her soul.

Still, I'm cautious as I enter the building. How could I not be? The last time Mom was alone here... I swallow hard, shaking away the image of the bloodstain on the studio floor that suddenly fills my mind.

"Hello?"

No sound comes to me through the darkness so I push on, entering the studio and turning on my customary light. I pause before heading for the barre, listening for anything unusual. There's nothing. Only the rush of my own blood pounding in my ears.

I must not have latched the door properly last night.

I push unease from my mind and rest my hand on the barre.

When I'm warm, I cross to the stereo and turn it on. An i-Pod is plugged into it. I pause for a second, staring at it. Did I bring my i-Pod down here? I thought about it, but I don't remember doing it. I shrug. I must have. Who else would have?

I swipe at the screen to choose something at random. I want to be surprised and to improvise to whatever might come up. The first notes trickle from the speakers. Something slow and melodic. Not ballet music, not anything I recognize. I like it, though. I start by simply swaying to the music, the movements so small they're less movements than tiny pulses or twitches. As the music builds, I let my muscles respond to it and my movements become bigger. My body and arms cut arcs in the air while my feet remain rooted firmly to the floor.

A vocalist joins the music. The lyrics are soft and beautiful, incomprehensible. I think it's a foreign language. I like it. The singing becomes another instrument, the lyrics meaningless to me. I let one foot slide forward, raising it slowly in front of me. Once it's as high as I can extend it, I rise onto the toe of my other foot and turn in a measured, deliberate fashion. I keep dancing like this, each movement considered and careful, one foot always in contact with the ground. I'm not ready yet to fly.

The song ends and is replaced by another, faster one. My feet catch the beat and follow it across the floor, my legs rising higher and higher with each step. Still I keep one foot on the floor at all times. This is Dad's dancing. Grounded and earthy, every movement connected to something solid and real. I should have bare feet for this, but I don't take the few seconds to untie my pointe shoes.

When the next song begins, I recognize it. I stand in the middle of the floor and stare at the stereo for a long moment. This is the piece Dad and I danced to at the theater. The piece I danced to with Zane, with Dad. My piece.

I'm confused by the sounds coming through the speakers. They don't belong in this place. This is Dad's music. How can it be here? While my brain struggles to make sense of it, my body recognizes the beat and automatically falls into the shapes and steps I choreographed. Tears fill my eyes as I remember first Dad, then Zane joining me, both of them falling automatically into step with me. I never needed to explain anything while dancing with either of them. They just knew where I wanted them. Where I needed them.

My heart aches for them both and I hate myself for being weak enough to miss them.

I leave the floor for the first time, crossing it on a diagonal in a series of jetes. It feels good to soar, to fly. But it feels as good to land. I slide across the floor, improvising where before there was a lift. I have to imagine my partner and mark the places he'd join me then go his separate way.

I feel hands on my waist and I am lifted, one toe still brushing the floor. My body tenses for a second, then eases once I catch his familiar scent.

"Zane..." I breathe, not quite believing he's actually here, not even sure if I want him to be.

"Shh..." He draws me close, spinning me so my back rests against his chest for an all-too brief second. It's long enough for me to feel the heat of his skin and the beat of his heart. Then I'm turning the other way, his hand caught in mine until the momentum of the pirouette separates us and sends me to the far corner of the room. I don't want to be apart from him. I don't want to be alone.

I stare at him, my chest tight, my throat thick with more emotions than I know what to do with. I want to kiss him. I want to hit him. I want to scream and cry and claw out his eyes with my fingernails. I want to laugh and hug him. I want to bury my face in his neck and breathe him in.

I do nothing but watch, the music flowing over me like a waterfall.

He stands in the circle of light near the barre. His hair gleams like oil and his eyes burn like two blue fires as he watches me. His face holds a mixture of hope and fear that does nothing to loosen the swollen lump in my throat. He's so damn beautiful.

He's a liar.

He lunges forward, one arm stretched toward me. I mirror the movement, sliding my feet across the floor until our fingertips are close enough for sparks to fly between them. We stand like that for several beats, the strings swelling to a crescendo behind us, the drums beating relentlessly onward. Being this close and not touching him is torture. My body screams for his.

I tip forward into an arabesque, bringing my hand closer now and grabbing his. He allows me to draw him to his feet, but won't come closer. He keeps our two arm-lengths between us, the space bridged only by our gazes.

My heart pounds, and it's not from exertion. It thumps, heavy and regular and strong against my ribs, following the beat of the music. My hands tingle with his touch. His fingers are strong and familiar, wrapped around mine. His skin is warm and rough, his nails ragged around the edges.

The music slows as it reaches the end of the piece. Zane lets go of one hand and spins me in toward him so suddenly I almost stumble and fall. I catch myself against his chest, reaching out one hand to brace myself. His heart beats as fast and hard as mine. Looking up, I find him gazing at me, tears glistening at the tips of his long, long lashes.

"Stas," he breathes.

"Zane." Every drop of hurt he's caused me fills the single syllable of his name.

"Stas," he says again, and this time it's an apology. I never knew my name could say so much, could mean so many different things.

He crushes me to him and my mouth finds his. We kiss like we're starving, not even coming up for air. He tastes like honey and cinnamon and I can't get enough of him. My shirt pulls up and his hands rove my waist. I don't care that I'm soaked in sweat, that his fingers skid along my spine. My legs shake with passion and exertion until Zane scoops me up and lowers me to the floor, his lips never leaving mine. He lies across me and I tug at his shirt. I want it off. I want to feel the lines and ridges of his body. I want his warmth against me, his skin.

He struggles out of it, our lips separating for the briefest moment. It feels like a year. He raises my shirt and buries his face in my breasts. I gasp as his tongue traces patterns across the fabric of my bra. My nipples rise and he catches one gently between his teeth.

"Zane," I breathe.

More music plays, but I can't hear it over the pounding of my heart.

"You're here," I manage, catching a fistful of soft, fine hair and pulling his mouth to mine again. "You're here."

He raises himself up so he can look at me, so I

can look at him. His eyes are clear and blue as he watches me study him. "Your lawyer called me."

Good old Frannie.

I knew she'd contacted him about the notebook, but hadn't asked any more. It never occurred to me he'd come for Dad's trial. I watch the way his throat moves as he swallows hard, the patch of stubble near his ear he must have missed while shaving.

The music changes again, something familiar I recognize from a show Dad did a couple of years back.

I glance toward the stereo cabinet and the i-Pod I now realize is Dad's, not mine. "Did you go to the theater?"

Zane nods. "I wanted to see it again. I loved being there with you so much. Plus, I had to pick up my car."

It was still there after all this time? I don't know where he parked it when he moved it away from the front of the theater.

"I know." And I do. Even though I was drowning in grief at the time, I remember being happy with him.

"What happened?" I get up and turn the music down a little. As much as I'd like to lie here and touch him all night, there's too much between us.

He sighs and runs his fingers through his hair in a gesture that's achingly familiar. "I didn't want to leave you like that," he begins. "You have to believe that, Stas."

I cross my arms over my chest, suddenly defensive. "Why?"

"Mom … Mom was kind of crazy that night. I guess she thought she'd really lost me or something. She drove all the way from Rosemont in less than three hours."

He chuckles and throws me a cautious look that I don't respond to.

"Whose house was it?" I ask suddenly, remembering the confused old lady and the basement I believed was his.

He flushes. "I dunno. I needed an address to enroll in school, so I used one. It seemed smart to hang around there, in case anyone came looking for me, or if any school notices got sent home. I was living in my car, Stas. That's why I had so much stuff in it. I couldn't tell you... When I took you into her house, it was the only time I ever went in there. If that door hadn't been unlocked..."

I stare at him. "Was anything you told me true?" I suddenly remember his mother calling him Ed at the hospital. I'm no longer certain I misheard her.

Zane steps toward me, stopping less than a foot away. "Everything was true," he says quietly. "Everything important, anyway. I just fudged some of the details."

"Your name?" I raise my eyebrows.

"Edward Zane Talbolt."

So that's why his mom called him Ed. "So..."

"I go by Zane. Ed's my Dad."

"The dad your mom divorced?"

Zane drops his eyes when he nods this time. "Everything I told you was true."

"So, why..." The lump in my throat chokes me so the words stick there. I look at him, hoping he can read them in my eyes.

"I begged to stay longer," he says, closing the space between us with a single step. He tips my chin up so I have to look into his face. "I even tried to get out of the car at the lights so I could run back to you at the hospital. But Mom was crazy that night. Kind of like your Mama K, but to the power of ten. No way was she letting me out of her sight. I guess I can't blame her. I'm sorry,

Stas. So, so sorry. That's why I wrote you that letter."

My face heats up. The letter I sent back unread. But would it have been better to have kept and burnt it, left Zane hoping day after day for a reply? "I'm sorry too," I whisper.

Neither of us speaks. There are so many millions of ways to hurt someone. But I have to believe there are also millions of ways to forgive those hurts. I just need to find the right one for us.

Suddenly I need to move. I push myself away from him. I run to the stereo and crank the volume until bass makes the floor rumble beneath our feet. I cross the room and run my fingers across the light panel, switching on every light in the place.

I reach for Zane's hand and we dance.

And we keep dancing, even after Mama K enters the room, followed by a sleepy-eyed Teddy.

When the sun comes up, we're still dancing. Zane, Teddy, Mama K, and me.

And we won't stop.

The End

Evernight Teen ®

www.evernightteen.com